Daisy's Christmas Gift Shop

Hannah Pearl

Stories that inspire emotions!
www.rubyfiction.com

Published 2021 by Ruby Fiction
Penrose House, Crawley Drive, Camberley, Surrey GU15 2AB, UK
www.rubyfiction.com

A CIP catalogue record for this book is available from the British Library

ISBN: 978-1-91255-054-8

Printed and bound in Great Britain by Clays Ltd, Elcograf S.p.A.

For my cousins and my children's cousins. Thank you for all the fun and long may it continue.

Also for my brothers. One day I might even be brave enough to tell them!

Acknowledgements

Choc Lit and Ruby have put together a fabulous combination of lovely staff and a supportive group of authors. It is such a wonderful family to be a part of and I want to thank you all for being there. Thank you especially to the Tasting Panel readers who loved Daisy's story and recommended it for publication: Dimi E, Sue H, Cordy S, Kath B, Isobel S, Hannah Mc and Susan D.

Chapter One

I didn't grow up wanting to be a princess. Instead I'd spent my formative years chasing after Ben, my twin brother, getting more than my fair share of skinned knees and ripped trousers. I didn't even spend my teenage years reading high fashion magazines or lusting after the latest pair of designer shoes. Admittedly, I may have read a few bridal magazines here and there. Mostly I'd spent that time thirsting after Ben's best friend since our first day of school, Elijah, or Eli to his admirers. And there were many.

Ben and I resembled each other closely, both barely a whisker over five-foot-six, with hair that shone golden in the sunlight but was positively mousey all winter, and green eyes which Dad always said showed our every emotion. We'd never been able to lie to him growing up, not that we had tried often. Ben, because he lived in a very clear-cut world of rules, and lying wasn't acceptable to him, and me because I thought that people didn't like liars, and I wanted everyone to like me. I still do.

I slipped the emerald-green silk dress over my head and shimmied until it dropped over my hips. 'Are you sure that this is suitable for a winter wedding?' I asked Lily, and not for the first time.

She handed me a pair of silver heels and I slid them on, wobbling for a moment before I found my balance. 'It's perfect,' she reassured me. 'It matches your eyes. Not that anyone will be looking that high.' She motioned at my cleavage, which, whilst fairly modest, was still doing its best to escape from the low-cut V of my dress. I tugged it up but Lily caught my hands. 'Leave it,' she said. 'Let Eli see what he's missing.'

'I don't want Eli seeing any part of me ever again,' I muttered, but Lily wasn't listening. She knew as well as I did that I was lying. Okay, I exaggerated earlier. On occasion I have been known to bend the truth, but I try not to make a habit of it, apart from when it came to Eli. 'I don't know why I'm asking you for fashion advice,' I continued, pouting as my best friend handed me my cream fake fur wrap. 'It's not like you wear enough clothes to know.'

Lily managed what she referred to as an adult boutique, but what the rest of the world knew was actually a sex shop. She spent her days selling handcuffs, vibrators and leather clothes with holes cut out for the very sections most clothes were designed to cover. Lily often tested her apparel before she sold it and despite knowing her for the last three years, I'd never plucked up the courage to ask if she tested out the rest of her products too. Today, she was wearing a black leather corset which laced at the back and a short deep red velvet skirt. Her shiny black boots ended just above her knee, and despite the heels being taller than I would ever attempt, she was still an inch shorter than me. I didn't know how she got into the top by herself, but with more of her ample charms outside of her corset than under it, she'd have no shortage of volunteers if she were to need help when taking it off. She looked amazing.

Lily handed me a lipstick and I opened the cap before peeking and handing it back. 'I think I'll go for something more subtle,' I told her. Lily shrugged and used it to paint her own lips scarlet. With her jet-black curly hair hanging loose to her shoulders, she could carry off such a bright shade. I stuck to a quick slick of lip gloss, all the easier not to smudge or lick off when I got nervous.

'Done,' Lily said, nodding at me in approval. She shooed me out of my cluttered bedroom at the back of my shop and up the wooden stairs to the section of the house where my dad and brother lived. The Tudor beams that criss-crossed the pale walls had bowed over the centuries, but they continued to hold firm, propping up our tall, thin home.

We followed the voices into the kitchen, where Ben and Eli were sat having a cup of tea at the table. Dad turned to face us and when he saw me in my dress a smile flitted across his face. It even reached his eyes, which was a rare occurrence, but just as quickly it was gone again. He placed a gentle kiss on my cheek. 'You look beautiful, Daisy, just like your mum did at your age,' he said and turned back to the counter where he was making himself a sandwich. His shoulders hunched as he buttered his bread. I hadn't meant to upset him by resembling my mother but his grief was unavoidable, even after all of these years.

Ben drained the last of his tea and stood up to place his mug in the sink. His navy-blue suit, freshly dry cleaned the week before in preparation for the wedding, was already creased around his knees. Eli, by contrast, looked striking. And what a contrast he made. He had plumped for a charcoal-grey suit and the black shirt he'd paired with it was only a shade darker than his eyes. He towered over the rest of us by a good six inches, and whilst this had never mattered to me, I knew that sometimes Ben felt that he looked boyish by comparison. Eli's black hair was shaved close to his skin, and I could smell his aftershave from across the room. Not that he had put a lot on, just that my brain was still alert to his scent, no matter how much I had tried to convince it not to be.

'Are you sure you don't mind me going out too?' I

asked my dad. 'I can stay if you like. We can watch a film together.'

He shook his head. 'You've got all done up to go out. Don't waste the effort on an old man.' He finished assembling his meal and sat at the table with it. 'Are you going too, Lily?' he asked. Her outfit may not have been considered appropriate for most weddings, but as Lily dressed this way for everything, from work to doctor's appointments, I couldn't blame him for needing to check.

'I've got to work this evening,' she said, kissing his cheek and turning to leave. 'Don't do anything I wouldn't do.' She winked at me as she passed.

'That probably doesn't leave a lot,' Eli replied and I shot him a dirty look.

'You can talk,' I said, and Ben quickly sprang to his defence. Within moments we were bickering like kids. Eventually Dad had had enough and banged his knife against his plate until we shut up.

'Lily, I'm glad that you can express yourself through your wardrobe, even if the rest of us are not as brave. Ben, be polite to your guests. Daisy, the same goes to you. Eli and Lily are visitors to our home. Even if they are here most of the time.' He stopped and sipped his tea. 'And you should afford them both more respect.' I knew that he wanted me to apologise to Eli but instead I just glared at the floor. 'Eli,' he continued, 'I believe there's a saying that your mother was fond of quoting, something about he who is without sin casting the first stone. That might be relevant here.'

Suitably chastened we all wished my dad a pleasant evening and filed out in silence. It wasn't until Lily had tottered off to work and Ben, Eli and I were stood on the main road waiting for our taxi that any of us spoke again. 'That was your fault,' Ben muttered.

'Was not.' I accidentally on purpose skewered his foot with my stiletto. He hopped around swearing, trying to rub his injured toe through his shoe.

'If she didn't dress like a tart—' Eli interjected.

'I thought that was your usual type,' I spat back. He didn't reply, just stared at me and I wondered if he was also thinking back to the night when we were newly sixteen and I had very much been his type. And he had been mine, albeit only for a few heady hours. We stood in silence after that until the cab pulled up, silver, sleek and shiny.

Eli opened the door and stood back so that I could climb in. It was a more gentlemanly gesture than he usually bothered with towards me, and I thanked him. As I slid in, my dress fell open, displaying the slit that ended high enough up my thigh that I'd had Lily check earlier in the evening that nobody would be able to see my knickers from any angle. At least I knew that I hadn't displayed more than I'd meant to, but it didn't explain why he was still staring.

'Cover up, Daisy,' Eli said, but I noticed that he hadn't looked away yet. It seemed that Lily was also correct about the effect of a strategically placed garter belt. I wanted to ignore him but I also didn't want to get folds in my dress so I shot him a dirty look as I rearranged my layers. Ben swung himself into the car and narrowly avoided landing on my lap. I shoved him aside. Eli closed the door behind Ben and took a seat in the front next to the driver. 'Sherrinford Hall please,' he said, and the car pulled away from the curb. Eli turned to offer me a chewing gum, but it was juicy fruit flavour and I didn't think it would go well with the wine I was hoping to drink shortly.

The happy couple had tied the knot officially at a town hall earlier in the afternoon in front of their families, but had chosen the beautiful and haunting gothic building on the fringes of the forest in Essex for their wedding reception. There were barely two weeks to go until Christmas so holly wreaths and simple golden lights hung from the stone porch. The fir tree on the left of the front door was lit up by a string of shimmering silver bulbs.

Inside, the decorations were styled to suit the age of the building, and were largely made of paper and lace. I hated to think of the risk of fire from all of the candles which sat in small glass bowls around the outskirts of the room. A Christmas tree, ornately decked in ribbons and baubles, was tall enough to skim the ceiling. We were handed a glass of champagne, and I sipped mine slowly as I took in the surroundings. It was perfect, and if I could bottle the romantic atmosphere I'd have been able to sell it and make my fortune.

Ben wandered off with his wine, leaving Eli and me in an awkward silence. Eli eventually broke it. 'You look beautiful.'

I stared at him, amazed that he had found something polite to say. I had been perfectly happy to wait without speaking. 'Thank you,' I said, taking another sip of my drink. 'Considering that you probably spent the last month hiding behind rocks in the desert or dodging assassins or whatever it is that you do, you've scrubbed up pretty well too.'

'I know,' he said, and the fleeting moment of truce was fractured.

'Of all the big headed ...' I began, but Ben chose that moment to reappear.

'We're seated at table eleven,' he told us, handing Eli a pint of lager. Eli handed me his almost full glass of champagne. I looked him in the eye as I downed it.

'Elegant,' he said, so I stuck my tongue out at him.

Ben either didn't notice or didn't care, or maybe he was just used to us arguing, as he tugged my arm to guide me to where we were to be seated for the meal. 'I'm here,' he said, pulling out a chair and sitting down. 'Erin is on my left. Where is Erin?' He got up and wandered off again. His bottom had been on the seat for less than a second.

'Looks like I'm here,' Eli said. He shrugged his jacket off, arranging it over the back of his chair and sat down. He reached across and picked up a small folded rectangle of ivory card and read it aloud. 'Eli's plus one. Looks like you're next to me.'

'I feel so honoured,' I said, laying on the sarcasm, given that he obviously hadn't told the bride or groom my actual name. 'I still don't get why you both needed to bring dates.'

'We didn't,' Eli replied. 'The invites said that we could if we wanted to, and you know your brother. He can fix or programme any electrical device you care to mention, but sometimes he misses subtleties. When he read that he could bring a guest he thought that meant that he had to, and before you know it he'd asked Erin. I never knew he had the courage.'

'So why did you ask me?' I said, finally making eye contact again and holding it this time.

'I know you love weddings, and it's been a while since you had chance to get dressed up. I figured that you could use a break. Ben said you've been working all hours in the run up to Christmas.'

I picked up my glass and clinked it against his, thanking him for the thoughtfulness. It really had been a busy few weeks and he was right, it was nice to have the opportunity to get out. The one drawback of having my bedroom at the

7

back of my shop was that it was hard sometimes to feel like I was off duty.

'Besides, you know what single women are like at weddings,' Eli continued. 'They get all drunk and emotional. I reckon I've got a decent shot of hooking up tonight even with you glaring at all my targets.'

I laughed, and Eli stared at me for a second before joining in. It was just what we needed to break the tension between us.

'As long as you weren't planning on hooking me,' I told him.

'Wouldn't dream of it,' he said, sliding his arm around my chair, his hand gliding a gentle trail across my waist as he leaned back to assess the talent in the room. He nodded in the direction of a woman who was laughing far too loudly at the bar. She slammed her empty glass down and was immediately handed another by the man on her left.

'Too drunk too early,' I said. 'If she carries on at this speed she'll be a mess by the end of the night.' Eli accepted my judgement and continued to scan. 'Too eager,' I said to his next potential target. 'She'll have texted to tell you that she misses you five minutes after you leave her bed.' That prediction was enough to put him off, just as I knew it would. Eli wasn't known for his love of commitment. 'Too skinny' I said, to the one after that.

'It's not like you to be jealous.' Eli smirked.

'I'm just scared you'll squash her, you and your massive man muscles.' He grinned even wider after that. 'My turn,' I said, and looked around the room for anyone who caught my eye. Whilst there was plenty of talent on offer, no one made me look twice. Eli noticed my reticence and began to preen. 'Okay, how about him?' I said, pointing at a man who was fiddling with his tie in the corner.

'Too self-obsessed,' Eli said, barely looking at him. I'd have complained but it was the same judgement I'd made.

'Him?' I said, pointing at a man who was chatting to the bride. His long, blond hair fell across his face and he raised his hand to sweep it aside as he spoke. Even from across the room I could appreciate the gesture as his eyes were the kind of azure you could lose yourself gazing into.

'I don't think you're his type,' Eli said, and I was about to protest when another man left the gents, walked over, greeted the bride too, before kissing my intended full on the lips. It was a lucky escape. He was stunningly gorgeous and I'd never have actually had the courage to chat him up.

I shrugged and turned my back to the room. 'I didn't need to find someone anyway,' I said, finishing my champagne. 'Weddings are about love, not just hooking up.'

'So says the queen of romance,' Eli said, reaching across the table until he snagged the bottle of white wine and refilling my glass.

'My business does very well, regardless of the success, or lack thereof, in my own love life.' This was lucky, I thought, as I was currently very, very single. Plus, my little shop had been doing well until recently. Dad didn't charge me rent but business rates and utilities had been taking an increasingly large bite from my takings. If things didn't start to pick up soon I'd be struggling during the dry spell that sometimes hit after the Valentine's Day boom had ended. I didn't want to give Eli the satisfaction of knowing that I might be in trouble. He had never quite understood the niche market that my little boutique of romance provided for.

I may never have been especially feminine or graceful,

but I've always been a hopeless romantic. Maybe it's because my parents were teenage sweethearts. My dad said that he'd fallen in love the first time he saw my mum. She'd just moved to London from a little village in North Wales. She'd wanted a break from the busy roads and had wandered down a quiet side street when she had spotted the shop and gone in to buy a sticky bun. My grandad ran a bakery from what was now my shop and had ovens in what was now my bedroom. They'd been married within a year, and though they'd always wanted children it was twenty years before they had any.

They'd given up trying in the end and busied themselves in their careers. Dad had taken over running the bakery and Mum had set up a studio for her painting in the attic. I don't think they wanted to be apart even for the length of a working day. They'd adopted a couple of puppies, and though they were sad to not have kids, they were happy to be together. Mum was four months pregnant before they realised that it was actually happening. Apparently when they found out they were having twins my dad didn't speak for several days. She'd told me that story many times when I was tiny, and I'd always hoped that it meant he was just excited. Mum's heart had given out when we were six. Dad hadn't spoken for a week after she died. And even now, twenty years on, he never smiled in the same way as I remembered him doing before.

He'd never baked again either. The house had been paid for many generations before I was born, and he'd got some insurance money to live on, so he'd closed the shop, claiming that he needed the time to look after me and Ben. I think he just couldn't bear to see any of the treats that my mum had loved so much.

The counters had remained empty until one day when I

came across their wedding album hidden in a cupboard. It was full of pictures of them staring into each other's eyes and laughing. I could barely remember a time that dad had seemed that alive. A couple of weeks later I'd cleared the downstairs rooms and launched 'Romantic Daze'.

I sold all the traditional accoutrements that you would associate with romance, such as luxury toiletries and chocolates. But I prided myself in going the extra mile. If your partner had a taste for a specific wine I would track down an importer and source it. If they liked a particular chocolate I would make up a beautiful gift basket containing it. Where Lily's shop catered to underwear with strategically placed holes, mine carried a range made of the finest and softest silk.

One of my biggest achievements had been when one of my favourite customers had wanted to find a piece of music that he and his wife had danced to at their wedding sixty years earlier. Very few recordings had survived, and those that did were in pretty bad condition. Eventually I'd hired a team of musicians from the local music college and we'd listened to as many of the recordings of the piece as we could find. The band rehearsed for a month, working out as much as they could from the fragments we could access. I'd booked a table at a local restaurant and briefed the chef to make the same food as the couple had eaten at their wedding reception, and then the band came out and played their song.

A florist friend had recreated their bouquet from a wedding photo which I'd given him, and though they were no longer well enough to travel on a second honeymoon, we'd recreated their trip to Blackpool inside the restaurant with sticks of rock and candy floss. The tip I'd got from my customer for the success had kept me solvent for the next six months, but the joy I'd felt at seeing them so happy together because of my work had lifted my mood for even longer.

I longed to find that kind of love for myself. Some nights I lay awake fearing that I would never find it. Other nights I tossed and turned fearing that either I'd had it already and lost it, or that I had fallen in love with someone who would never love me back as I wanted him to. I was liable to be in an awful mood the day afterwards. Not solely due to the lack of sleep, but also because I'd be fuming with myself for being so weak.

I was stunned out of my reverie by the banging of a small bronze gong, announcing that dinner was to be served. My brother reappeared with a timid looking lady next to him. He introduced her as Erin, a colleague from his office. Her blonde hair, similar in colour to mine and Ben's, fell in waves to her shoulders, which were raised in tension. She clasped her hands together as she stood beside Ben. Her pink floral dress fell to an unflattering length, ending mid-calf and giving the impression that her legs were both shorter and chunkier than was probably true. But her blue eyes sparkled as she gazed at my brother.

I wanted to take the opportunity to get to know her, not least to ask how she managed to get my brother to ask her out. He didn't often notice the human interactions going on around him. Unless they impacted on him attempting some complicated technological feat, in which case he was liable to be pretty grumpy. So when he topped her glass up and she blushed when their hands touched, I was really proud of him.

The tables began to fill, and next to me Eli reached into the centre of the table and helped himself to a bread roll. He tore it open and began to cover it with butter. Erin had to stand and lean in to reach the basket, but when she could finally reach she grabbed two and passed one to Ben. I shot Eli a look, and he shrugged at me pretending not to understand. I rose, about to reach across myself and grab a bun, when a hand rested briefly on my shoulder.

'Allow me, please.'

I turned to see who had spoken. The baritone belonged to an imposing figure of a man. His golden hair was cut short, and his stubble was almost the same length. His blue eyes sparkled in the candlelight, and his shirt was stretched tight across his broad shoulders. He stood and picked up the basket, which he held out to offer me the contents.

'Thank you,' I said, as I helped myself.

'I'm Taylor,' he said, reaching his broad arm out to offer me his hand to shake. He didn't explain if that was his first name or his surname, and I didn't know how to ask, so I took his hand, mine feeling tiny by comparison, and made to shake it, before he gently drew my wrist towards him and kissed the back of my hand. I could sense Eli glaring at me. I ignored him.

Taylor let go of my hand eventually and walked around the table to take the empty chair next to Erin. Even seated, it was easy to see how much taller Taylor was than Eli. Maybe he felt jealous. It wouldn't do Eli any harm to be brought down a peg or two, though. I leaned back to look past Taylor, meaning to check if he had also brought a date. He must have read my mind. 'I came alone,' he reassured me. 'And you? Are you a friend of the bride or the groom?'

'Neither,' I said, before realising that I should probably explain why Eli was sat beside me shooting daggers at Taylor with his smoky eyes. 'My brother and his friend work with them. They kindly brought me because they know how much I love weddings.' I didn't mention what it was that my brother and Eli did for work. Largely because it was supposed to be a secret, but also because I was never entirely sure of the details. I had once told one of Eli's prospective hook-ups that he claimed to be a real-life James Bond type, hoping the suggestion of womanising would put her off. But this only seemed to aid his pick-up efforts so I had never repeated it again. Plus Eli had been cross with me for saying so much. Maybe I'd accidentally got too close to the truth.

Waiters began to bustle around the room delivering plates. My starter was placed in front of me. Taylor picked up his knife and fork and began to tuck into his pâté and crackers. I fussed with my food, arranging and rearranging it until Eli leaned over me, took my plate and scooped the pink quenelle onto his own. He swapped it for his salad and handed it back to me.

'Clearly my brother forgot to mention to them that I'm vegetarian,' I explained to Taylor. He nodded in understanding. 'So what do you do?' I asked. He began to fidget and finger his burgundy bow-tie. I doubted the fabric had been designed with a neck as broad as his in mind but his discomfort seemed to have more to do with not wanting to answer the question. 'You work with my brother and Eli, don't you?'

He nodded and sipped his wine before he whispered quietly out of the side of his mouth, as if he were trying to give away secrets as discreetly as he could despite the hubbub. 'Do you realise that there are probably dozens of people having similar conversations in this room right now where they attempt not to give away anything they shouldn't?' He winked at me as he spoke, and I found myself smiling in return. Next to me Eli huffed audibly as he ate my food.

'So are you in the computer department with Ben, or the International Relations department with Eli?' I asked.

'Ben *is* the computer department,' Taylor said, as he took the bottle of wine and leant across the table to refill my glass.

In no time at all the waiters began to remove the empty side plates and replace them with the main course. When my plate arrived laden with creamy mashed potato, fresh asparagus and the rarest lamb I've ever seen outside of those running around a field, I groaned and cursed Ben's lack of thought. Eli rescued me once more, swapping my lamb for his sides.

'Aren't you going to feel ill after a dinner of just meat?' I asked him.

He washed his mouthful down with a glass of red wine. 'I'm far too manly for that,' he said, and began to stare, unblinkingly, at Taylor.

Whilst Eli was often prone to displays of his masculinity, he didn't usually do so casting me in the role of his femme fatale, and I began to feel uncomfortable. Eli gripped his cutlery hard enough that I could see his muscles bunch beneath his shirt. Finally, I gave a small cough. Taylor broke eye contact, at last, and turned to smile at me.

Eli leant past me to speak to Ben and began to discuss which women he was going to dance with that evening. I felt sorry for Erin, with Eli talking as if she weren't there, but Taylor successfully kept me distracted when he removed his bow-tie and unbuttoned the top two buttons of his shirt. 'That's better,' he said, and I wondered how constricted his neck had felt.

'Do you play rugby, by any chance?' I asked him.

Taylor launched into a long and detailed description of the fitness regime which led to the physique before me. 'So, are you going to tell me what you do for work now?' I asked when he finished telling me about the marathon he had recently completed. He shook his head. 'Because if I knew you'd have to kill me?' I asked.

'Nothing so clichéd,' he replied. 'But if you were ever to find yourself in need of bodily protection, give me a call.'

Chapter Two

As the last of the dishes were cleared from our table, Taylor pushed back his chair and asked me to dance. We made our way through the crowds of guests out of the dining room, with its brocade curtains and mahogany window frames. We passed through the grand entrance, with its sweeping staircase and chandeliers, which gave way to an even more impressive ballroom. A Christmas tree bigger than any I had seen outside of Trafalgar Square twinkled with so many fairy lights that they could have lit up my entire flat.

A four-piece band finished their warm-ups in the corner and launched into a rendition of Louis Armstrong's 'Wonderful World', as the groom led his bride onto the floor for their first dance. By the time they finished I was blinking back tears and excused myself to use the bathroom before Taylor noticed. Inside, I took a minute to use the facilities and pull myself together. Then I did what I always did in a time of emotional crisis and rang Lily.

'How's the wedding?' she asked as she answered her phone.

'Beautiful,' I sighed. 'Her dress is ivory lace, with the most fabulous train I've ever seen. And her bouquet has roses of the same colour, shot through with pearls. I think I'll have to see if I can offer something similar for Valentine's Day.'

'Sounds perfectly lovely, if you go for that kind of thing,' Lily said. 'I'd have gone for red, myself.'

'Because you make up in vitality what you lack in subtlety,' I told her, 'and I love you for it.'

'It sounds quiet for a wedding. I don't hear any music in the background there.'

'I'm ringing from the loos,' I explained.

'You don't need to call me every time you spot a machine selling lube,' she said. 'They're not going to put me out of business, I promise.'

'I only did that once.' I laughed. 'Or maybe twice.' I fell silent for a moment.

'So how come you're hiding out in the bogs?' Lily asked. 'I thought you'd be happy to be there. You look at weddings the same way I look at a fabulous handbag, or a new vibrator. We just got this one in stock that has—'

'Lily!' I shouted, 'I don't want to know.'

'It might relax you.'

'I prefer my—' I paused to think of the correct word '—entertainment, to come with a heartbeat, and not batteries.'

She sniffed at my lack of willingness to try new things. 'So how is Eli behaving this evening?'

'Like he's in heat,' I told her.

'So what's new?'

'He's acting that way towards me. Usually it's me admiring him from a distance, and kicking myself for it. I don't know how to react now he's paying attention in return. It makes me feel like I'm ...'

'Dinner, and he's hungry for you?' Lily suggested.

'That's disgusting.'

'Only if he does it wrong. I sell a DVD that could teach him what to do.'

'He already knows,' I told her, sighing as I remembered how skilled he'd been, even ten years previously. 'But I met this hulk of a man at dinner. You'd love him, Lily. He's twice your size, easily, and I reckon I could see his six-pack through his shirt. He's waiting for me to dance.'

'So go and dance with him. Make Eli good and jealous. I need to go anyway. One of my regulars went into the changing room with a new corset half an hour ago and I can hear strange noises. Either he's stuck, or he's already enjoying it way too much. Either way, he's not leaving without paying for it.' She hung up before I could ask her whether it mattered that despite Taylor being gorgeous, I wasn't sure if I wanted to dance with him.

I gave my hair a quick flick to add some volume, slicked on some more lip gloss and left the room. I was about to head back to the ballroom when I heard my name being called. Turning around, I found Eli lounging against the wall next to the ladies.

'I think the bathroom you need is just up the stairs,' I told him, pointing to where the gents were located.

'Don't fall for Taylor,' he said, with no preamble.

'I don't see that it's any of your business.' I made a move to pass him and head back to the music. He grabbed my arm and I tugged it away angrily. 'You have no right to tell me who I can go out with,' I told him. 'You threw that privilege back in my face years ago. Now, if you'll excuse me, I'm going to dance with a man who does want to be with me.'

'He wants to be with lots of women,' Eli explained.

'Which is so different to your approach?' I scoffed.

'He isn't right for you.'

'I'm old enough to find that out for myself.' I walked off, my heels beating out a staccato on the tiled floor.

Taylor greeted me at the entry to the ballroom with a kiss on the cheek and a fresh glass of champagne. I noticed Eli making his way back into the room, flirting outrageously and laughing as women stroked his arm or touched his cheek. I emptied the glass and placed it back on the tray of a passing waiter. 'Will you dance with me?' I asked Taylor. The room was beginning to spin around me anyway, I might as well be turning with it. Either that or slow down on the drinking, which would be hard with Eli acting the way he was around me.

Taylor swept me into his arms and twirled me around the dance floor. He was surprisingly elegant for such a big man, and I felt weightless as he held me. The hour grew late, and the band switched to slower numbers. I excused myself and sat to catch my breath, smiling as I saw Erin lead Ben onto the dance floor. It wasn't his natural environment, and he was out of time with the music, but they both looked radiant as they swayed together. At least until Eli interrupted.

I couldn't hear his words from across the crowded room, but I could see him pointing at himself and Ben and then back to a pair of young women in skirts far too short to be polite for a wedding who were stood at the bar.

Ben shook his head, but Eli gestured some more. Eventually Ben whispered something in Erin's ear and followed Eli meekly towards the girls. I was about to go over and help my brother. It was clear to me who he wanted to be with, even if his best friend couldn't see it, but I was distracted by Taylor. He asked me if I wanted one last dance, and as Eli was leaning in to the tall blonde girl, I took Taylor's hand and walked with him back onto the dance floor.

The final number was slow and tender, and I found myself pressed against Taylor's chest, my hands around his waist, as we moved. The band finished playing, and we all stopped to applaud them. Taylor's eyes raised to the ceiling, and I saw that we had come to a stop underneath a bunch of mistletoe that was strung up above.

I hadn't decided if I wanted to kiss him, but it seemed

rude to leave him hanging, so I closed my eyes and leaned forward. Just as our lips were about to touch, I was pulled away yet again.

'Ben!' I shouted. 'That was rude, even for you.'

'I need to go into work,' he said, ignoring how cross I was with him. 'Erin just called to say that there is a problem with the servers and they need me to fix it. She's driving me in her car. Our cab is due in a minute anyway so I asked Eli to make sure you get home safely.'

'I'm a big girl,' I told him. 'I can get home by myself.'

'I promised Dad I'd look after you,' he said, blinking behind his glasses.

'And I promised that I'd look after you,' I added, completing our family motto. I kissed his cheek and told him to be safe. He ran his hands through his hair, ensuring that any last vestige of its previous styling was gone, and made his way out of the front door.

I turned back to Taylor. Though the mood for a kiss was undoubtedly broken we were still stood underneath the mistletoe. Eli was next to him, shoulder to shoulder. Well, Taylor's shoulder to somewhere near the top of Eli's head anyway. Taylor's breadth contrasted with the compact power promised by the energy that seemed to be humming through Eli. I looked from one to the other. Finally Taylor took a half step back and bowed to me. 'I'll ring you?' he asked waiting for me to nod before turning and leaving. I hadn't given him my number but he worked with Ben and Eli. He would have methods to find it now that I'd told him it was okay to do so.

Eli and I were silent for the car ride home. I was fuming at him, but I had no idea why he seemed to be just as fed up with me. As we pulled up outside my house, he got out of the taxi too.

'I'm sure I can get home safely from here,' I told him, somewhat sarcastically as I was stood right on my doorstep.

He gestured at the mistletoe that I'd hung outside my shop the week before. I gulped. It had seemed like such a light-hearted tradition when I'd put it up. Half an hour earlier I'd nearly kissed Taylor. But now did Eli really want to kiss me as well, even though he had been so rude for most of the evening?

'It's bad luck to refuse,' Eli said, sensing my uncertainty. So I stepped forward and placed a chaste kiss on his lips. He stood still, waiting for me to finish. I wondered if I had mis-read him somehow, but surely that was what he had wanted? I stepped back, confused. He closed the distance and kissed me back, but there was no mistaking his intent. His kiss was more sure than mine had been and I met him gladly, enjoying how it felt to be so close to him for the first time in almost forever. His arms slipped around my waist and it felt as though I fitted perfectly against his chest. I wondered if he'd be able to feel how hard my heart was beating.

'I didn't realise that you enjoyed Christmas traditions so much,' I said as he moved his head back and stroked my cheek with a cold hand. I waited for the cool air to take the blush from my cheeks where his fingers had touched me.

'That's the only decent one,' he said. Was that why he had kissed me? Just because of the mistletoe? He'd given so few signs that he saw me as anything other than his friend's sister and yet that kiss, *that* kiss. Ah, I could still feel the tingle on my lips.

'So you're not looking forward to Christmas? It's only a few weeks away now.'

'It's not so much fun on your own,' he said. Not that Eli

was usually on his own at Christmas. He'd joined us every year since his mum had died, but I knew what he meant. Holidays could be a painful reminder of those missing from the celebrations.

I stood on tiptoes to kiss him one more time, trying to take his mind off the path I had set it on by the mention of Christmas, but it was too late. My lips touched his but the heat of a moment ago had passed already. He didn't make eye contact again. I settled for thanking him for taking me to the wedding before letting myself in to my flat and closing the door behind me.

Chapter Three

I didn't sleep well that night for thinking about Taylor and Eli. The next morning I had to drag myself out of bed in order to open my shop on time, thankful for my lack of commute. A shipment of bath oils and scented massage lotions arrived, and I kept myself distracted by arranging and rearranging a new display in my window. This was mostly for my own benefit and to make the room look pretty. Most of my business was referral by word of mouth. It was lucky because the shop opened onto a tiny cobbled street, reminiscent of those which had existed in London for hundreds of years, and there wasn't much footfall, though we were barely a hundred yards from one of the busiest touristy roads in central London. I often commented that we ought to try and reinstate the old gas lights for a more authentic and ethereal experience. Ben would huff at me and point out the fire hazard. Most of the light that Ben was used to came in the form of computer screens.

Lily turned up at noon, yawning and rubbing her eyes. Her shop didn't close until after midnight, with lots of her customers passing through after the nearby restaurants and pubs closed, so we often met midday for a meal. I made her a coffee and waited until she'd drunk it before offering her some pizza. She wrinkled her nose.

'How can you eat pizza for breakfast?' she asked.

'I'd be having it for lunch,' I pointed out.

'Let's go out to eat. Then we can both order what we need.'

I checked my phone one final time before we left, but

there were no texts yet from Taylor, and the battery was almost flat so I plugged it in to charge and let us both out. It seemed to be the only way I'd go more than thirty seconds without checking to see whether I'd received any messages.

London can be ridiculously expensive, especially when you live right in the centre, as I did, but there were one or two hidden gems that only local residents would know. Lily wound her way through the crowds that flocked down Tottenham Court Road until we came to our favourite café, tucked away down a quiet side street not dissimilar to my own. I was glad it wasn't further, even though I'd wrapped up against the chill in my thickest navy wool coat. Lily must have been freezing in her bright blue PVC mini skirt and vest top, even with the leather jacket that she wore over the top, but she didn't show any signs of it.

Inside, Lily ordered herself a gigantic fried breakfast, and I wondered where she was going to put it all. It didn't stop me from ordering the same however, but this time with veggie sausages and no bacon. 'I thought you wanted lunch,' she said.

'There was a lot of alcohol last night. It turns out my tummy needs some grease to soak it up.' We ordered two more mugs of coffee, and sat quietly sipping until our food came. By the time we'd finished, Lily was fully awake and bouncing with energy again.

'There's a trade sale at the conference centre in the Docklands later,' she said. 'Do you want to go with me?'

I shook my head. 'I had nightmares at some of the things I saw there last time. And I didn't sleep well enough last night to risk it.'

'Too busy having fun with the dreamboat?' she asked. I shook my head and she tsked at me. 'Too bad. You could do with some action. Before you forget what your "lady parts"—' she waved her fingers in air quotes as she spoke, '—are for.'

'I don't call them lady parts. I'm more grown up than that at least.'

'So what do you call them?'

'Neglected,' I said, picking up the bill and going to pay for our meal.

Lily came back to Romantic Daze with me and spent an hour telling me how vanilla my selection was. I pointed out that she was welcome to go back to her own shop, but she had an hour before she was due to go to the trade show and she wanted to spend it with me.

I set her the task of doing a stock take on my supply of camisoles and dressing-gowns. 'They're so modest,' she complained, but she counted them and noted the remaining sizes nonetheless. I was just about to set her off to refolding the lingerie when there was a disturbance outside.

It was unusual to hear a crowd on this road, so we both stopped what we were doing and hustled to the window. Eli and Taylor were stood outside. Ben was in the middle, glancing nervously between them. I couldn't blame him. Whilst they weren't exactly nose to nose, given their height difference, the tension between them was palpable. Eli's eyes had hardened, and Taylor's hands were tightly clenched at his sides.

I opened the door and walked out, Lily right on my heels. 'Taylor,' I said. 'This is a pleasant surprise.' It sounded sarcastic as I said it, but I hadn't meant it to. He took one final look at Eli, then turned to face me and smiled.

'I tried to ring you. I wanted to thank you for a lovely evening yesterday. Your brother answered and said that you were at work so I thought I'd pass by and say hello.'

Eli shot Ben a filthy look which clearly made him feel guilty as he shuffled from foot to foot. 'I left my phone here when I went out,' I explained, before thanking Ben for answering it, even if he'd not then realised it might be useful to pass the message on when I got home. He seemed to feel calmer after that and stopped wriggling. A group of young women walked down the high street and paused by the top of the road as they saw Taylor and Eli. They crowded in together and began whispering. I saw one of them point at Eli.

'Come inside and have some tea,' I said to Taylor.

'That sounds lovely,' Eli replied, and before I could clarify who I meant, everybody followed me back inside. A moment later I could hear the sound of laughter and chatting outside the front door, and when the group of girls entered the shop after us, it was too crowded to move. They were too busy smiling at Taylor and Eli to care, but I began to feel claustrophobic. I didn't often have more than one or two people inside usually. A personal service was important to my customers.

'Lily, please can you take Taylor, Eli and Ben up to Dad's kitchen please?' I asked, hoping that I wasn't sending Dad up a fight that was waiting to happen. Lily was impervious to the tension, or perhaps she was thriving on all the testosterone floating around, as she shepherded my guests up the winding stairs.

The girls turned out to be a group of twenty-somethings from Italy, taking an early Christmas break to do some shopping. Thankfully they didn't disappear the moment they realised that the show was over. I introduced them to my range of handmade necklaces and silver drop earrings. By the time they left, clutching their parcels of heart-shaped wooden photo frames, silk scarves and candles, wrapped

27

up in tissue paper and tied with ribbon, I'd made more in one hour than I usually cleared from walk-in custom in a week. I wondered how good business would be if I hired Taylor and Eli to stand outside more often, then I remembered how they'd looked as though they were about to kill each other. I locked the door behind the girls and sighed, before going up the stairs myself to see who was still standing.

'Sorry Dad,' I said, as I let myself into his kitchen. I handed him a packet of biscuits from my kitchen to replace the ones that had been demolished from his supplies. He gave me a brief hug and shuffled off. A moment later I heard the TV switch on in the living room.

'I'd better be off,' Taylor said, handing Lily his empty cup. 'I've got a meeting at work. Got to see a man about a thing.' That was about the same level of detail as I was used to hearing from Ben and Eli about their jobs too. He thanked Lily for the tea and kissed her cheek. I had accidentally positioned myself in a corner next to Ben, so he couldn't get very close to me and settled for a wave from across the room.

'Did I do something wrong?' Ben asked, looking at me nervously.

I gave him a squeeze and told him how much profit I'd just made thanks to their luring in the female customers. He looked relieved.

'At least he's useful for something,' Eli scoffed.

'I could use him for a few things,' Lily commented, and fanned herself with Dad's discarded newspaper.

'Were you here for any reason?' I asked Eli.

'I thought I'd come over and see if you needed any help,' he said. 'I thought you might need a hand putting up Christmas decorations or something.'

I thought back to him asking for a kiss underneath the mistletoe the night before. 'That's really kind but I think I have more than enough up already. Lily and I are off on a buying trip this afternoon. I need to re-stock.' Lily leant over to high five me, and I wondered just what I'd let myself in for.

Chapter Four

The trade show was fantastic, though I did come away feeling like I'd learnt more there than from any sex ed class I'd ever had in school. There had been hundreds of stalls spread over four floors of the conference centre. I'd seen a greater variety of adult toys than I would ever have believed possible. The ones that were neatly in their boxes were daunting enough. Those that had practical demonstrations terrified me, and Lily had given up trying to persuade me to go in with her after I'd watched the first one with my hands over my eyes. The underwear had been a similar story. There had been some beautiful and elegant pieces on display. Some on racks, and some on stall holders, and some items that covered so little flesh I couldn't see the point of making them at all, let alone trying to persuade people to buy them. It was a little outside of my usual experience, and I got home feeling exhausted but wired at the same time.

Lily carried a stack of brochures into my flat, where she curled up on my bed, folding over the corners of interesting pages and circling items on others. For my part, despite my prudishness at some of the more exotic displays, I'd found a new supplier of luxury bedding. I also had a box of naughty teddies. Not the underwear kind, the soft toys. I'd fallen for them because the one they'd had on display was a plush, white, furry bear clutching a satin heart. The stall holder had told me that he'd actually got one final box with him and that I was welcome to take them with me. Having haggled over the cost and paid for them, he'd brought out a carton emblazoned with teddy bears in various fetish costumes. I'd tried to change my mind but he'd refused to take them back.

Lily had laughed for the entire ride home on the train. Several of the other passengers had not, and I still felt guilty about the look on a little toddler girl's face when her mum dragged her away from me. 'Can't you sell some of these in your shop?' I begged Lily.

'People don't exactly visit me to buy cuddly toys,' she said.

'They don't come to a specialist romance boutique to buy things like this either.' I lifted out a teddy bear with a suspicious bulge underneath its leather trousers. 'Why would a toy ever need to have something like this?'

'Maybe he met a lady teddy he liked the look of. Or a cute boy one. I wouldn't want to limit his choices.' I threw it at her and she caught it one handed. 'Maybe I'll take this one home,' she said. 'Reminds me of an especially hairy boyfriend I had once.'

'I'll wrap it up for you for Christmas,' I told her. I was about to offer to make tea when I heard the letterbox rattle. 'Bit late for the postman,' I said, getting up to see what had arrived. There was a thin white envelope laying on the doormat just inside my shop. I ripped it open and read the letter inside before handing it to Lily.

'Intriguing,' she said, raising one eyebrow at me.

'It's not that exciting.'

'You're just jealous because you can't do this,' she said, lowering that perfectly shaped eyebrow and raising the other one. 'Besides, it just says that a new boutique is opening, directly across from you. I wonder what they're going to sell.'

'It's called "Picture Perfect". That sounds pretty romantic. I really hope that they don't offer any of the same services that I do. I mean, I know that most of my clients are pretty loyal, but I'd still be upset to lose them.' I took the letter back from her and read it again. 'It doesn't say exactly what they'll be offering. It only has a name at the bottom. Cody Rainbow. Is it a man or a woman, do you think?'

'Probably one of the two, or someone in between,' Lily said. 'Let's take a leaf out of Ben and Eli's books and go all super spy on them.' She put down her catalogue and used her fingers to make binocular shapes around her eyes. She was joking but it got me thinking. It wouldn't take much of a drop in sales to make me feel the pinch come spring. Should I be more worried about having a new shop on my little road?

'I think you may have had enough caffeine for today,' I told Lily, and fetched us each a glass of wine instead. Later, after Lily had gone I let myself upstairs to Dad's house. My floor comprised of my bedroom, the shop and a tiny alcove which just about sufficed as a kitchen given that I rarely cooked. I also had a tiny bathroom which was barely big enough for a loo and a shower, and so I retreated upstairs any time I needed more space, or a hot bath.

I decided to use my pamper time to do some research, or at least that was what I told myself, as I tipped a generous helping of new lavender-scented bath oil that I was thinking about stocking into the tub and lay back to relax. Afterwards, I dried myself with my giant fluffy towel and opened the package of treats I'd bought myself from the trade show. Inside was a red silk camisole and matching French knickers. If I were to choose to stock these I'd probably order them in ivory or pale pink, but Lily had insisted that for my personal set, I choose a more dynamic colour.

I'd forgotten to bring my dressing-gown, so I put my baggy jumper on over the top, opened the door and was met by silence. Dad was probably asleep already and I assumed that Ben was out with Eli, so I let myself out and made for the stairs. I was half-way there when there was a noise behind me and I jumped.

'Sorry,' Eli said, 'Ben and I were watching a film in his room. I was just going to get us a beer. I didn't mean to startle you.' In his black sweater and jeans, he had melted into the shadows until he spoke.

'You didn't,' I lied, pulling my jumper down as low as I could, which really wasn't far enough. For once I was glad that Lily had dragged me to visit her favourite waxing salon, though at the time I'd sworn that they were sadists and that I was never going to go back.

'See you soon, Daisy,' he said, turning away again. 'By the way,' he called out over his shoulder, without turning around. 'Nice pants.'

I blushed and hurried down the stairs, grateful that in the dark he wouldn't be able to tell that my cheeks were as red as my knickers.

When I got to my flat I closed the door and locked it behind me. I treated myself to an all over application of a hideously expensive moisturising lotion which I'd been thinking about selling. Even making a hot chocolate and curling up in bed with a novel didn't help. No matter how pampered I felt, I was no nearer to being able to sleep. I grabbed some jogging bottoms and pulled them on over my underwear.

Letting myself back into Dad's house, I paused outside Ben's room and made sure that I could still hear the film running. His laptop was on his desk in the living room, and it played a tone as I opened the lid. I tried to quieten it by hugging the machine against me but it was no use. I held my breath for a moment, but Ben didn't come out of his room so I set it back on the desk and began to type.

Ben was a stickler for secure passwords. The wi-fi in the house had a sixty-four digit randomly selected key. No one hacked it, but it was a nightmare every time I got new device that needed to connect. This was an old family laptop though, and Ben had got so fed up trying to get my dad to remember the code every time he wanted to check the football scores, that the password to unlock this computer was simply our surname, Kirk.

Ben frequently reminded us that if anyone stole the laptop they'd be able to log in fairly easily. He himself refused to use it and tended to grumble when anyone else did. It hadn't stopped him, however, from loading a bunch of intrusive and probably highly illegal search programmes onto it. Maybe he spent so much time running programmes like these at work that he forgot that some of us still had the illusion that we had some privacy left online. I wasn't sure how much of Cody Rainbow's privacy I wanted to invade, so I started off with a good old Google search.

After skimming through page after page of photos of American high school students, who seemed to be split approximately fifty/fifty male and female, I was still none the wiser. I opened the first of Ben's programmes and entered the name, but with no gender or date of birth, I was still left with far too many options. I groaned with frustration and sat back. Unsure what to do next, I stared at the screen until I felt hands on my shoulders. Eli began to massage them, and I groaned again, but this time in pleasure.

'For someone who looked so relaxed after her bath an hour ago, your shoulders are all kinds of tense now,' he said. He continued to rub the back of my neck and I didn't ask him to stop.

'There's a new shop opening on the road. All I have is the owner's name and the shop's so far. I need to know if this is going to impact on Romantic Daze.' Eli began to stroke the top of my arms. 'I can't lose my business,' I said to him, finally admitting that perhaps I did have a reason to be nervous about my shop after all.

'I thought you said you were doing well.'

'I am,' I told him, 'but I always do at Christmas. Then I get just enough birthdays and anniversaries to keep me ticking over during the summer, but if the rates go up again and I lose some of my sales, who knows if I'll be able to make it through until next Christmas. I can't lose my shop.' Eli might not have understood why my customers meant so much to me, but he knew what it felt like to lose someone you loved and he understood why I wanted to work in a building that had meant so much to my parents.

'So why don't you find out more about this Cody person?' he said, reading the name from the screen.

'I don't know how,' I told him, gesturing at the list of possibilities.

'Use your imagination. How else could you investigate?' he asked.

'I'm not a secret agent like you, remember?' I said, rolling my eyes at him.

'You could have been,' he said, and I turned away and began to puzzle over the screen once more. 'You never looked at your aptitude scores, did you?'

'I didn't need to. You and Ben needed something to occupy you once you finished university, and I love my brother but there are a lot of roles he wouldn't be suited to. I only took the tests so that he would come with us and take it as well. My shop was already set up downstairs.'

'I got Ben to hack the system,' Eli admitted.

I swiped his arm. 'You'd lose your jobs if they found out.'

'Your brother is the only person who would be able to spot that we'd ever broken in, so the chances are we were safe. Your scores were higher than mine. You could have walked into a job if you'd wanted one.' Eli loved what he did, though I doubted that I would ever know exactly what it entailed.

'I know you think my shop is silly, but I love it,' I began.

Eli stopped what he was doing, pulled a chair over and sat in front of me. 'I never said that.'

'You didn't need to. I can tell from your face whenever I talk about it. You don't understand why I need it so much.'

'I know how to make a woman feel good without resorting to generic chocolates and half dead flowers,' he scoffed.

'Is that what you think I sell?' I asked him. He didn't answer so I closed the laptop lid and made him follow me downstairs. The lamp-post outside filled the front of the shop with a yellow glow, so I left the overhead light off as we walked around. I showed him the necklace that I had waiting beneath the counter for Mr Sellis to pick up the next week for his wife. It was a replica of one he'd bought her that had been stolen in a burglary the year before. The original had been a gift from him on the birth of their second child and apparently she'd cried for hours when she realised that it was gone.

Next, I showed him the box that Arthur and I had been putting together for him to surprise Janet with on their second honeymoon. I'd tracked down CDs with some of the songs on that they'd danced to at their wedding. I'd ordered a bottle of her favourite perfume from a department store in New York, and together we'd been to visit her favourite jeweller where I'd helped Arthur choose a beautiful eternity ring. 'Arthur was seriously ill last year and Janet nursed him through it. This is his way of thanking her and celebrating the fact that he's still here to go travelling with her.'

Eli didn't reply, but as he walked around the shop, opening drawers and running his finger down the shelves, he seemed finally to be paying attention to what I said. 'I love what I do,' I told him. 'I like helping people to be happy. What happens if this Cody person puts me out of business? These are tough times for small businesses. People aren't spending money freely right now. No one knows what the economy is going to be like next year, and I'm kind of a niche service. In a few years' time I'm nervous everyone will be tech savvy and they'll all be able to source their own romantic products. What if one day they won't need me any more?'

'I'm pretty sure we'll always need you, Daisy.' It was the nicest thing he'd said to me in a long time. Then I remembered that he'd also told me I was beautiful at the wedding. Was he thawing towards me, finally? Did I want him to? I waited in case there was a stinging punchline but none came. He got up, walked over to me and stretched out his arms. I hadn't been so close to him in years until we'd kissed the night before, but it didn't stop me from walking straight towards him and letting him draw me in for a hug. 'I think I get it,' he said finally. 'You're selling memories to people who were happier in the past and need to remember what it used to be like.'

The fact that he truly thought that this was the answer

was infuriating. I shoved him away. 'How can you find so many women to like you when you don't have the first clue about what we need to be happy and to feel desirable?' I asked him.

'It worked for you, once upon a time,' he responded.

'But not enough to keep me,' I pointed out. 'Not that you were ever bothered about that.'

He didn't reply, but set the earrings he'd been looking at back in their box and stowed it back behind the counter. He walked towards the door to the stairs but stopped before he headed back up. 'For what it's worth,' he said, 'I was bothered.'

He walked away, and I began to tidy up the last of the boxes that we'd taken out when he popped his head back round the door. 'Also, I forgot to say, the lingerie here is nice, but I prefer you in the red ones.'

Chapter Five

Eventually the anger I felt at Eli faded and was replaced by sadness. Every time I helped a couple to make a special memory for their future, I gave myself the opportunity to keep believing that love could last. It reassured me that one day I would find love just as my parents had, and that health allowing, my chance at love might last for the rest of my life. I wondered if Eli accepted that he could ever feel that way, or that a woman might feel that for him.

Then I got to thinking about Taylor. Love at first sight happened for some people, but I believed that for most of us, love grew over time until neither of you were whole without the other. It didn't scare me, therefore, that my feelings for Taylor weren't stronger. It had felt wonderful to dance with him at the wedding. I knew that I ought to ring him and thank him for coming to see me the day before, especially as I hadn't been able to talk to him properly due to Eli's public display of machismo, and yet all of sudden I could find a million jobs that I needed to do first.

One of my customers had suggested that I place an ad in a magazine that he read for senior gentlemen. He'd told me he always found shopping for his wife very stressful, and that she did all of their gift buying. The only person he had to think of was her, but this placed him under extreme pressure as he wanted to show that he appreciated the thought she went to for everyone else. He recommended that I offer my services as a personal shopper to source unusual and romantic gifts for men like him. I rang the advertisers at the magazine and realised that not only was

I far too late to advertise for Christmas, but in fact I only had a couple of days to send them the information I wanted in time for them to include me in their new year edition. Hopefully it would leave me in prime position to pick up customers who were starting to look for Valentine's Day gifts.

I dusted shelves and ordered new rolls of paper for the till. I even dug out all of my receipts and boxed them up neatly to deliver to my accountant, a woman around the corner who had been doing my books since I first started in return for a new item each birthday and Christmas for her husband's collections. He had a myriad of interests and it had become one of my favourite tasks. I had discovered a variety of amazing little auction houses where I merrily bid on bottled ships and snuff boxes. The year that I'd found a mint collection of cigarette cards featuring old *Doctor Who* memorabilia, not only had my tax return been completed for me, but Mrs Derwin had spent several evenings helping me set up savings accounts and start a pension. At the time Ben had teased me for being old and boring before my time, but I loved the security of knowing that my business might provide for my future as well as my present, if I could keep it going.

I'd already sourced a hand-crafted Victorian pipe for Mr Derwin for Christmas and was having fun searching on eBay and placing one or two bids for other items which would be useful in future, when my mobile rang. 'Have you had breakfast?' Lily asked me.

'Hours ago, but I'm about to take a huge culinary leap and make beans on toast for lunch if you want to join me?' The phone cut off abruptly in my ear, and a second later my front door opened.

'I brought coffees.' Lily handed me a takeaway cup

before tossing her jacket onto my bed. 'So when do we start snooping on Mr or Mrs Cody Rainbow?' she asked, as she pulled the bar stool out from behind my counter and sat herself by the till.

'How did you know that I was worrying about the new shop and its mysterious owner?'

'Because living with secret agents was bound to rub off on your somehow. Plus my boss was moaning about how much the overheads had gone up this year so I guess you'll be feeling the pinch too?'

I nodded to let her know how right she was. I took the five steps it needed to reach my kitchen and emptied a tin of beans into a bowl so that we could eat as we plotted. The microwave beeped as I set it to heat. As the bread toasted, I ran upstairs and fetched Ben's old laptop. 'For the purposes of making our research manageable without a trip to the States, which seems to be where most Codys live, I've narrowed it down to these five people.' I showed her. 'I'm making a huge assumption, any of the others could have come to the UK recently to set up "Picture Perfect".'

'We've got to start somewhere' Lily agreed. 'And if we do need to go to America there's this shop I've always wanted to go to. It has to be seen to be believed I'm told. They custom make movies that you can—'

I threw my hands up over my ears before she could finish the sentence. I didn't need to learn about anything that Lily had never seen before.

As we ate we took turns to run the five Codys through Ben's various databases. I suggested that we could safely ignore the fifteen-year-old girl who was in a Scottish boarding school while her mum worked as a CEO in London. Similarly, Lily felt that we were probably safe to exclude an eighty-five-year-old man whose last known address was a nursing home in Manchester.

'That leaves us with three Codys,' Lily surmised. She sent the files containing their previous addresses to the printer in my room. 'Do you want to split up and investigate them now, or shall we go together?'

'Don't you have to work?' I asked.

She shook her head. 'I broke up a fight over the last copy of a new reality show sensation's latest sex tape without anyone getting hurt and no stock being broken. The manager gave me a day off to say thank you. Word is that the stars made a fortune off the first one. I'm fairly sure we'll hear from him when the next one is ready to go too.' I waited for Lily to suggest that making a tape might be an easy way for me to solve my financial worries but luckily she didn't. Perhaps I'd finally convinced her it wasn't going to happen. 'This Cody is in London,' Lily said, shoving a piece of paper at me. 'Why don't we go?'

I wasn't sure what we planned to achieve exactly, but I knew spending time with my bestie was exactly what my state of mind needed. Plus it would take my mind off Eli. Who knows, maybe Lily was right and we'd discover who Cody was. I'd be a step closer to knowing just how worried I needed to be about Romantic Daze's future.

After we'd washed up I texted Ben to let him know our plans so that he wouldn't worry if my shop was shut at an unusual time. I locked the door and we headed for the tube. 'Are you sure you don't want to wear something more inconspicuous if we're trying to go undercover?' I asked, for at least the third time. Lily's leopard print skirt and boob tube were currently hidden under the black parka that I'd insisted that she borrow, more to ward off hypothermia than anything else, but her legs were still bare but for a pair of patterned tights which were more hole than fabric, and a pair of gold spike heels. My own clothing choices of a pale grey pinafore dress and lacy cream blouse were positively modest in contrast, but they made me feel professional. And just a little cute. Even if they too were hidden under a thick coat. There was a bitter wind despite the crystal-clear blue December skies. I took the red stripey elf ears off her head and we were ready to go.

Lily marched off at a speed I could barely match, even in my flat shoes. I hustled to keep up. 'So what's the plan now?' she asked as we got off the tube an hour later on the other side of town. 'Do we ring on the doorbell and give them a lecture about setting up on your turf?'

'No,' I told her. 'We cut down on the number of gangster films you watch, and then we wait here discreetly and see if we can catch a sight of Cody, work out what he or she is up to and find out whether it's going to impact on Romantic Daze.'

'I can be discreet,' Lily said, leaning against the wall until her coat fell open. A car driving past swerved, narrowly missing taking out a post box, as the driver took in her ensemble. I reached forward and buttoned the jacket up. Lily didn't notice and launched into a description of the brief relationship she'd had the previous year with a well-known politician to pass the time. 'I'm telling you, Daisy, if I weren't good at keeping secrets, the papers would have had a field day.'

'You got caught on film in a car in front of the Houses of Parliament,' I pointed out. 'The MP had to resign. In fact, the last I heard he had started working in a country with very limited internet access.'

'You have no idea what we got away with first though,' she said and winked at me.

It was tricky to be inconspicuous on a deserted residential street. The terraced houses were set back from the road behind tiny front gardens which on the whole contained more bins and gravel than they did actual plants. I wanted to peek through the lace curtains of Cody's house but I didn't dare in case any residents were to spot us and call the police. An hour later, the soles of my feet were beginning to ache and I needed to pee. 'Let's go and grab a drink,' I suggested.

'I know just the place,' Lily said, and led me to a pub around the corner.

'How did you know this was here?' I asked her. Not just because I'd never been to that part of London before, but also because it was so dark inside it was almost as though it were underground. I ordered a hot chocolate to warm myself up, and Lily asked for a double brandy to do the same. Her drink looked more tempting than mine when it came. The 'hot chocolate', if it could really be called that, had lumps of powder still undissolved floating on the surface. I pushed it away and bought us another round of spirits instead.

An hour later we arrived back at the house, in better frame of mind but a little too tipsy to be capable of melting into the background. Lily hoisted herself up onto the wall and sat there, kicking her legs. 'Maybe we should go,' I said. 'Even if Cody turns up, what are we going to say? Please don't sell anything I do. They'll laugh me into bankruptcy. Come on, tell me some stories and cheer me up. I'm drunk enough to cope with the details this time.'

Lily jumped off the wall, slung her arm around me and we walked back up the road towards the tube station. 'Let's go. For all we know Eli and Taylor will be wrestling naked outside your shop to win your hand.'

I turned and stared at her. 'I'm not sure either of them really wants my hand. Anyway, why would they be nude? It's freezing out.'

'It's your fantasy,' she said, shrugging her shoulders at me.

Chapter Six

'I didn't drink enough to be this hungover,' I groaned, as I woke up to find that my head was pounding. I tried to go back to sleep but it didn't happen. No surprise, my body was busy complaining about how badly I'd looked after it that afternoon. I murmured a silent apology and hoped it would forgive me with a minimum of further pain.

Lily and I had come back to my flat after our drinking session in the pub and had apparently collapsed top to tail on my bed for an impromptu nap. I shoved Lily's feet out of my face and sat up. The world had gone dark whilst we had slept. The oak trunk that functioned as my bedside table was covered in biscuit wrappers and empty mugs. We'd obviously had the munchies before we'd passed out too. I shifted them aside and switched on the little hurricane lamp which I'd found at an auction the previous spring.

Lily sat up and began to rub her eyes. Her curls were a little more dishevelled for the sleep and her skirt had ridden up even higher, though there hadn't been much of it to begin with. 'What did we interrupt?' said a voice from the doorway. 'Ben, I told you we should have come down five minutes ago.'

'Get out, Eli,' I shouted, picking up a teddy bear from the floor and throwing it at him.

'You have classy toys,' he said, catching it one-handed and using the other to poke at the toy's lacy underwear. 'We came to see if you needed any help with your reconnaissance, but I can see it's been going well.'

'We got cold so we went for a drink to warm up,' Lily explained.

'Then we had another because it turns out that hanging around waiting for someone to show is really, really boring,' I added. 'How do you do this all the time?'

'You think this is what we do for work?' Eli asked, his eyes shining as he laughed. 'So what's your next plan, Cagney and Lacey?'

I groaned, pulled a pillow over my head and laid down again.

'I'll help you investigate,' Ben offered.

I put the pillow back down and got up to give him a hug. 'You're the best little brother ever,' I told him.

'I'm literally two minutes younger than you,' he said, pushing me away. I tussled his hair until he shooed me off. 'I'm going to get my laptop.' He stomped off up the stairs and back to his own room.

Eli pointed at my bed. 'So is this a private party or can anyone join in?'

I stuck my tongue out and he headed off, grinning to himself. Lily yawned and stretched. Her tummy rumbled. She clearly felt less nauseous than I did.

'Why don't you head upstairs? I'll get us all some dinner.' Maybe the grease would help ease my hangover. Or it would kill me. Frankly either seemed okay at that point.

I went to fetch us all some fish and chips, grabbing a veggie burger for myself, and we reconvened a few minutes later in Dad's kitchen. 'Field surveillance isn't going to work,' I told them all. This was largely because Lily and I had no idea what we were doing, but also because it was nearly Christmas and I didn't like to leave my shop for too long if I could help it.

'I'm just going through their bank statements,' Ben said, without looking up from his screen. 'If any of them have used their cards locally we might be able to pinpoint which one is moving here.'

'Is that legal?' Lily asked. No one answered her, and she shook her head. 'Can you look anyone up? There's this guy who comes into my shop, he's got the biggest—'

'I don't want to know!' I told her. 'Don't investigate any strange men for Lily,' I ordered Ben.

'Spoilsport,' she said, taking a huge bite of her battered sausage.

Ben's mobile rang. He tore his eyes from the laptop to check the screen but didn't answer it. I'd have found it odd except that Ben generally preferred to text than to talk and rarely made calls himself. Eli noticed it too though.

'That was Erin ringing. Do we need to head into the office?'

Ben shook his head. 'It wasn't work. Don't worry.' He didn't say any more and didn't make eye contact with us so I didn't feel like I could ask about it, and I had a lot of questions, like why his friend from the wedding was ringing him? He was acting as though it wasn't unusual for him to be receiving calls from women that weren't about his unique and in-demand computer skills.

'No purchases nearby in the last few weeks,' Ben continued, as if nothing odd had happened.

'That doesn't mean anything,' Eli added. 'They might just be old-fashioned and prefer cash.' The doorbell rang. Eli opened the window and stuck his head outside. Leaning back in, he closed it and turned to me. 'I think you'd better go and answer it.' I assumed that meant it was Taylor. Eli didn't usually scowl at the thought of more guests.

My flat and Dad's shared a bell but we had our own front doors. It made it easier for us to receive deliveries yet retain our privacy. It took a moment to decide which home to let him in to, but eventually I decided on mine, more for the lack of audience than for the need to be alone with Taylor.

'Just passing again?' I asked him.

He grinned. It had started to snow, and it should have been romantic, him stood there in the dark clutching a bunch of flowers, and yet somehow it wasn't. Perhaps it was because on this occasion that Eli was correct that a bouquet didn't always equal romance. These flowers appeared to have been bought as an afterthought from a petrol station and were half dead. Then again, maybe the romantic gesture fell flat because everyone else had followed me downstairs and were now waving at Taylor over my shoulder.

'Come on in,' Lily bellowed. 'We've got more chips than we can eat.'

'Don't mind if I do,' he said, shaking the snow from his collar as he stepped inside. I moved back, accidentally landing on Eli's toes. He swore and stepped back too, knocking Ben onto his backside.

'Upstairs. Now,' I commanded. Back in the kitchen Taylor handed the flowers to Lily who hunted through Dad's kitchen until she found a jug which would suffice as a vase.

'I thought that given you were into all that romantic stuff I ought to make an effort,' he said. I wanted to tell him that he really shouldn't have worried, but I knew Eli was listening in so I didn't say a word.

'That's really thoughtful,' Lily told him, flashing him the smile, and the view of her bounteous cleavage. He tipped an imaginary hat in her direction and she fluttered her eyelashes in his direction. It took him a good few moments to turn his head back to me, and I realised that I didn't mind one bit.

'I'll hack into the council's website and see if I can find any requests for permits or licences,' Ben said.

'I'll pretend I didn't hear that,' Taylor muttered.

Ben was soon absorbed in his searches again. Eli slipped his hand into the pocket of his jet-black jeans and pulled out a shiny mobile phone. Not to be outdone, Taylor pulled out his own and soon all three men were lost in their work. I shrugged at Lily and handed her the bottle of ketchup. When Dad's football game finished on the TV and he shuffled in to find some food, they didn't even notice when I put the last of the dinner on a plate and handed it to him.

He sat with us at the table to eat, taking in the presence of a new fellow without any comment. He noticed, as did I, the occasional surreptitious glances that Eli would shoot across at Taylor, before tapping away on his phone again. Dad coughed gently to clear his throat, and rubbed his forehead with his hand. When he finally summoned up the courage to ask Lily how she was, I realised why he had been nervous. He wanted to be polite, but the last time he'd asked, she had launched into a spirited description of a new toy for gentlemen that she recently sold. Dad had gone so red in the face I was scared he'd have a heart attack. Thankfully today Lily was distracted from her tales as she was busy staring at Taylor.

Taylor wore tan chinos and a pale blue short-sleeved shirt. It was a simple outfit, but the trousers were a similar colour to his hair, and the shirt complemented his eyes. Of course, I suspected it was the combination of his sheer size and powerful physique that held my friend rapt. Quite how Taylor managed to get his muscles to flex when the only movement he was making was the tiniest of taps with his finger, I had no idea. I wouldn't have put it past him to know exactly what he was doing though, not least because it was two degrees below freezing outside, he hadn't bothered to wear a jumper and his jacket was over the back of a kitchen chair.

Lily muttered something about stakeouts being more interesting when you're drunk. Dad looked at me for an explanation but I shook my head. He must have decided that it was easier not to ask, as he looked down and continued to eat. Shortly after he'd finished the last chip, Ben closed his laptop with a decisive slam.

'Whoever this Cody is, either they're very good at covering their tracks online, or they're a ghost.'

'A what?' Lily asked.

'Someone who is as good at avoiding leaving a trail of breadcrumbs behind them online as I am, but that's doubtful. Very few people are that good.' If anyone else had said this I'd have called them egotistical, but in Ben's case it was most likely true.

'Maybe it's just someone who is too old to bother with all that internet nonsense?' Dad suggested. Ben looked at him as if he'd spontaneously spoken in Greek.

'Do you have an email address?' Taylor asked me. He handed me his phone and I tapped my details into it. 'If you hear a helicopter overhead don't worry. You'll get the report of the infra-red detection scan first thing tomorrow morning. Ditto for the drone fly over.' That was presumably the result of Taylor showing off in front of Eli, but if it got me answers I wouldn't say no.

'I've set up alerts on various sites that should let us know if this street is mentioned online, anywhere. Also if it's mentioned on various other ... erm—' Ben looked at Taylor before he finished his sentence '—totally legal and non-hacked websites.'

I began to pile up the dirty plates. Sometimes it was better to be able to deny any responsibility later. Like the time that I'd first launched my store and Ben had tried to help by hacking a competitor's website and redirecting all of their customers to my site instead. When their lawyers had tracked me down, I'd been able to prove that I was at a music festival with Lily with no internet access. There had also been no showers or clean toilets, but they weren't as upset by that as I was. I'd got home to find a very angry woman on my doorstep, who had thankfully accepted my confusion as genuine, and who was put off enough by my smell that she hadn't even wanted to come inside my flat and discuss it further. Ben had undone his promotional work and I'd escaped without legal action. That was my brother through and through, occasionally apt to make mistakes but only ever to try to help people he cared about. He had the biggest heart of anyone I knew and I loved him for it.

Taylor lifted his jacket from the back of the chair and pulled it on. 'I'd better go. Early start tomorrow.'

'At the gym?' Lily asked, licking her lips.

'Tracking down and assassinating enemies of the government?' I asked. Taylor winked at us and left without another word.

'I'll come over tomorrow morning and we can plan what action we're going to take,' Lily said. I put my head in my hands, dreading what she would come up with.

'And I've booked a week's holiday for us.'

'To Wales?' Ben asked. 'My favourite cottage might be free.'

'Only because the weather there will be freezing,' Eli pointed out. 'This is our chance to get some sunshine. If Ben gets any more pale he'll start glowing in the dark.' Eli put his phone back in his pocket.

'And how is that going to help Daisy?' Lily asked.

'I thought I'd get out of her hair for a little bit' he replied. So clearly Eli had noticed that he had been getting to me even more than normal, but I wondered if he could tell that the bickering felt a little different recently. I hadn't forgotten that he had called me beautiful or the way he had angled for a kiss under the mistletoe. Was he running away rather than letting us grow close again?

Chapter Seven

Lily said goodnight just as I ran the hot water in the sink and announced that it was time to do the washing up. Apparently she needed time to get her outfit sorted for work the next day. I didn't like to ask for any more detail than that, so I gave her a quick hug and told her that I'd see her in the morning. Dad looked exhausted too so I sent him to bed with a book and a mug of herbal tea. He complained that I was fussing, but he went anyway so I knew that he must have been really tired. Ben disappeared off claiming that he needed to plug his laptop in to charge, but a moment later I could hear what sounded very much like computer game noises coming from his room.

I dropped the last of the clean plates onto the rack to dry and rolled my shoulders to try and ease out the knots. 'You need a beer,' Eli told me. He crossed to the fridge and peeked inside. 'You need to buy some beer. Also some food, unless you can live on butter, gherkins, and jam.'

'I'll go grocery shopping in the morning,' I replied. 'Shortly before I get illegal intelligence on a random stranger who may or may not put me out of business.' I sighed and wondered how on earth I'd got myself into this one.

Eli shepherded me downstairs to my flat. There I fetched a couple of beers from my slightly better stocked selection and handed one across. The only chairs in my flat were a couple of bar stools set behind my glass counter so we perched on those. They weren't overly comfortable but it was that or sit on my bed, and that felt a little too intimate.

'So where are you off to on your holiday?' I asked. I could hear the resentment in my voice but Eli ignored it and answered me anyway.

'I thought about going to Magaluf.'

'Shagaluf?' I retorted. 'Figures.'

He continued to ignore my petulance. 'But I checked and it's only around ten degrees at this time of year. So I booked us a week in Cyprus. We'll be back in plenty of time for you to get ready for Christmas.' Not that my dad or Ben bothered much with decorations but I usually put a little Christmas tree on the kitchen counter and some tinsel around the TV. It was a token effort but my dad wouldn't have managed much more cheer. 'It won't be sunbathing weather,' Eli continued, 'but it'll be warmer than here. I can't wait to feel some sunshine on my face again.' He lifted his chin as if he were catching the rays from my ceiling light. 'I need it, Dais,' he said, and I looked at the exhaustion on his face and the tension in his body. He did need the break, but it didn't mean that it would be easy on those of us left behind.

'Have fun,' I told him. 'I'll just stay here, try and keep my shop open, look after my dad ...'

'Oh, I booked for your dad too,' Eli said. 'He looked so down at tea-time.'

'I didn't realise you'd noticed,' I said. 'He's been pretty down all the years you've known him to be fair.' Eli reached across and squeezed my hand quickly for reassurance as I spoke. I could feel the warmth even after he's let go again.

'I should have checked whether he had a passport before I booked, but I know someone who works in that department who should be able to speed things along if not.'

'He got one last year when he went to Canada to see his sister,' I reminded Eli.

'Did he enjoy that trip?'

'He didn't pack a warm enough coat, and wouldn't let Auntie Jean buy him one until he'd spent half a day in hospital with suspected pneumonia. Also, he didn't sleep on the plane, in either direction, so when he got home it took him a fortnight to recover from the jetlag. Don't you remember Ben looking like a zombie for most of last February because Dad woke him up by watching films at three a.m.?'

'I'll get Ben to assign our seating,' he said. 'I'm sure he'll be able to ... persuade ... their system to find your dad a decent seat.'

'And you too,' I scoffed.

'I'm happy in a regular seat,' he replied. 'Even though they don't have a lot of leg room for guys my height.' He stood up and did a slow circle, in part to show how tall he was, but mostly I was sure to draw my eye to his body. If so, it worked. He sat back on the seat. 'Ben's just been a bit quiet lately. I figured what he needs is a few days in the sun with his best friend. Then I saw your dad this evening and thought that it wouldn't do him any harm to come too. I got a bonus for a job well completed last month. I thought I'd treat them.' That must have been the job that had left him looking so drained.

I set my empty bottle on the counter top and threw my arms around him. It surprised me as much as it did him I'm sure, being such a change from our usual bickering, but I was touched by his kindness, and recent days had brought a definite thawing in our relationship. Or lack of relationship.

'Thank you for being so thoughtful,' I said. My nose

was an inch from his. I noticed a small graze under his chin where he'd nicked himself shaving. Before I realised what I was doing, I leant forward and placed a gentle kiss against it. I felt his hands drop lower onto my waist, encircling me tightly with his arms, and as they grazed my bottom, he froze and pulled back. 'I'll get us another drink,' I said, hopping off my stool and dashing to the kitchen.

Opening the door of the fridge, I waited for the chilled interior to take the heat and redness from my face. 'Don't fall in,' Eli called out, so I reached inside and grabbed the last two bottles. I stood back to close the door and bumped straight into him. 'Sorry,' he said. 'I didn't mean to make you jump.'

He stood, toe to toe with me, our chests pressed against each other. My hands were full, but his arms were empty and he took me into them once more. This time it was his turn to kiss me, which he did gently and sweetly. Also, frustratingly quickly, and before I could react, he'd taken his drink from me, opened it and begun to walk away.

I opened my own bottle, and took a long swallow. Despite his reticence, Eli hadn't left, and was now wandering around the shop again, looking in drawers and boxes. I turned back to my cabinet and found a box of snacks. Slamming a package in the microwave, the kitchen was quickly filled with the sound of popping and the smell of buttery popcorn.

'Do you want to watch a film?' I asked Eli. I didn't wait for an answer but walked into my bedroom and began to boot up my laptop and hoped that he would follow. I didn't want him to leave, despite having no idea what was going on between us. In all the years since we'd been intimate, he'd shown no signs of wanting to be close to me again. More than that, we'd spent the time sniping at each other. I wasn't sure now whether he was just testing his luck again, or whether this was something more. I'd seen Eli in action, stalking women at bars and clubs as if they were prey, and more often than not his elegant and striking predator mode was successful. I'd never seen him hesitate before. Watching a movie seemed to be a good way of spending time with him but without putting any pressure on either of us.

There was a beeping in the kitchen, and I heard the microwave door open and close. And then Eli was stood at the door to my room, bowl in hand. 'Sorry,' I told him, patting my bed, 'there aren't any chairs.'

'Budge up then,' he said, sitting next to me. He kicked his shoes off, and we lay, side by side, socked feet up by the pillow and heads resting on hands, arms bent at the elbow. 'You're going to make me watch something really girly now, aren't you?'

'Was there ever any doubt?'

'I could go upstairs and borrow an action film from Ben,' he suggested.

'He'd probably come and watch it too,' I pointed out. Eli made a low grunting sound, but he stayed where he was. I wondered why he suddenly wanted to be alone with me, but tried to concentrate on the film and not obsess about it. I'd wasted a lot of my teenage years on that topic already. It was no use though, and I spent the next hour and a half conscious every time Eli moved of how close he was to me.

By the end of the film, the heroine was safely married to her dream man. I was wiping tears from my eyes and Eli was staring at me with a look of shocked incomprehension on his face. 'That was …' he began.

'Beautiful,' I supplied. 'Heart-warming'.

'I was going to say cheesy and predictable,' he complained.

'How can you say that?' I asked, moving the now empty bowl to the floor so that I could swipe his arm.

'She spent the entire film dodging disasters. I've never seen a character be so unlucky.'

'She overcame obstacles in order to have the wedding of her dreams,' I responded.

'The dress got burnt, the venue got flooded. Even the groom only arrived just in time and minus his eyebrows. Honestly, why didn't they just admit defeat and give up? Or failing that, just fly to Vegas and get married by Elvis?'

'I guess guys don't dream of having the perfect wedding,' I muttered.

'Not all women do either,' he pointed out. 'Just the ones that you meet here. No wonder you're biased to believe all that true love crap.'

'And you're not biased?' I scoffed. 'Don't you think that there's a chance that you might settle down one day, once you're done sowing your wild oats, obviously. You might fall in love and have your own happily ever after?'

Eli sat up and swung his legs over the side of the bed until he was facing away from me. 'I'm glad that you believe, and I think you'll find love,' he told me. I didn't tell him that I had once before and it hadn't made me happy, but he continued to speak. 'You're beautiful, any man would be lucky to have you. But me, no, I can't see any happy ever afters in my life.' It was both astounding to hear him saying such nice things about me, and heart-breaking that he didn't predict the same happiness for himself. I decided to provoke him further and see what happened.

'And if that man were to be Taylor?' I said.

He turned to face me. 'Do you actually fancy Taylor?' he asked. I didn't answer, and he began to grin.

'I didn't say no,' I told him. He laughed, stopping only when he reached over to tuck a strand of hair behind my ear. When he kissed me again, this time without holding back, I stopped talking too.

Chapter Eight

I woke up to an empty bed, but Eli had left me a still steaming cup of coffee on the trunk. He couldn't have been gone long. A million thoughts spun through my mind. What had I done? Well, I could remember that, vividly, in several different positions. But why had we slept together after all of this time? And what did it mean that Eli had left, but not without doing something thoughtful first? I reached for my mobile and checked the display, blinking as the screen lit up the dimness of the room.

No messages. I took a sip of coffee and got up, telling myself that it was because I was hungry, and not just in case Eli had left a note anywhere else in the flat. He hadn't. I wanted to soak in the bath, but I didn't want to risk Ben and Dad seeing me first if I were to go upstairs. Not that they could tell from looking at me what I'd been up to. Well, Ben wouldn't anyway. Instead I took a long, hot shower, trying to ease the ache from my tired muscles.

Afterwards I got dressed in comfy old jeans and favourite hoody. I sliced a couple of bagels and dropped them into the toaster. I chopped some fruit and grabbed a yogurt too. I needed it. We'd burnt a lot of calories over night. I was just smothering the bagels in butter when my front door opened. 'Daisy?'

'I'm in the kitchen, Lily,' I called out, though by the time I finished saying it she'd taken two steps into the flat and could see me. She looked at me and shook her head.

'You've got enough breakfast here for two people. Where's Taylor?'

'No idea,' I told her.

'Hence the baggy clothes. Is this covering up some weird reaction to finally getting lucky again?' I blushed, and she whooped loudly and gave me a huge hug. 'I always know when people have done it. So, how was he? Tell me everything, and I mean *everything*. Is he as big as he looks? And I don't mean his height.' She swiped half a bagel from my plate.

'It was amazing,' I admitted, taking a sip of my drink.

Lily stretched up and waited until I hit her hand in a high five. 'I knew it, but he left first last night. Did he come back? Did you booty call him? You dawg. I didn't know you had it in you. Well, I could tell from the satisfied expression on your face that you'd had it in you, but you know what I mean.' Her eyes were shining with excitement. In fact, I hadn't seen her buzzed so early in the morning since the last time she went clubbing and she stopped by for breakfast before she went home to crash.

I spun away, suddenly gripped by the need to find a jar in the depths of the cupboard. 'It wasn't Taylor,' I said, my back still turned. I waited whilst she absorbed this, taking my time, spreading peanut butter on my breakfast. I was on my third bite before she spoke again.

'Eli?' she asked.

I nodded. 'Still want me to tell you all the details?' I asked. She waved her hand at me as if she were wafting away a bad smell.

'I thought you swore off him ages ago? He's so ...'

'Handsome, thoughtful?' I remembered how he'd swapped food with me at the wedding so that I had something to eat.

'I was going to say that he doesn't exactly buy into the same monogamous lifestyle that you dream of,' she said, which was more gentle than I expected her to be. Hell, if she'd hooked up with a guy who had broken her heart ten years earlier I don't think I'd have pulled my punches.

I finished my coffee and stomped towards the bathroom to brush my teeth, but as that only took about two minutes, it didn't make much of an impact. Afterwards Lily made me swap my baggy sweatshirt for a cute jumper, then she French plaited my hair to make me look a little more grown up and professional. Finally she nagged me until I put on lipstick and mascara, claiming that I still looked like a teenager.

'What are you doing here so early?' I asked her.

'What with the men all going so high-tech last night, I thought maybe you and I could go old school.' She shook a rucksack off her back. It was made of camouflage material and didn't coordinate with anything in her wardrobe. 'I bought it on the way here,' she explained.

'And you thought you'd melt right into the jungle background of a busy city street?'

She ignored my sarcasm and started to unpack it. 'Binoculars,' she said, handing me a pair. 'Refreshments.' She took out cans of soft drinks and bars of chocolate and stacked them on the counter.

'So where are we going on our stakeout?'

'That's the best part,' she said. 'Right here. We don't even know whether we had the right Cody before so there's no point trekking half way back across London again. It could be a wild goose chase, so I figured instead of trying to find Cody, why not wait here for Cody? Whoever it is, they'll turn up sooner or later to get their shop set up I thought I'd take the first shift, pull one of those bar stools over and watch out of the front window.'

'And that won't be visible at all,' I said snarkily. Lily

63

ignored me. She deserved to. Hers was probably the most sensible idea I'd heard yet.

'It'll be great. We won't get cold, we have access to a bathroom whenever we need it.'

'I can see the advantages,' I admitted. 'Do you think we'll find out anything useful?'

'Won't know until we try it,' she said, turning to look at me without lowering the binoculars. 'I think you have stubble rash on your cheek.'

I was bent over my bathroom sink trying to see if Lily was right when my front door opened again. 'Hello, sir. How may I help you today?' Lily seemed to have my customer in hand, so I took the time to dig out an ancient tube of concealer. By the time I emerged, Lily was putting his credit card details through the till, before wrapping his purchases up into a stack of boxes and tying them into a pyramid with a red ribbon.

'Was that Mr Robinson?' I asked.

'He told me to call him Bert,' she said.

'He's been in every year since I opened. Never bought more than a box of chocolates.'

'This year he decided that he also needed a pair of leather gloves, a scarf and a tray of those expensive truffles you showed me. Though of course you only let me eat one.'

'That box costs as much as a week of groceries,' I said. My mouth dropped open as she handed me the copy of the till receipt. 'Feel free to help out in here while you're doing your surveilling,' I told her.

Two hours later we'd eaten all the chocolate that Lily had brought with her, finished the cans of pop and emptied my fridge. 'I'm going to the supermarket,' I told her, giving her a quick one-armed hug.

When I got back home with so much shopping that I'd

had to call a cab, Lily was rearranging the night gowns. 'I sold quite a few of these this morning. Did you have more in stock?' I shook my head and began to put packs of vegetables away. 'You could try ordering some from that stall you liked the look of at the trade show. I have their card somewhere.' She began to paw through her purse to try and find it.

'For the record, I didn't like those knickers. I was just trying to work out which were the leg holes and which were the bonus ones.'

She grinned and I threw her a box of truffles. 'They're just the supermarket version,' I apologised, 'but if business carries on like this I'll be able to afford the posh ones for you next time.'

I took a shift at the window after that while Lily had a rest. She was supposed to be having a nap as she'd be working in her own shop until midnight, but she was obviously wide awake as she asked me every thirty seconds whether I had heard from Eli yet and if I was okay. The answer to both questions was no, but I didn't want to admit it out loud so I just told her to go to sleep and continued to stare out of the window. I was almost comatose myself when a car pulled up outside.

I shouted for Lily, and she was next to me in seconds, yawning and rubbing her eyes. I pointed at the sleek black BMW that had parked right outside my door. 'Do you think it belongs to Cody Rainbow?' I asked.

The back door opened and Eli stepped out. 'Maybe he's come to whisk you on a romantic date?' Lily suggested. 'Maybe he wants to take you out for a fancy dinner and these are his wheels?'

I surprised myself by hoping that she was right, but I was cruelly disappointed when instead of knocking on my door, he knocked on my dad's. When Ben came down with a holdall, I pulled my boots on and left the flat.

'Hi,' I said, wanting to ask more but not wanting to give away how confused I felt. 'Where are you going?'

'Holiday,' Ben said, opening the boot and dumping his bag into it. 'Eli booked it yesterday, remember? You were there. And you think I'm oblivious.'

'I didn't realise that you were leaving so soon,' I said, glancing from Ben to Eli. Eli looked down at his shoes for a beat before walking round to face me. He was about to speak, when Dad called him in to help carry his suitcase down. I wasn't sure that Eli needed to sprint off quite so quickly to help, but perhaps he didn't know exactly what to say to me either.

'The Boss said she wants Eli fresh and ready to go on a new project in January so she said better to go now and get it over and done with,' Ben said, as though a holiday was something to be endured rather than enjoyed. I hoped that Eli would enjoy it, because as much as I wanted answers about what had happened the night before, I knew he needed a break. I ducked back into my flat and put the snacks that I'd bought for Ben and Dad into a bag. I added some bottles of water and made it back out just as Dad was climbing into the car. He stroked the shiny roof as he slid onto the leather seat next to the driver, and I was shocked to see that he was grinning.

I walked round to the back of the car and opened Ben's door to hand him the bag of snacks and a packet of his travel sickness tablets. 'Make sure you look after yourself til you get back.'

He rolled his eyes at my worrying, but he completed our saying nonetheless. 'Look after yourself too. Seriously, Dais, we're not going to the Moon.'

I kissed his cheek then dodged out of the way before he could shut the door on me. I crossed my arms around myself, partly against the wind and partly against the feelings of loneliness. I knew that they all needed the break though and so I tried not to let them see that I was anything other than happy for them. Eli checked that the boot was closed and ran through his checklist with Ben. Passport, credit card, no illegal programmes on his laptop in case they got stopped at customs.

My teeth started chattering but I wasn't ready to wave them off yet. As he walked towards me I could see the fine lines of tiredness around Eli's eyes that I hadn't noticed the day before. As hurt as I was that he was leaving before we had chance to talk, I tried to reassure myself that perhaps it wasn't me he was running away from. He'd woken several times in the night and though we'd made the most of being awake together, I had wondered if it was stress as much as passion that had contributed.

'Are you sure that Ben won't get into trouble for taking time off at short notice?' I asked.

'I promise you I cleared it with the office for him too. Besides, they have separate rules for Ben at work,' Eli said, walking towards me. He took the scarf off from around his neck and wrapped it around mine. 'You know everyone else in the office wears a suit to work?'

I shook my head. Apart from the recent wedding I'd never seen Ben in anything smarter than a T-shirt with no swear words on it. 'They do,' Eli continued. 'The men all wear ties.' I looked at his choice of holiday outfit – a pale grey shirt and blue jeans which had been perfectly ironed. Even his casual clothes had an elegance about them. 'The women,' he continued, 'can choose from trousers or skirts, but they are worn with tailored blouses and jackets, not sweaters. We got a new boss last year. We were sitting down for a team meeting when she noticed that Ben was wearing a Sonic the Hedgehog T-shirt. She asked where his suit was. He stood up, walked out without another word, and when he got back an hour later, dressed in a new suit that he'd just gone out and bought, he walked in to the middle of the meeting as if nothing had happened and sat down. She shouted at him so loudly afterwards that I could hear it from outside the room with the door shut. The next day he turns up in an Iron Maiden T-shirt. She walks into a meeting room half way through his presentation. When he stops to take questions, she asks where his suit is. He walks out, goes home and gets it on. That time it took him an hour and a half. He gets back to work, goes into the meeting room and doesn't understand why no one is still there.'

I shook my head. 'Some days I can't believe that he hasn't been fired yet.'

'The third day,' Eli continued 'it's a *Monty Python* T-shirt. By lunchtime, he's installed a code that he's written that makes the bank accounts of a group of terrorists look to other agencies as if we've frozen them. Our American colleagues have been pressuring us to do this but we'd been resisting because we wanted to trace where the money was flowing to and from. Ben's code was amazing. It has a second level which made it appear to those using the accounts that their money was arriving and leaving, but it was a ghost, a shadow. No money ever changed hands, but we could see every transaction that they were trying to make. A suspicious transaction took place that afternoon, the boss organised an impromptu raid. We scored the biggest cache of weapons ever found on British soil.' By this point I was grinning in pride at my brother's achievement. I loved it when other people got to see how amazing Ben was too. Anyone who judged him on a few socially awkward behaviours missed seeing what an enormous heart and incredible mind he possessed. It was their loss. I felt very, very lucky to have him.

'So on the fourth day,' Eli told me, 'the boss turns up, hands Ben a bag with a bunch of *Doctor Who*, *Star Wars* and *Star Trek* T-shirts in it, tells him to keep up the good work and never questions him again. But if it makes you feel better, I sent her an email yesterday before I booked the tickets saying that we needed a break and got her authorisation before I booked a thing.'

I threw my arms around him and hugged Eli close, before realising that he might take it the wrong way, or maybe it was the right way, but whichever, I let go and stepped back again. I was about to wish him a safe trip, when Ben wound the window down. 'Come on,' he shouted. 'You said on our last holiday that you liked to be by the pool with a drink in one hand and a girl in the other by dinnertime.'

My heart sank. It was my own fault though. It was barely twelve hours since he'd told me that he didn't believe in happy ever after love. I shouldn't have got my hopes up that he had changed his mind already. I spun on my heels and walked back inside my shop. Sinking to the floor, I dropped my head onto my hands and sobbed. Lily sat next to me, put her arm around me and rocked me.

Chapter Nine

Lily offered to call in sick and stay with me instead of going to work, but I didn't want to get her into trouble. She was reluctant to leave, and promised to call later that evening, but I told her that I was going to keep busy and not wallow in self-pity any more. She didn't believe me. The red eyes and sniffly nose were probably a pretty strong clue that I wasn't at my best, but nonetheless she left without another word when I shooed her out the door.

Back inside, I turned the sign on my shop to read 'closed', stripped the sheets off my bed and took them upstairs to Dad's house to wash them. I treated myself to a long hot bath at the same time, and after setting the laundry to tumble dry, I went back down to brave my own flat again. I remade the bed with a batch of the new sheets that I'd bought at the trade show. I shouldn't really have used them, they were Egyptian cotton and hideously expensive, but I wanted to remove the scent and memory of having Eli in my bed.

Seeing the bed looking luxurious and clean made me realise what a muddle the rest of the room was in. I straightened piles of books, folded clean clothes and put them away, and found a discarded mug under a nightie on the floor. I couldn't remember how long it had been there, and it kick-started me into a full cleaning binge. By the time Lily phoned me a couple of hours later, I'd scrubbed my flat and was wondering what to clean next.

The doorbell rang just as I was bleaching my tiny bathroom. I bumped my head on the sink in surprise, and peeked out the window to see who it might be. There was a young man in motorbike leathers stood waiting, and for a split second I wondered if Lily had sent him to cheer me up, though it was the kind of surprise that she would prefer more than I would. Finally, I realised that he was holding a flat box, at least eighteen inches from side to side.

I stripped off the yellow gloves I'd been wearing and sprinted down to open the door. 'You have the wrong address,' I told him, but as the wafts of cheese and tomato hit my nose my mouth began to water and I wished that I had been organised enough to phone in an order.

He reached into his pocket for a piece of paper and read my address from it. 'Super large Veg supreme,' he said. 'Already been paid for, receipt says it was ordered by a Miss Lily?'

I thanked him and took the box. Lily answered her mobile on the third ring, though I presumed that she wasn't talking to me when she said 'The strawberry dick lick will be all you need for dessert, trust me.'

'And there was me thinking that I'd be full after this giant pizza.'

'It arrived then? I wanted to make sure that you weren't too heartbroken to eat,' she said, and I spent so long telling her how thoughtful she was and how much she meant to me, that she had to remind me to eat it before it got cold. I offered to bring the pizza to her shop so that she could share it with me, but she told me not to bother. 'It's a full moon tonight,' she said by way of explanation, then added when I didn't understand, 'people get up to all sorts at full moon.'

I had thought that the whole point of her shop was that people got up to all sorts all of the time, but I still wanted to check she was alright being there. 'Are you sure you're okay at the shop?'

'Are you kidding? I've racked up enough sales tonight that if we didn't open again 'til next week we'd still have done well.' She began shouting to another customer to stop using up all the batteries, and I thought she'd forgotten that I was still there, until finally she came back on the line, apologised and said that she'd call me again soon.

Truthfully, if she hadn't have sent the pizza, I wasn't sure that I would have got round to feeding myself properly, but given that there was food in front of me it took less effort to make myself eat. It felt quiet without Dad and Ben in the house, even though usually we had at least one supposedly locked door between us, so I went upstairs to their flat, switched the TV on and curled up in Dad's favourite armchair. It smelled of his aftershave and made them feel just a little closer. I wondered whether Eli had made good on his plans to be hooked up with alcohol and women already, but it made me feel sick so I turned the programme up louder in case it could drown out those thoughts. It didn't work.

Perhaps having my dad there would make him tone down his game. It was hard to look suave when your company was a prematurely aged senior citizen, who had been depressed for around twenty years, and who was likely to ask girls if they were cold if he saw one in a short skirt. Ben wasn't the most reliable wing man either. We were at a club once, and Eli was midway through reeling in a striking blonde woman who was six-feet tall and could have been a model. Ben walked over, handed Eli a beer and asked whether this was the woman he'd been talking about bedding the day before.

Eli had taken the slap to the face without spilling a drop, I had laughed until I almost wet myself and we'd ended up back at Lily's bedsit trying to agree on a drinking game and attempting to ignore how grumpy Eli was. Lily had wanted to play 'I have never,' which is when you take a shot whenever anyone suggests an act that you haven't tried. Ben and I usually ended up wrecked when we played, Lily often grew more sober throughout the game, and I tried not to get upset when I found out just what Eli had been up to. So we'd watched a *James Bond* film instead and downed vodka every time he'd drunk on screen. It had been two days before we'd all felt human again.

Thinking of how my dad and Ben might hamper Eli's plans cheered me up. I managed to demolish half of the pizza and put the rest in my small fridge. Back in my room, I was glad that I'd cleaned up. The bed, with its new pale pink sheets covered in tiny embroidered flowers looked suitably different from the night before when Eli had been with me, and I surprised myself by managing to fall asleep quite quickly.

My phone woke me early the next morning, and I reached for it, hoping that it might be a message from Eli before I came round enough to berate myself for being weak. To test my resolve, I made myself shower, drink a coffee and eat a slice of cold pizza before I looked at my text. I'd apparently slept through various other beeps too. Lily had written to me at three a.m. to say that she had just gotten home and wouldn't be with me until later that day. The message that had woken me was from Taylor, and I felt guilty as I opened it.

It was hard not to compare the men in my life. Taylor, with his muscles and his easy smile. As opposed to Eli and his more compact form. Still strong and hard-bodied, but his power hidden beneath his elegant clothes. Darkness and light. Taylor's sparkling blue eyes. Eli's smoky, the colour of jet when he was angry. Eli who set my heart racing when he touched me, who flew away from me without a backward glance. Taylor who seemed keen, with his half-dead flowers and offers of help. We hadn't even kissed, let alone been on a proper date, yet I still felt dishonest.

I knew that I should talk to him and try to clarify our situation, but I wasn't sure what to say. If I cared about Eli this deeply, was it dishonest not to let Taylor down gently as soon as I could? I clicked his message open, and was relieved to find that instead of confusing me further, he'd simply forwarded the report from the fly overs that he had arranged.

The UV sensor hadn't detected any unusual displays on my street, but apparently had registered some interesting findings on its approach, leading to the police going in and finding a marijuana farm in the roof of a building two roads away. With that success, Taylor offered that he could request a further study if I wanted him too. I took a few moments to compose my reply carefully. I thanked him for his help but told him not to worry. I didn't think we were likely to find out much more about the mysterious Cody from the air.

It was signing off the email which stymied me for the longest time. Taylor had signed off with just his name, and I was tempted to do the same but it felt too formal. I added a kiss, then deleted it again. Finally I settled on adding a smiley emoji and sent it before I could worry about it any further.

My phone beeped again before it even got as far as my pocket, and I was hesitant to see whether Taylor had been waiting for me to reply. Instead it was my dad. A man of few words these days, he'd sent me a photo. He and Ben were sat by the pool. The sky was a beautiful cerulean blue, but Dad had learnt his lesson from Canada and had his coat on regardless. Ben was wearing a Hawaiian shirt and holding a glass of something pink. The drink appeared to be filled with so many pieces of fruit and umbrellas – and even what looked like a sparkler – that it would be a miracle if he could get close enough to the glass to drink it. I Googled to check what the time difference was. Cyprus was only two hours ahead, so it was barely lunchtime there, but they were on holiday and I was glad to see them looking relaxed.

Eli wasn't in the photo so I couldn't see whether the lines around his eyes had already softened for being away. I hoped that was because he was taking the photo, and not because he was already busy with a hook up. I couldn't stop thinking about him. Time to open the shop and hope for a day busy enough to distract me.

I checked the online calendar where I tracked my appointments. Noting that I had Mr King due in shortly, I cleared the remains of my breakfast away, straightened my black skirt, smoothed the front of my turquoise roll neck, and put the kettle on. As always, he was punctual, arriving at ten on the dot, and dressed as sharply as ever in a blue pin-stripe suit with pink shirt and white collar. His hair, slightly more grey than it had been at his previous visit six months before, was cut with a military precision. I made him a cup of coffee and let him browse the store. Half an hour later, I made him a second drink and tried to help him narrow down what he was after.

'Have you thought about buying Mrs King a new handbag for Christmas?' I asked.

'Got her one for her birthday,' he said, flicking through the pages of my new bedding catalogue.

'Perfume?'

'Says it makes her nose run,' he said.

75

I remembered why I usually planned his appointments for the end of the day, so that I could go to the pub afterwards to unwind, but he had meetings at his bank all afternoon and insisted that I squeeze him in.

'Jewellery?' I got a blue velvet tray out from underneath the till. 'I found this antique silver brooch just a couple of weeks ago. I've polished it until it shines. It's set with rubies.' I showed him the small pin in the shape of a harp with sparkling stones set in a line.

He barely glanced at it before he shook his head. 'She prefers gold?' I asked. 'No problem. How about this?' I showed him a ring, set with a pearl, surrounded by golden leaves.

'She says she has more rings than fingers to put them on,' he said, waving away my suggestions.

'Earrings? I have some beautiful diamond studs. Chocolates?'

'Diabetes.'

'A silk dressing-gown? I carry a range of sizes and colours.'

'She's got several.'

I shook my head and began to wonder whether I could get away with making myself a drink like Ben's. We'd looked at and rejected my range of porcelain figurines, candles and toiletries, when Lily arrived. She kissed Mr King on the cheek, and I wondered briefly whether she was being polite or whether she already knew him from her place of work too, though I suspected that if she did, she wouldn't have seemed so pleased to meet him again. Helping herself to a cup of coffee and a slice of pizza, she pulled her stool up to the window and dug out her binoculars again.

Mr King began to look through the range of romantic

CDs and vinyl that I stocked. My stomach rumbled and I offered him a sandwich as I wanted to make one for myself. I tried not to groan when he thanked me and said that he'd love one, knowing that it meant that he was nowhere near finished yet.

After an hour of watching an empty road, Lily gave up her surveillance and joined in trying to help me sell something, anything, to Mr King. As much as I felt that online stores lacked the personal touch that my customers valued, I could suddenly see the advantages of their approach. Finally, I asked him whether he was sure that he had even come to the correct shop, given that he'd looked through everything but the teddy bears without finding anything he liked.

'Teddies?' Mr King said, putting his empty plate back on the counter.

'Oh, they're not what you think,' I said, wishing I could take back my hasty words.

'I want to see them,' he said, sitting back on his stool and crossing his ankles and his arms. His tone of voice left no room for dissent.

I went into my room and pulled the box out from where I'd hidden it under my bed. I looked inside. There were twenty bears, several were wearing leather, a couple had some wisps of lace. The rest held a variety of sex toys. They were unsuited to my product range, and I was nervous that Mr King would be too scared to ever come back to my shop again.

That decided it, and tucking the box under my arm, I carted it back out to the counter. Setting the toys out one by one, Mr King began to smile when he saw the first, and by the time I drew out the last one, he was laughing so hard he was holding his sides.

'I'll take them,' he said.

'These are a specialist item,' Lily said. 'And the last of Daisy's stock. It won't be cheap.'

He shot his arms out in front of him and straightened his cuffs. I took in the gold cufflinks with diamond inlays. It was his subtle way of telling us that price was not a factor for him. Lily got it too, as she began to type numbers into the till whilst I wrapped each bear into an individual gift bag.

'Gladys will love these. They'll appeal to her sense of humour,' he said, handing over a gold credit card. I nearly yelped when I noticed what Lily was charging him, it was at least five times what the bears had cost, but when she passed him the keypad he entered his PIN number without blinking. 'I'll see you in February to buy her a Valentine's present,' he said, picking up his bags. Lily opened the front door for him, and he struggled out, his arms full of parcels.

'I think we overcharged him,' I said, tidying up after our working lunch.

'How many hours did it take to make that sale?'

'Three,' I told her. 'Though each felt like it lasted an eternity. What on earth can I sell him for Valentine's Day?'

'There's another trade show in Birmingham in a few weeks,' Lily said, 'though this one is a little more wild.' I thanked her for the thought but suggested that she go without me next time.

'I still think you earned the money,' she said.

'Couldn't have done it without you,' I told her, opening the till. I counted out a bunch of notes until I had half of the profit from the teddy sale and handed it to Lily.

She squealed and hugged me. 'How long before your next appointment?' she asked.

I glanced at my watch and panicked. 'About three

minutes,' I said, sweeping crumbs into my hand and dropping them into the bin. A few dropped to the floor, and as I reached down to pick them up, I noticed one last teddy that must have fallen on the floor when we'd unpacked the box. We hadn't charged Mr King for it, so I tucked it into my handbag and decided to keep it as a good luck mascot. Plus, it had a huge furry boner, and there was really nowhere in my flat that I wanted to put it in case anyone else were to see it.

The door opened, and we both turned to greet my next customer. Where Mr King was all about crisp lines and ironed creases, Arthur came in wearing a brown woolly jumper, baggy cord trousers that were thinning at the knees and hiking boots. He apologised for the trail of mud that he left behind him. I offered him a pair of slippers, and Lily brought him a stool whilst I grabbed a dustpan and brush. Arthur had first stumbled upon my shop a couple of years earlier after attempting to shop alone on Tottenham Court Road on the last Saturday before Christmas to buy a gift for his wife. He had wandered down my road hoping to find a quiet pub to rest and recover after failing to find anything and becoming overwhelmed by the crowds. I'd given him a glass of my dad's brandy and let him sit down for half an hour without saying more than a dozen words. Finally, he had begun to talk about how important it was that he find the right gift, but that he never wanted to experience those hordes again. Eventually he had calmed down enough to look around him, and after helping him choose a new nightie, a box of chocolates and a floral bone china cup, he had hugged me goodbye and promised to come back next time he wanted to buy his wife a gift.

On this visit he oohed and ahhed over the pearl ring, before admiring a silver topaz brooch in the shape of a cat and a bottle of rose-scented hand lotion. He told us that roses had been their special flower since their first date when he had turned up with a single yellow rose. When he told us that it had been all that he could afford, but to make up for it, on their anniversary he bought a bouquet with one rose for every year that they had been together, even Lily had to wipe away a tear. He said he couldn't wait until June when he would get to finally give her a bouquet of fifty. I showed him an 18-carat gold rose-shaped brooch that I'd found in an antique shop in Covent Garden and he put the cat down and picked that up instead.

Lily showed him the sheets with roses embroidered on it and he ordered a set of those too. When he showed her the photographs of his grandchildren, she showed him the range of photo frames made from reclaimed wood that I stocked. I rang his purchases up at the till, though Lily was having such a good time I suspected that she wouldn't have dreamt of marking his sales up as highly as she did for Mr King. This time, I knocked five per cent off for what I liked to call my 'nice client discount'.

Arthur sat down to put his shoes back on, huffing and puffing as he leant over to tie the laces. 'So what do you lovely ladies have planned for this afternoon?' he asked. I bit my tongue before I could explain that I'd probably spend it wondering and worrying about Eli. Instead, Lily showed him her binoculars and explained that we were watching the road to find out about my new neighbour.

'I promise that no matter what opens up nearby, I'll always come back to you, dear,' Arthur said to me. I smiled and wrapped the slippers he had borrowed in tissue paper before tucking them into his bag.

'Little Christmas present from me,' I told him.

'See you in February. I'll be back to pick up a little

something special for the missus,' he said, tugging the collar of his jumper up against the chill.

'I'll be here, unless the mysterious Mr or Mrs Cody Rainbow and "Picture Perfect" have put me out of business by then.'

Lily chuckled, but Arthur stepped away from the open door and back into the shop.

Chapter Ten

'Cody Rainbow?' he asked. 'Are you sure you don't mean Cody Ray?'

I shook my head and showed him the letter. 'It doesn't say what he or she will be doing, but "Picture Perfect"? That sounds pretty romantic. I'm not really scared that he or she will be direct competition, but it doesn't give away much and I must admit it's got me nervous. I do okay here but it wouldn't take much to put a serious dent in my business. I don't get a lot of walk-in trade as it is.'

'Apart from me,' Arthur pointed out. 'You saved my bacon and I won't forget it.'

I kissed his cheek.

Arthur pulled the stool back out and sat at the counter, not even noticing the mud that followed him again this time. I wanted to sweep up, but I wanted to hear his information first. 'Cody is a photographer, made her name as a journalist. You know that iconic picture from after the bombing in the embassy? She took that. Then a year later she burnt out.'

'Alcohol?' I asked.

'Drugs?' Lily said.

Arthur shrugged. 'I don't know, stress I think. I just remember my wife reading a story about her in a magazine not long ago. She was in rehab for a while, and the piece was advertising her relaunch. It said she was thinking of changing her name but I didn't know what to. I'm sure it's her though.' That would explain why Ben hadn't been able to track her down online. I assumed that she had changed her name for that very reason, to give her some space from whatever had led to the career break.

Arthur continued, 'The shop is called Picture Perfect? It has to be her. She's an artist with her camera. She had a series of landscapes. They were beautiful. There was this one of the sunset, reminded me of our honeymoon. We only went to Bognor, but one night, we were walking up the beach and the view was outstanding. Never thought I'd see anything like it again until I saw her photo. Now if I could buy one of those ...' He stopped and realised what he was saying. 'I'd still shop here too, of course,' he said, picking up his bags and wishing us a merry Christmas.

'We did it,' Lily squealed. 'Take that spy boys with your techy gadgets and your hacking skills. We solved the mystery with good old-fashioned conversation.' She fanned out the notes I'd handed her earlier. 'Time to celebrate?' she asked.

'How long do you have before you have to be at work?'

She glanced at the small silver dial set into a black leather strap around her wrist. 'Two hours, but if I go in slightly tipsy it's okay. The boss reckons I get a bit flirty when I've had a drink, pushes sales up.'

I checked the time on my own watch. 'I've only got an hour before my next client is due, and I've two more in after that. It's going to be a long day today.' Just what I'd told myself I needed this morning, though now I was wishing I could take off again. 'How about we sneak to the patisserie and I treat you to a cream cake?'

In the end Lily paid for her choux bun and my slice of gateau. She said that she felt flush with so much cash in her pocket. Afterwards I hugged her farewell and retreated to my boutique, opening up again just a couple of minutes before another of my favourite customers turned up. Albert had seen the advert that I'd placed in the London newspaper three years before. He'd turned up, all five-foot-four of him in his camel-coloured mac and tweed flat cap.

He'd spent ten minutes choosing a diamond necklace and a hamper of his wife's favourite snacks. We'd spent another hour chatting over a cuppa as he told me about how they'd met at a tea dance when they were teenagers. After Christmas I'd got a thank you card from his wife. She had been grateful for the difference from his previous attempts of jumpers which didn't fit, or even worse, the year that he had bought her a new armchair because she had complained about the old one. She came in herself three months later to buy his birthday present, and explained that the chair was very much his, and that the new one that he had ostensibly bought for her had remained covered in his old newspapers and very quickly smelt no better and looked no smarter than the old one.

These days they both phoned me separately, usually one after another. They would plan a shopping trip to London, and each claiming that they needed time alone, I'd schedule their appointments with an hour clear in the middle to avoid them meeting in my shop by accident. I usually used the time before her appointment to hide the things I knew that she would like so that she wouldn't see them and ruin the surprise, and the time before his appointment getting everything back out again and adding to the pile anything her eyes had lingered on as well. Albert and Doris also received my five per cent nice customer discount. And given that after they left I could usually bask in the happiness that they shared, I benefited from seeing them too.

That afternoon I made sales, wrapped packages and served tea and cookies. By the time I closed the door, I'd had one of my best days ever, and looked forward to curling up on Dad's sofa with a plate of junk food and a film. It was a huge relief too to feel less nervous about my new neighbour. I began to feel just a little more hopeful about the future of my special shop. First I just had to tidy up the debris of the day. I swept the floor again and washed it to get rid of any last traces of mud. Then, I carted mugs to the kitchen, ran a sink full of hot water and began to wash up.

I heard the door to shop open and close and I called out. 'I thought you had work, Lily. Did they let you out early?'

There was a gentle cough, and I placed the last mug on the draining board and turned around. There was a woman wearing a long, rainbow-coloured cotton shawl over black linen trousers and a maroon floaty shirt. I wanted to point out that the shop was closed for the evening, but I'd made a point of never turning away a customer who needed my help. Goodness knows if I did, I'd have turned away Mr King before I sent this lady packing. Not least because she was at least six inches taller than me, and probably weighed twice as much. She wasn't fat, not by any stretch of the imagination, she was simply statuesque. Her figure was topped by a crowd of ginger curls that tumbled freely down her back.

'Welcome to Romantic Daze,' I told her, gesturing with my arm to let her know that she was free to browse. 'I'm Daisy.'

'Sorry I'm not Lily,' she said.

'No problem,' I told her. 'I thought that I had locked up and my friend is one of the few people with a key so I assumed it was her.'

'I can come back tomorrow,' the lady said, wandering around my shop and running her fingers through the selection of silk scarves. I couldn't blame her, I often found it comforting to do the same.

I assured her that she was welcome to browse and she took me at my word, spending an inordinately long time gazing at the photo frames. I used the time to study her, as discreetly as I could. She appeared to be in her late forties or early fifties, though there wasn't a streak of white in her hair yet, just a scattering of laughter lines. It was hard to tell if any of the rings that she wore on each of her fingers were from a significant other. She carried with her an aura of peace. Perhaps it was in the slow yet deliberate way that she moved, graceful but sure of herself. I loved how when she was drawn to something, like a scent bottle or a bar of fragrant soap, she would hold it, feel it, smell it, just as I did. I knew that anything she chose would mean something to her. Finally she chose a CD of piano concertos and brought it to the till to pay. She explained that she had just moved across the road and had been out exploring when she'd seen my light on. She stretched her hand out for me to shake. 'I'm Cody.'

I gulped and hoped that she couldn't tell from the look on my face how guilty I felt. I'd never have snooped if I'd known that she would be so nice, and there was no way I'd have let Ben try and investigate her online. I hate to think what he'd have been able to tell us about her if he had found out who she was.

Cody announced that it was only fair that having seen my shop, I come back to see hers. Where my house demonstrated its age in its bowed walls and crooked roof, hers was modern, with straight edges and perfectly aligned sparkling windows. She took a key from a pocket of her trousers and let us in. This time it was my turn to be lost in wonder. The front opened directly into what in any other house on the road might well have been a living room. Every wall had been painted in white gloss. The furniture had been removed, and the only hint of Cody's colourful approach to dressing was evident in the light shade, which was box like and made from red paper so thin it was translucent, especially in the face of the wattage glaring out from it.

I stood, speechless, absorbing the intensity of Cody's landscape prints. The walls were dominated by a series of photographs, enlarged to be the size of regular posters and framed in glass, edged with white borders. The image of the woods in a thunderstorm had me pulling my jacket tighter around myself to stay warm. As I was drawn into the photograph of a deserted beach at sunset, Cody handed me a glass of cold, crisp white wine, and I imagined the feel of the breeze on my face as I sipped it.

'These are incredible,' I told her. 'They're so powerful, so emotive. This one,' I gestured at a shot of an old-fashioned sailing ship alone on the ocean, 'if this is for sale I know of a lady who would kill to buy this for her husband for Christmas. And I wouldn't mind the one of the beach myself. It reminds me of holidays when I was a kid.' I took a sip of wine, trying to work out when I went from being nervous that she would put me out of business to being so overwhelmed by her talent that I couldn't stop myself from admiring her work.

She laughed and sipped her own drink. 'I don't want to steal your customers,' she said, and I immediately stopped worrying about the impact of her moving here. 'I suppose I could give you a commission for anyone you send my way.' She tapped her glass against mine in a toast. 'It'll be a pleasure doing business with you,' she said. 'I've got a pan of soup on the hob. Fancy a bowl?'

'I'd love some but I'm veggie,' I told her.

'Me too,' she said, leaving me to take in the pictures as she went to prepare the food. The walls of the hall were covered in smaller prints, these in a variety of frames. They included close-ups of flowers, long exposures of starry nights, and here and there a wildlife shot or two.

I was still singing Cody's praises as she led me to the kitchen and handed me a steaming bowl of soup. 'You're too kind,' she said. 'It's been strange for me to reinvent myself. It's reassuring to hear that it hasn't been a mistake.'

She didn't go into any more detail about the breakdown that had led to her leaving the world of journalism, and I didn't ask, but as I tucked into the fragrant mixture of tomatoes and beans at the bottom of my dish, I hoped that this might be the first of many evenings that I spent looking at her work.

Instead of talking about herself, she asked about the history of 'Romantic Daze', and I told her how I'd come to open my shop. When she asked about the state of my own love life I decided it best to follow her lead and skimp on the details. If she noticed then she was too polite to press for more. The only outward sign of her former life was an invitation to an award show, printed in a calligraphy style font on ivory card. It was blu-tacked near to the shelf holding the spare toilet rolls and bleach next to the loo in a tiny bathroom under her stairs. Whether that was any indication of whether she had attended at all, or won or lost, I had no idea.

When I got back home, I made sure that I locked the door this time, before kicking off my shoes, brushing my teeth and going to bed. I stayed awake just long enough to text Lily about my evening and to wish her good night's sleep, before the wine and the busy day combined to leave me unable to keep my eyes open any longer.

Chapter Eleven

The day dawned crisp and bright with the promise that you'd be chilled to the bone if you attempted to enjoy the winter sun for longer than a few moments, but that wasn't what woke me. Ben had emailed in the middle of the night to say that he'd found a credit card in the name of Rebecca Cody Ray which contained the charges for groceries at the local organic store, and several to a company which specialised in printing and frames. He thought he had tracked down my elusive competitor and said that now he had her full name, he'd be able to supply me with a file of information by the next day. Given that I'd now met Cody and really liked her – in fact I'd probably eaten the food paid for with that card – I'd quickly emailed him back and pulled him off the search. I'd then spent another chunk of the night feeling guilty that I'd intruded into Cody's business and hoped that I had gotten in touch with Ben before he'd read anything too personal. I'd finally fallen asleep again just before my alarm went off.

Dragging myself out of bed, the sun felt too bright as it shone through my thin net curtains, so I locked myself in the bathroom and showered until I felt a few more brain cells kick in. Coffee helped. Not enough, but it allowed me to get dressed and open up on time. I dealt with the first couple of customers on autopilot. I hated feeling like I was going through the motions. The ethos of Romantic Daze was to offer a personal service, to not only carry the stock items that you might expect in a store of this nature, but also to get to know my clients and discover unusual gifts that they would never have found by themselves. Luckily this approach meant that I'd done my research already, and had the prospective gifts under the counter waiting to be inspected. My clients seemed thrilled with my finds, no matter how much I knew I wasn't my usual smiling self as I served them.

Waving Mavis off with a signed record of her husband's favourite singer under her arm, I locked the door and decided that if I wanted to do a better job that afternoon, I ought to take the hour that I'd set aside for lunch and use it for a nap instead. I gobbled down a cereal bar, shut my door and was asleep again in minutes.

I woke up, for the second time that day, and swore when I glanced at my phone and saw how long I'd slept. My client had been due in ten minutes earlier, and I hoped that I hadn't slept so deeply that I'd missed them knocking on the door. Tying my hair back into a ponytail, I slipped my shoes back on and opened my bedroom door.

Lily was behind the till and was busy talking Keith through his selection from the silver-edged glass bottle collection that I'd arranged on the window sill. 'Daisy,' Lily greeted me. 'I was just explaining that you were unpacking the last of the Christmas stock in the backroom.'

Keith had been coming to my shop for several years and no doubt knew very well that the only thing behind the door was my bedroom, but he was too polite to mention it.

I kissed Lily's cheek and offered to put the kettle on. Carrying a tray of hot chocolate and biscuits back out to them, I assured Keith that his wife would love the antiques he had chosen. He promised to be back again before long and went on his way, whistling as I showed him out.

'You saved me, yet again,' I told Lily.

She pointed out the lines on my cheek where I'd slept

on the crease on my pillow, and I hoped that Keith hadn't noticed. 'You look different,' she said, assessing me.

'I look a lot better than I did before my nap.'

'That's not it. You're less jumpy than you were.'

'I'm not scared that Picture Perfect will spell the end of this place any more,' I explained. 'In fact, I can see us referring clients to each other. It could be a good thing. Though I don't think she'll ever come close to being my favourite colleague.' I fetched a small box from the fridge and handed it to Lily. 'There's only four in there so savour them. These are the most expensive truffles I could find.' I'd decided my friend more than deserved them.

Luckily Lily was too distracted by her chocolates to ask me how I was feeling about Eli. I hadn't made any more decisions about him, but I still had another five days before he was due home, so at least I knew I wouldn't be bumping into him before I'd had chance to think through what I wanted to say. Then I'd have another few days before Christmas, at which point I'd no longer have work to distract me and we'd doubtless have to spend the whole of Christmas Day upstairs in Dad's flat eating and pretending to be cheerful together. I'd have to find a way to cope with being in such close proximity to him again if I didn't get any answers when he returned.

I had four more appointments back to back after Lily left for work. Locking up after my final customer, I headed into my kitchen and immediately walked out again. Grabbing my coat, I locked my door and turned to walk towards Lily's shop. She could usually take a break for dinner and I had decided to take her out for a treat to thank her for looking out for me.

I was passing under the streetlamp when I heard Cody call my name. She was wrapped up, with a fake fur hat on top of her auburn ringlets. Her trousers today were burgundy linen and her coat had a patchwork design. It shouldn't have worked, and yet her height and poise gave it an elegance the outfit would have lacked on anyone else. She looked amazing.

'I'm just off to see if I can persuade my friend to join me for dinner,' I told her.

'That sounds jolly.' She dug into her pockets to try and find her key, and I noticed that she stopped for a moment longer than she needed to before she let herself into her new home.

'Would you like to come with us?'

Cody closed her door, tucked her key back into her pocket and looped her arm through mine. 'I would love to,' she said.

'We'll have to go to her shop to ask her if she can take a break,' I explained.

'I love checking out other people's businesses.'

'It might not be quite what you're expecting,' I warned her. I explained a little more about the products that Lily specialised in selling. Cody giggled and kept on walking, but I noticed that she held on just a little tighter.

When we got there, Cody seemed excited to go into Lily's shop and it was me taking an extra moment first to pull myself together. Usually I peeked through the grill on the door to make sure that there was no one inside that I knew before I went in. I'd made that mistake before when I burst in only to come face to face with my dentist. I'd had to find a new one after that. Not that going to Lily's shop was a bad thing, but I'd seen what he was buying and found it hard not to giggle through my next check-up.

Lily didn't need asking twice when she saw us. She yelled to an unseen person behind a black curtain that she was taking her break, grabbed her handbag from the drawer and followed us outside.

I slept better that night, with a belly full of food and having had the company of friends. Waking up, I felt more positive. Even when I went to the loo and found that I'd got my period, I was able to spend ten seconds feeling relieved that the condoms had worked before I groaned and wrote the rest of the day off to a fog of paracetamol and hot water bottles.

Over the next few days Dad sent me a series of photographs. He wrote a brief note on the last one, that it had been a quieter holiday than he had expected, especially with Eli for company. It was off season in the town they were staying in, and having spent some time wandering around the various sites, he'd grown bored until Eli had signed him up for a cookery class in the hotel kitchen.

Ben sent me a photo of himself in the sea. I could see goosebumps all over his torso, but as he was temporarily away from any electronic devices, I figured that the holiday was doing a good job of drawing him out of his shell too. I didn't hear a word from Eli.

When the same silver car pulled up outside the house the following Saturday to drop them home, I was still staring at my phone waiting for a text to say that they'd landed.

'You could have just checked on the airport website,' Ben scolded me when I told him off. He scowled some more when I hugged him and I wondered if he was just acting like a teenager, when I noticed that he seemed to be particularly guarding his right shoulder. He picked up his bag and let himself into the house.

Eli climbed out of the car in one fluid movement, pulled himself up to his full height, glanced round to make sure that Ben was safely inside before dropping a quick kiss on my lips and following him in. 'Where's my dad?' I shouted. Chasing after to get an answer, I found them stood in the kitchen. Ben was pouring himself a glass of juice and Eli had the kettle boiling. 'Thanks for getting the groceries Daisy,' I muttered.

'Thanks Dais,' Eli said, spotting the loaf of fresh bread that I'd bought the day before and raiding the fridge to make himself and Ben some sandwiches. 'They didn't feed us on the plane. I've been gasping for a decent cuppa.'

'Tell me you didn't eat my dad,' I said, handing Eli some cheese so that he could make my sandwich too. Ben shot me a look.

'I signed your dad up for some classes at the hotel,' Eli said, ignoring my brother.

'He e-mailed me. I think he was enjoying cooking again.'

'Did he tell you that he got chatting with the manager and they asked him to stay another week to run some baking sessions for a coach load of pensioners? Their regular teacher is having a baby and the chef had the ... wrong temperament for teaching those who were a little slower at picking up new techniques,' Eli explained. Clearly Dad had left some fairly pertinent information out of his messages. 'He'll be back in time for Christmas so he knew you wouldn't mind.'

And I didn't, but I was surprised, though happy for my dad that he had found something to keep him busy. It would be good for him. Despite my confusion over our personal relationship, I was grateful for how well Eli was looking out for my family, so I took the plate he offered me and hugged him again to say thank you. It seemed like he held on for a few seconds longer than he needed to, but it was hard to tell for sure. It might have been wishful thinking on my part. I hugged Ben again too, but this time he squawked when I touched his arm. I definitely wasn't imagining that. I ordered him to take his jacket off, which he did. Then his jumper. Again, he complied. When I told him to roll his sleeve up though he reverted to petulant teenager mode again and wouldn't make eye contact with me.

'Ben,' I ordered. He stood up, glared at me and lifted his T-shirt over his head. There on his right bicep was a tattoo.

'Don't blame me,' Eli said, raising his hands in a gesture of mock retreat. 'He did this by himself.'

'And I like it,' Ben said.

I stepped closer and took another look. 'What is it?' I asked, staring at the circles and lines. 'Did you get a tattoo of computer wires? And have you been working out?'

Chapter Twelve

Ben began to unpack after lunch and set the washing machine off on what would be the first of many loads. The one advantage of having such an orderly mind was that he was able to take care of cleaning up after himself at least. Eli said that he had better go home and do the same, so I followed him down as I had a customer due soon. At the front door, Eli turned and called out to Ben that he'd be over again that evening. Ben was upset that we'd not been more enthusiastic about his tattoo and didn't reply.

'Will I see you later too?' he asked me.

I thought about what Ben had said about Eli's plans for the trip, of drinking and picking up women. Then I looked at him. The skin around his eyes was line free and he was clean shaven. The holiday had been good for him, and it hurt to think what he might have been up to that had him smiling again. His fingers reached out and stroked a gentle trail up and down my arm. Then I remembered that I still had my period and felt achey and bloated. 'I can't sleep with you,' I blurted out. His eyes hardened, and he stepped back. 'I mean ...'

'I think I understood what you meant,' he said, turning and walking away.

'Eli!' I called, but it was no use. He didn't stop, and my client strolled around the corner, heading for my shop, so I had to watch as he left me, yet again. Part of me wanted to run after him, and part of me was angry that he could walk away so easily. But then, whatever the connection was between us, it was so undefined that even if I'd caught up to him, I had no idea what I'd say.

I couldn't clear my head even when dealing with my customers. Trying to persuade an eighty-year-old man that whilst his wife might like naughty lingerie, she would probably also appreciate a warm dressing-gown to go over the top was little distraction. After he left with a robe from my shop and directions to Lily's, I locked the door, poured myself a glass of cold white wine and went upstairs to talk to Ben.

He'd finished with the laundry and had started giving the flat a good clean, pausing only to glance at his phone whenever he thought that I wasn't watching. It was odd. Ben didn't usually seem so keen to hear from anyone except a contact who hooked him up occasionally with new computer games, but he didn't tell me who it was he was hoping to hear from so I didn't ask I left him up to his elbows in suds and began to fix us some dinner. I craved comfort food, so made bangers and mash. Veggie sausages for me and meaty ones for Ben. The potatoes were bubbling away whilst I set the table. Mum and Dad had been given a set of fine, white china plates when they'd got married. When we were little Ben and I had broken so many that Mum had invested in a set of sturdy, blue-rimmed thick crockery, but today I wanted to make an effort so I used the good china. It was a nice way to feel closer to her and I needed it right then.

Fetching the rest of the wine from my flat, I poured us each out a glass and began to steam some broccoli. Ben finished vacuuming the living room just as I set the dish of sausages on the table. It felt lonely, just the two of us there without our dad, but then some days even with three of us you could feel the gap where Mum should have been. I asked Ben about his holiday, hoping that he would tell me what Eli had been up to and not wanting to know at the same time, just in case he had hooked up with someone and I ended up crying into my mashed potato.

I didn't want to let Eli get to me, but it was hard not to. I had thought that my crush on him was a thing of the past, until it was centre and present in my bedroom again just a week earlier. Ben didn't notice my inner turmoil. Even if I'd pointed out to him that I was stressed about something he wouldn't have known what to do or say, so I listened instead as he told me how much Dad had enjoyed being bumped up to first class on the flight. Eli had kept to his word, and he and Ben had flown in economy, so I didn't feel too guilty about their subterfuge. Ben promised me that he had checked before he made the switch and there had been plenty of empty seats. He was a little put out that Eli had stopped him upgrading them both too.

Seeing Dad's face when they disembarked and he told them about the free champagne had calmed Ben down. He was as relieved as I was anytime we saw that Dad could be happy still. Now that he was safely home, Ben was trying to put the trauma of a week of virtually non-existent wi-fi behind him but clearly his idea of a holiday and Eli's had been a little different.

He helped himself to another huge spoonful of potato, and was smothering it in gravy when the doorbell rang. 'That'll be Eli,' he said, making no move to get up. 'He said he'd be back around tea time.'

'Nice of you to let me know' I muttered, pushing my chair back and going to let him in. I knew that any subtlety of statement would be lost on Ben, and sure enough when Eli and I made it back upstairs, having not said a word to each other on the way up, Ben greeted him with a complicated handshake and stood to fetch him a plate.

'There was supposed to be enough for you to have for

lunch tomorrow,' I told my brother but he shrugged and said that he'd just have a sandwich. Eli noticed my displeasure, but just grinned at me and tucked into the food.

'You'd have loved the beaches, Dais,' Ben said, as he handed Eli the last of the wine I'd bought. 'The water was so clear, freezing cold though.'

'The locals thought this one was crazy,' Eli said, gesturing at my brother. 'No one else was on the beach, let alone in the water. We'll have to go back again when it's warmer.'

'I couldn't help it,' Ben said. 'I've never seen a shade of blue like it. I had to go in.'

'What did Dad make of the trip?' I asked, aware that he must have enjoyed it more than I'd ever have predicted given that he had actually stayed on voluntarily.

'He was pretty quiet the first few days,' Eli admitted. 'I was starting to get a bit nervous that I'd pushed him into coming, but the fresh air and good, local food seemed to help. He found a few dishes that he liked and got chatting to the chef. I'd seen the cookery classes advertised in the lobby, so I signed him up.'

'He'd been a bit moany on our trips, to be honest,' Ben said.

'So had you,' Eli added. 'I quote, "why would I want to go and look at old temples when I can just type it into Google and see pictures from here?"'

'I would have been able to if they'd had fibre installed. Honestly, I was just lucky that they weren't still using dial-up.' Some days I wondered how my brother would have managed if he'd been born before the internet existed. He'd probably have become fixated on steam trains instead.

'And the nightlife?' I asked, unable to help myself even as I dreaded hearing the answer.

'The bars were pretty cool,' Ben answered.

'You're just saying that because they were half empty so they weren't too loud for you, and because we didn't know anyone there so it didn't matter if all your drinks were served with more fruit decorations than actual alcohol,' Eli reminded him. Ben smiled at the memories.

'So it wasn't the heaving masses that you were hoping for?' I asked, relieved at the thought that they hadn't been stumbling around drunk surrounded by bikini-clad babes for the entire trip.

'We found a few places that were okay,' Eli said. 'The bar by the seafront was nice. Mostly locals, but they were happy to have some company during their quiet season.'

'Plus the hot girl behind the bar totally had her eye on you,' Ben said. He reached over to high five Eli again, but I pushed my chair away from the table and barged him out of the way so that I could drop my empty plate into the sink.

'Your turn to wash up,' I told them. Eli smirked when he saw my reaction, so I accidentally trod on his toes as I reached across the table. I opened a second bottle of wine from my dad's stash and filled my glass to the top.

'Have you had a good week?' Eli asked. 'Busy selling more soppy presents and frilly pants to old men?'

I glared at him, and Ben began to glance nervously between us. Without my dad there to referee, the tension quickly rose. We had sniped at each other over the years but Ben hated loud voices and so we'd generally kept it to a level of using angry words rather than high volume. Now though I was really cross. I'd waited for a week to find out whether our night together had meant anything to Eli and he seemed to be enjoying making me squirm. 'You mean, did I help people find meaningful gifts for their loved ones, yes I did. And now I have a well-earned day off tomorrow, followed by a busy day on Monday going to pick up some more supplies.'

'Are you out of pink soap? Can't you just go to the supermarket then come home and write new labels for twice the price?'

'Stop,' Ben begged, but it was too late. I was fuming. Eli owed me answers but instead he was lashing out, rehashing arguments that we'd had a hundred times before, only this time I didn't hold back.

'You're just jealous because you can't form a deep enough emotional bond to want to buy a girl something thoughtful,' I spat back. Ben lifted his hands to cover his ears. I knew that I should stop shouting and yet I didn't. 'You're upsetting my brother,' I yelled. 'Why did you even come over again?'

'Because he asked me to,' Eli responded, standing up and leaning forward until we were nose to nose over the table.

'I wish you'd both just stayed away, you're supposed to care about me, but you're shouting. You know I hate shouting. It makes my ears hurt and my tummy ache. Why can't you ever just talk to each other like friends are supposed to? I hate that you can't be in the same room without being mean,' Ben shouted, picking his plate up and dropping into the sink hard enough that it landed on top of mine and smashed. 'Now look what's happened. This was supposed to be my safe space. This was where I could come when everything out there was too much. Where am I supposed to go now?' He turned and ran from the room. A moment later the front door slammed shut.

Chapter Thirteen

Eli and I continued to stare at each other until eventually I folded. 'I'm going to look for Ben.' I headed down to my flat where I wrapped up as quickly as I could in hat and scarf and gloves before slamming my own door behind me. My mobile rang as I trudged down the road towards the station. Taking it from my pocket, I read Taylor's name on the display. I slipped a glove off so that I could use my finger to swipe the screen, cursing as I did so at how quickly my hand felt frozen.

'Hi,' I said, as I began to run down the stairs to the underground. 'I've been meaning to call.' And I had, I just hadn't worked out what to say and so I'd been avoiding ringing him. 'This isn't a great time but I meant to say thank you for the emails.' There was no reason to take my current foul mood out on Taylor, though having a normal conversation felt alien when all I could think about was Ben.

Taylor didn't reply, and I glanced at the display. Out of signal. We'd been cut off. I'd reached the barrier and had to decide whether to go back up the street to call Taylor again, or continue to search for Ben. Apologising to Taylor out loud, though he wouldn't hear it, I slipped my phone back into my pocket and touched my card to the sensor to get through the gates.

Running to catch the tube as it pulled into the station, I stood with my nose in the armpit of a tourist who had evidently wrapped up too well for the weather and was now rather unpleasantly fragrant. I cursed my haste, thinking that I could have walked to most destinations within zone one almost as quickly if I had only thought my plans through. Still, when the tube pulled into Leicester Square station, I found myself climbing onto a second train to complete my journey. If Ben was looking for a safe space then all I could think to do was try the places that he visited most often.

At Covent Garden, the hordes exited the train, and I was swept along with them. The queues for the lifts were a good ten metres deep, so this time I decided to eschew technology and headed for the stairs. One hundred and ninety-three steps later I was cursing myself for making the wrong decision at every opportunity.

I'd barely got my breath back as I skirted the cobblestones around the market, making my way for the pub that Eli and Ben often visited after work. It was busy, and I fought my way to the bar. I asked the pierced and tattooed leather-clad man behind the counter if he had seen Ben. He stopped serving for long enough to give me a look that spoke of my stupidity for asking if he knew any customer by name. I ordered a drink that I didn't really want in case that made him more willing to talk, but instead it served to further piss him off as it gave him more work to do. I offered to buy him a drink and tried flashing the photo that Dad had e-mailed me the day before of Ben by the pool, and finally he took a brief look before walking away without another word to sell overpriced soft drinks to a dad of two screaming toddlers. I couldn't blame him, I wanted the crying to stop too. Probably not as much as the parents did though. I hoped that they didn't feel judged by the grimaces around them. The kids' volume was admittedly impressive, but they were just giving the service in the pub the feedback it deserved.

I left my glass, still half full on the counter and walked back out into the darkness. The snow began to fall, and I dug my woolly hat out of my pocket and jammed it on over my head. By the time I reached the next pub on my list, my ears were cold anyway. The skinny guy in drain-pipe jeans, slung low enough to show off the top of his grey boxer shorts, glanced at my phone as he handed me a bottle of Appletiser. 'This one I remember,' he said, winking at me as he tapped Eli's picture. 'He's cute. Him,' he gestured at Ben, 'not so much. Don't think they've been in recently.'

He handed me some change and began to serve the lady next to me. 'Should have at least worn nice pants,' I muttered as I sipped my drink.

'Did you ask for something?' he asked, turning back to me. I shook my head and left my bottle on a table on my way out.

My bladder and depleting purse told me to stop ordering drinks just to try and get people to talk to me, not that it made much difference. There was no sign of Ben at the next couple of pubs either. I began to walk home, cursing at the hordes that meant I had to walk down the roads as if they were a slalom race, weaving from side to side to avoid bumping into people. I loved living in London, but occasionally it grew frustrating that walking took so much concentration.

I tried a couple of Eli's favourite post-drinking takeaways, but as Ben had eaten just before he'd left, and he evidently hadn't been drinking since, I knew even as I went in that they'd be a bust. I stopped into Lily's shop to see if she had any ideas.

As usual, she pulled no punches. 'Those are places you or Eli would have gone. You need to try and think like your brother, you silly moo.'

'So I should go home and see if he's back there again on his laptop?' I asked.

'And maybe think about returning Taylor's call?' she said. 'I mean, I know Eli has that whole dark and brooding thing going on, but Taylor is smoking. Have you seen the size of his thighs?'

On that note I gave her a quick hug and walked the rest of the way home. There was no sign of Ben in his room and no note from Eli telling me where he had gone or what he was doing. I thought about calling the police, but wasn't sure that they'd take me seriously, especially as he had only been gone a couple of hours and was a grown man, physically at least. Also, I didn't want to do anything that brought Ben to the attention of the authorities just in case it ended up messing up his security clearance for work. I hoped that my brother would come home soon and tried to make myself relax. I didn't think I'd be able to sleep, but sometime around midnight I must have nodded off.

Eli woke me at eight, knocking on the door of my flat until I got up and let him in. 'I've looked everywhere,' he said. 'I really hoped he was back but he just wouldn't open the door.' Eli walked past me to my little kitchen where he put the kettle on and began rooting through my cupboard to find the coffee. 'Have you been up to check?'

I shook my head, feeling guilty that I'd been asleep and hadn't thought of it myself. 'Have you been to bed yet?' I asked, realising that the black jeans and grey wool sweater that he was wearing were the same ones he'd had on the day before. There was a fine layer of jet-black stubble on his chin, and his shoes were scuffed. On the bright side, my period had finished, and I felt a little less grumpy than I had the day before.

'I've been ringing him but no answer. I tried every club I've ever taken him too.'

'You've been looking in all the places you'd have gone.

You have to try thinking like Ben,' I said, pretending that I hadn't done exactly the same myself until Lily had pointed it out.

'Looks like you thought he'd show up in your flat,' Eli retorted. He reached for the kettle and missed.

'You're not going to be any use to him even if he does show up,' I told Eli. 'You go and lie down. I'll wake you up in a couple of hours if he's not home and we can start looking again.' The truth was I wasn't sure exactly how worried I ought to be. Ben was a grown man, but I'd always seen myself as his protector, as had Eli, and it was hard to let go of that. Especially when he had stormed out so upset at us both. After Mum had died Dad had started making us promise to look after each other and I felt like I was letting them all down by not doing more to find Ben and make sure he was okay.

I left Eli kicking his shoes off as I went upstairs to check Ben's room. There was still no sign of him. I tried his laptop but couldn't crack the password. I went to the living room and found the old one where I'd left it next to the sofa. I wanted to check Ben's social media pages, not that I was expecting a tweet saying where he was given that he hadn't texted us, but just to feel like I was doing something. Ben, however, deemed any social networking site that was popular as being for civilians and refused to use them, which ruled out ninety per cent of the methods that my peers used to communicate, so I didn't know where to start. After Googling his name and getting nowhere, I remembered how little luck I'd had finding information about Cody that way and closed the lid.

By lunchtime I'd done another walk around the local area with no luck. I made some sandwiches then woke Eli with more coffee. He looked better than I would have on four hours sleep which was annoying, but not by much. 'Could he have gone to work?' I asked. 'I've tried everywhere else I can think of.' Eli sipped his drink and yawned. I waited until he set the cup down and tossed him a clean towel. 'Why don't you take a shower. It'll help you wake up.'

Eli's stress levels were evidently high as he didn't make any comments about me wanting to get him naked and didn't even bother to ask me to join him. My nerves I could have put down to being an over-protective sister, but the fact that Eli was worried too had me even more anxious.

Eli showered and then we ate quickly and were soon on the hunt for Ben once more. A quick tube ride had us stood outside of the towering grey concrete block where Ben and Eli worked. 'There shouldn't be anyone in here on a Sunday,' Eli said.

'I thought spy business would be a round the clock activity,' I commented, but Eli shot me a look so I stopped talking. 'Shouldn't it be harder than this to break in, if you're all top secret super spies?'

'Technically I'm just a civil servant, albeit one with a job description you'll never find in writing.'

'Because you have a licence to kill?'

'Because if they wrote down everything I do for this country they'd have to pay me an awful lot more.'

'So why isn't your building hidden away in a secret cave or something?'

'It would be a bugger to recruit if we were out past zone six. You're not supposed to come inside and during the week there would be no way I would even try. In fact, once we find Ben I'll get him to delete any sign of our visit from the logs. And the CCTV.'

'Now I really want to go in,' I told him, trying to figure

out myself whether or not I was being sarcastic. Eli swiped his ID card and opened the front door. Inside, there was another door that was accessed with a nine-digit security code. I glanced around me, taking in the white marble chips that had been used to make a tile floor. The walls were painted an institutional shade of green. Then I noticed all the cameras and turned my face away just in case anyone was watching.

'If you're looking for posters warning that loose lips sink ships, they took those down sixty years ago,' Eli whispered into my ear. His breath was warm and sent a shiver down my spine.

We rode up in the lift, and I tried to commit every detail to memory, knowing that these were the walls that Ben saw every day and that I'd likely never be inside again.

Reminding myself why I was there, I poked Eli to move him forward. 'Don't worry, we're just one government department hidden inside a whole building of them. Most of the others are fairly harmless.' That suggested that his wasn't. 'This makes us much harder to spot, if anyone were to try.'

'That's why there are no retina scans or complicated password systems, much to Ben's annoyance I'm sure?'

'That, and the final door to our department has a fingerprint scanner built into the handle. I suggest you don't touch it unless you want a cage to rise from the floor and keep you trapped until Monday.'

I wasn't sure if he was trying to spook me or if that was a real security measure but I didn't want to risk finding out. Eli reached for the door handle and I pressed myself against his side and squeezed through after him without touching it. 'Let's check Ben's desk and get out of here,' I whispered.

Eli laughed, and the sound echoed in the empty corridor. 'There won't be anyone here. Except your brother hopefully.'

I followed Eli into the room and looked around it. There was a black metal desk, set with its back to the wall. The surface was clear but for a keyboard and an infra-red mouse. There wasn't a post-it or a pen to be seen. There were no photos on the shelves, only a few books about cracking the Enigma code and one about some computer techniques so advanced I didn't even understand the title. There was a coaster on the windowsill, but no dirty mug left waiting to be washed. The only sign that a person had ever used this room for work was a screwed up chocolate bar wrapper in the bin.

'This is Ben's office, isn't it?'

'It's his kingdom,' Eli confirmed. He reached forward and began opening desk drawers.

'Should we be snooping in his space?' I asked, feeling guilty for invading Ben's privacy, although he had none of the same concerns with regards to other people.

'What else did you have in mind? Did you think you were here to sit in his chair and do some sightseeing from his window?'

I didn't like Eli's tone of voice, but he made a good point. I put the snark down to him being as worried about Ben as I was. I opened the top drawer where most people would keep their assortment of half-chewed biros, paper clips and expired photocopy cards. Ben's drawer held a stub from when we'd been to see *Star Wars* and that was all. Eli came over to see what I'd found. 'I was sure Ben had left his phone charger the other day. He must have stopped in already to collect it. He bugged me so often to borrow mine on holiday that I had to buy him another. I don't know what he was doing on his phone all week to empty the battery so much. It's not like he's answering now to let us know that he's okay.'

The second drawer down held a supply of cereal bars. 'He must be trying to look after himself a bit better,' I said, feeling reassured that Ben was learning to eat when he got engrossed in his work.

'I put them there six months ago,' said Eli.

The bottom drawer was empty. 'I've never been able to do that,' I said, staring at the scratched wood lining. 'If I ever see an empty space I can immediately think of a thousand things that could fill it. How can Ben have a useful opportunity for storage and nothing to put in here?'

'Everything that was important to Ben was stored on here.' Eli tapped the computer. 'And we'll never be able to get into it.' He swore and kicked the bin. It clanged so loudly that I jumped. After that, I held my breath waiting for the security guards to come and find us and arrest me, but thankfully they must have been having a lazy Sunday, if they existed at all, as no one showed.

'Feel better?' I asked. Eli swore again.

'Let me ring Erin,' he said, reaching for the phone on Ben's desk. 'They work together pretty closely. She might have an idea where we can look.'

'But what happens if she tells your boss and Ben gets into trouble for disappearing?'

'It's the weekend, he's allowed out. I'll pretend he left his phone at home and I forgot where he said to meet.'

He dialled a number from memory. It seemed that he must know Erin pretty well too, and I hoped that she would be able to help us, but as I pressed my ear next to Eli's so that I could hear the call, the only sounds was a ringing tone which went unanswered.

'I'm just going to get a jacket from my room,' he muttered, leaving Ben's office with his head down.

'Is that our cover if we get found out in the office?' I asked.

'If you get caught you won't need cover as much as you will a lawyer,' he responded, his voice drifting down the hall towards me. I jumped off Ben's chair and hurried to catch up with him. His long legs had carried him almost to the end of the corridor and it was lucky that I had peeked or I'd have missed seeing him turn into another office.

Eli's set-up couldn't have been more different. The basic furniture was the same, presumably all supplied by the government. Eli's desk though was buried under a mountain of paper, he had maps fastened to one wall and a pot plant on his windowsill. The soil was dry and the long leaves which tapered to a point were brown around the edges. A small silver photo frame sat at the back of his desk. Inside was a picture of Eli and his mum. He was in his late teens, his image captured half-way between the cheekiness of his youth and the serious and contoured planes of the present day.

'I miss your mum,' I told him, remembering her warmth. I didn't remember cuddling my own mum, but I could close my eyes now and feel Amelia's soft arms and enormous pillowy bosom encompassing me. 'She gave the best hugs.' And she gave them so freely, every time you said hello, goodbye, that anything had upset you, and sometimes just for the sheer joy because you were close and because she could reach. I blinked back a tear and wondered how Eli managed. I thanked my lucky stars that I still had my dad, and promised myself that when Ben came home I'd be more patient with him. 'Let's go home,' I suggested. 'For all we know, he's cooled down now and he's back there wondering where we are.'

But he wasn't. The dishes from our dinner the night before were still in the sink. After wrapping Ben's broken plate in newspaper and throwing it away, I ran in some hot water to wash the rest, as Eli made us a cup of tea. 'So what do we do next?' I asked.

Eli set our drinks on the table. I set the final pan to soak, the potatoes having stuck hard overnight. Perhaps there were benefits to Ben's fastidious approach to tidying up. It was rare to find the kitchen so messy. I just wished that he would be so careful about letting us know where he was.

We wrote lists of all the places that we'd already tried, and anywhere else that we thought Ben might go. Eli researched online to make a list of all the shops nearby which specialised in top range electronics, and we added those to our places to search.

'There's only one drawback,' Eli pointed out. He tapped his watch. 'This time on a Sunday, they'll all be shut.' He yawned and rubbed his hand over his chin. His five o'clock stubble was now more of a nine o'clock length.

'Why don't we take a break?' I suggested. 'I don't like Ben being out there by himself, but he's old enough to look after himself, at least for a few more hours. You can sleep in his room and I'll get a few hours downstairs. We can split the list over breakfast and work out where we're going to look next.'

Eli must have been exhausted because he accepted my idea without complaint. It was hard not to worry about Ben, but it had been his decision to walk out. I would never forgive myself if anything happened to him after he had left feeling so upset and alone but if he'd managed to look after himself all night and not come running home, he must have had a plan. I tried to reassure myself that he would be okay until we caught up with him and brought him back. I rinsed my mug, set it on the draining board and headed down to my flat. I heard the pipes clanking and guessed that Eli was taking a shower. I couldn't blame him, I felt grubby myself after all of the running around. The gurgle of the drain signalled him finishing in the bathroom. I picked up my towel and headed for my own wash.

I took a few extra minutes to wash my hair and shave my legs, lying to myself that it was because I hadn't done them since I'd been on my period all last week and couldn't be bothered, and not because Eli was currently naked or close to it upstairs. And I definitely didn't use the expensive rose shower gel that left my skin feeling all soft and fragrant because of him either, it was just because I loved the scent. I almost pulled on a little black nightie that I'd been saving, but when I found myself daydreaming about Eli seeing me in it, I put it back in my drawer and took out my oldest and tattiest pair of pink fleece pyjamas instead. They were covered in teddy bears, had holes in the knees and were definitely not designed to get a man in the mood.

I was buttoning the top when there was a knock at the door by the stairs. I took a second to decide whether I should have gone with the black nightie after all but then there was a second knock so I opened it. Eli looked at my pyjamas and nodded. 'Nice.'

I wondered whether he was being sarcastic, but when I looked down I realised that several of the button holes were ripped and Eli could see my tummy button. Amongst other things. I turned and found a dressing-gown. It was red silk and clashed awfully but I slipped it on and belted it tight. 'You need something?' I asked.

'I went to borrow a clean T-shirt from Ben's drawer ...' he began.

'When you realised that you were twice as broad and they wouldn't fit?'

'Over my muscles? Yes. So I took one of your dad's. If he minds please tell him I'll buy him a new one.'

'He won't mind,' I assured him. It was true. Dad was convinced that Eli looked after me and Ben and consequently he was liable to forgive Eli anything. We'd never tested it by telling him that we'd slept together when we were sixteen. There were some things a dad never needed to know.

'Anyway, I was going to say, I think Ben has been home. I wanted some shorts to sleep in so I raided Ben's drawer in case he still had those Bermuda shorts he bought for Spain last year that were too big for him.'

'When you remembered that we were relieved that they didn't fit because Ben had been planning to wear them everywhere and they were hideous?'

'Can I finish? They're still there, but his holdall is gone. I'm sure it was there this morning.'

I pushed past Eli and bolted up the stairs. He was right though, the signs of a visitor to Ben's bedroom were subtle, and if we hadn't known him so well we'd have missed them entirely. Pulling out a drawer, I noticed a gap where there should have been pants and socks. 'Are you sure this isn't just the stuff that's in the wash from your holiday?' I asked.

Eli shook his head. 'I looked yesterday and those drawers were full.'

I sat back onto Ben's bed. 'So where is he? We always row a bit, Ben knows we don't really mean it.' Maybe it was the sheer volume that we'd reached the last time that had pushed Ben to leave. Eli must have been thinking about our fight too.

'So why do we argue?' Eli asked, sitting next to me. I rested my head on his shoulder and closed my eyes. I wanted to answer but I was scared that he wouldn't like what I had to say and that we'd end up yelling all over again.

'How do we find Ben and bring him home?' I asked.

Eli put his arm around me and I leant against his chest. It didn't feel like being pulled into a soft pillow, like hugging Amelia had been, but there was a comfort in the strength Eli offered instead. I closed my eyes and stayed pressed against him until I realised that it was getting weird. I coughed gently and eased away again.

As I sat back, my eye-line shifted and I noticed something on the floor under the desk. It was the leopard print passport cover that Eli had bought on their last holiday. It read 'I scored in Shagaluf' in diamante. I hated it.

'Where would Ben go?' I asked. 'It looks like he's packed for a few days. We're not going to find him hanging out in the computer game department in HMV if he's taken clothes with him.'

I was about to pick the passport up, when there was a ring on the doorbell.

Chapter Fourteen

Cody stood on the doorstep wearing a red woollen coat and a turquoise crocheted beanie that had slipped back so that more of her hair was now out of it than under it. There was a small bubble-wrapped parcel under her right arm.

'Sorry to stop by so late,' she said, taking in my pyjamas. I'd have mumbled something about my choice of outfit but given that her trousers were bottle-green and her blouse was orange, I didn't think she'd mind that I wasn't colour coordinated. 'I saw your lights on and I wanted to bring you something.'

She handed me the package and I unwrapped a frame, about the size of an A4 piece of paper. Turning it over, I saw it was a print of the beach photo that I had admired at her house. 'I wanted to thank you for your company last week. I'd been nervous about moving here and opening a gallery. It's been a long process for me to feel ready to engage with people again, and meeting you was a big help.'

I gave her a hug and promised that I'd hang the picture in my room. She turned from the door, and I called her back so that I could hand her a gift bag that I'd had ready under the counter too. 'This is a little "welcome to the street" present,' I explained. She unwrapped the tissue paper to find a circular polished steel tray. There were three tea light holders in ascending height from one inch up to three. 'You can change around where they sit to get the lights how you want them,' I pointed out, 'and there's a bunch of candles in the bag too. I've put lavender, rose, lemon and jasmine. You can choose whichever scent matches your mood.'

Cody thanked me and was gone in a twirl of layers and a cloud of sandalwood.

'Did you buy her that because you feel guilty for spying on her?' Eli asked, emerging from my room to join me by my shop counter.

'I didn't spy. Much. Mostly it was Ben and Taylor.' Lily and I proved to be too inept at subterfuge to find much by ourselves.

'What's the deal with you and Taylor?' he asked. I shrugged. I'd have answered more fully except that I had no idea what to say. I didn't want to risk losing whatever spark it was that had reignited between us by admitting to finding another man attractive, but equally if Eli had moved on on holiday I didn't want him to think that I was sitting around pining over him.. The detente between us felt fragile, and Eli bounced between being flirtatious and cross with me rapidly. I wouldn't have accepted behaviour like that from anyone else, but I knew what Eli had been through and so decided to wait until I could work out what was going on in his head.

Picking up the photograph that Cody had brought, I carried it through to my bedroom. 'You know he's more muscle than brain, don't you?' Eli called as he followed me into my room.

'Lily thinks he's gorgeous,' I pointed out.

'And you?'

I shrugged again and lifted the photo to see how it would look against my wall. 'I haven't decided whether I go for brain or brawn.'

'You could have both,' he said, flexing his biceps. I laughed, but found my eye being drawn back to the print from Cody. It brought back so many memories.

'The first few years after we lost Mum, Dad was too

wrapped up in his grief to go on holiday. But the year that we turned nine, I heard all my friends talking about where they were going that summer. I came home and nagged my dad until he booked a trip. He took us to Wales. We stayed in the village where my mum grew up. My uncle had a holiday cottage that he let out. Ben was so car sick and the traffic was awful. The cottage was tiny, so we were all sleeping in one room. I don't know if Dad had a good time. Thinking back it must have been really tough on him, but we were just a few minutes drive from the beach. Ben and I had the best holiday ever. We spent the week swimming in the sea and eating ice cream. It was the first time we'd been happy in ages. I find myself dreaming about it occasionally.'

'Do you think Ben would have gone back there?' Eli asked.

'It's possible,' I said. 'He suggested it before you booked to go to Cyprus, remember? London is huge but he never goes to most of it. We've checked all of his favourite places anywhere near here. We talked about that trip for years. Dad ended up taking us back a couple of times when we were teenagers. My uncle sent us a key eventually and said we could use it whenever it wasn't booked but it was too far to go very often. It was kind of our happy place when no one was very happy. I remember drooling over the boy who worked on the farm next door for a whole year, then going back determined to catch his attention. I got there, and he'd changed so much since the year before, he was a foot taller, but he'd had the most awful haircut and developed a real attitude. I'd swanned in wearing these tiny shorts and a crop top. I changed my mind quick smart, only for him to spend the rest of the trip following me around with his tongue hanging out.' Eli laughed, and more happy memories began to flood back. 'I can see Ben going there, now that you mention it. Do you remember the year he broke his foot?'

'He came back with a cast on and using crutches,' Eli joined in. 'He thought he was top dog at school, stomping about. Told everyone he'd done it working on a farm.'

'We'd gone to see the cows. The farmer offered us the chance to milk one, he took pity on us city folk having no idea where our food came from. I took one pull on a teat and the cow stepped back and landed on Ben's foot. We spent the rest of the day in A&E. That can't have been Dad's favourite holiday either.'

'He limped for a month, even after the cast came off,' Eli said. 'He told the story anytime anyone drank milk near him forever. Let's go and look. We've looked everywhere that we can think of near here, and we need to get him home before your dad gets back next week. Do you think your dad still has the key? Let's go and check.'

So we let ourselves back into Dad's flat and searched but it was useless. Dad, unlike Ben, was not orderly. He had a bunch of old keys in a drawer in the kitchen but none of them were labelled. There was no way of knowing if the cottage key was still there or if Ben had taken it.

'Dad will kill us if we let anything happen to him,' I agreed. Not adding that he wouldn't need to. Eli and I would never forgive ourselves if our fight was the reason that anything happened to Ben.

I rang my uncle to try and suss out the chances that Ben was there, but didn't want to tell him too much for fear of him worrying and calling my dad to ask what had happened. Luckily he seemed too distracted to ask much. I told him that we'd been thinking of taking a trip and wondered if the cottage might be free. He said that he thought it was but he was away himself, making the most of being single and child-free by taking a cruise to Iceland in search of the Northern Lights. He'd left a key under a rock in the front garden in case a neighbour had needed overflow space for guests over the holidays. We were no further forward with finding Ben but we certainly couldn't discount the very strong possibility that he was in Wales.

'I need some clean clothes,' Eli said. 'I didn't mind sleeping in this T-shirt but I'm not wearing it in public.' I looked and realised that he'd found a faded old one that I'd bought for Father's Day once which read 'You can't scare me, I have twins'. I couldn't blame Eli for wanting to go home.

'Don't forget to pick your car up if you're going home,' I told him.

He groaned. 'It's a five hour drive, at least.'

'And I don't have a licence.' There was never much point learning to drive a car when it was cheaper and more convenient to go everywhere I usually went to in London on foot or by tube.

'I'll be back in an hour,' he sighed. By the time he returned, his black Audi pulled up on a single yellow line outside, I was ready to go. Lily had promised to nip in to the shop and keep it ticking over whilst I was away. I'd left her copious notes of who would be popping in and what items they'd need but I had no doubts that she would be fine. She had handled far more exciting customers than my little shop generally brought in.

I checked the display on the map on my phone. 'Only two hundred miles and we'll find out if my hunch was correct.'

After that, Eli didn't speak again for the rest of the journey, even after I offered to sing to keep him awake. When I tried to sing anyway, Eli wound the window down and threw the CD out. 'That was your music,' I pointed out, and after that he didn't even look at me. Finally we left the motorway and I guided Eli through the twists and turns that led up into the hills.

'Turn right, then you can park on the drive,' I said. Eli stayed silent. 'You'll feel better when you get inside and find Ben,' I told him.

'Phew.' He pulled in and hit the handbrake. His neck cracked as he rotated all the tired muscles back into place after our long journey.

He stared at me and I wondered if he regretted travelling so far just to check up on my hunch, but when he opened the boot I noticed that he picked up my bag as well as his own. I led the way to the front door, noting that the outside light was on. I ran up the path, hoping that I'd find Ben asleep inside, especially given that we'd driven half the night to get here, but the door was locked. I used the torch on my phone to find the rock my uncle had described and lifted it to find the key. I opened the door and we were met by that particular brand of silence that only exists in an empty house.

Chapter Fifteen

Eli dumped our bags on the floor. He was so exhausted that his eyes skimmed straight over the slate floor tiles and Elizabethan timber fireplace. I told him where the bedroom and bathroom were, not that he'd have had any trouble finding them as they were the only two rooms upstairs. The realisation that we'd driven for five hours and Ben wasn't here took the shine off being back in a place that held such happy memories. The red afghan rug on the living room floor was the same as the one that had been there on our last trip, as were the cream-coloured curtains.

'What shall we do?' I called out.

Eli stuck his head out of the bathroom door, toothbrush in the side of his mouth. 'I'm not going anywhere until I've slept. I can't drive back another five hours now, it'd be dangerous.'

I gave him a few minutes to get changed, and then headed up myself. By the time I got in the bathroom I could already hear a gentle snoring. I had to admit, though it was disheartening to get out here and not find Ben, I needed to sleep too before I'd be any good to investigate further. I carted my bag upstairs so that I could get ready for bed.

The shower felt like one of the best I'd ever had, even though it never went much above luke warm. Drying off quickly in the chill of the bathroom, I dug into my bag to find some pyjamas, only to find that the only ones I'd packed were some that Lily had made me buy once. I'd probably shoved them in the holdall so that there wasn't a chance that anybody would spot them in my drawer. I considered sleeping in the T-shirt I'd worn in the car, but it already felt grungy so I pulled the pyjamas on then pulled a jumper over to make sure there were a few bits of me that were actually covered up. I could still hear Eli snoring upstairs but I was wired from the journey. Deciding to treat my city lungs to some proper fresh air, I took a blanket from the sofa, wrapped it around my shoulders and let myself out the front door. The air outside was so clean without the petrol fumes of the traffic that I was used to at home that I could almost feel it cooling and filling my chest as I breathed it in. That wasn't the only difference. With no street lights, the view of the stars was incredible. The constellations were probably obvious to anyone who knew the first thing about astronomy, but growing up with near constant light pollution I hadn't seen them enough times to have learnt the names. Ben would have known. He'd grown up fascinated, first by the concept of an infinitely large universe, and later by the technological and mathematical developments which were helping us to slowly understand it a little better. As I watched, a tiny streak of light flashed by and was gone within a few seconds. A shooting star. I closed my eyes and wished to have my brother back safely.

Not trusting that my wish would be enough, I tried to get myself back on track. Bed. I should sleep so that I could wake up tomorrow and think what to try next. I switched on the torch on my phone and used it to light my way back towards the house. Checking the path as I walked to make sure that I didn't trip over any tree roots, I spotted a wrapper caught in a bush next to the front door. It was the same as the brand that we'd seen in Ben's desk drawer at work.

Recharged with hope, I went back in, stripped back down to my tiny pyjamas, then stood at the foot of the bed, trying to work out whether I should climb in with

Eli or try and keep warm on the sofa covered in blankets. The cottage walls were probably the best part of a foot of stone thick but the heating had clearly been off when the cottage was empty, and I started to shiver as I stood there. Eventually my teeth started chattering too, so I gave up worrying and climbed in next to Eli.

When we woke the next morning, his hand was on my bottom. I'd have complained but both of mine were on his. 'Well this is a delightful way to start the day,' Eli said, yawning without letting go of me.

In contrast, I pulled my hands away as quickly as I could and sat up. Eli's eyes dropped to my neckline. 'I forgot to pack my PJs. These were all I could find in my bag.' The top was more translucent than I had realised when I'd put in on in the dark. 'Lily made me buy them,' I explained.

'I'm starting to approve of your product range after all,' he said. I waited until his eyes reached mine, eventually, before I spoke again. I told him about finding the wrapper the night before.

'That proves Ben was here, don't you think?'

'It might,' he admitted, sitting up. The duvet fell to his waist, revealing his bare chest. This time he had to wait for me to tear my eyes away before speaking. 'But we can't get carried away. Ben hadn't told your uncle he wanted to stay in the cottage, so we can't know for sure.'

'I wish I could hack his e-mails or track his phone position,' I moaned, falling backwards onto the bed and closing my eyes as I spoke. 'I bet if Ben were here he'd have loads of ideas of how to find a person like himself.'

'He didn't find Cody,' Eli pointed out. 'You did that.'

'Not me, I can't take any credit. Arthur told me who she was.'

'Because you gave him time. You make people

comfortable, get them talking. I bet you Arthur was in your shop at least an hour, wasn't he?'

'Forty-five minutes,' I told him. 'I already knew some of the items he'd like and had them pre-wrapped ready for him to take.' I yawned. Waking up with Eli had felt lovely, but we were only here because we were on a mission. It wouldn't do to get distracted by his biceps. Even if they looked impressive in the morning light. 'I'm going to put the kettle on.' Realising that my legs needed shaving again, I pulled my jeans on too so that Eli wouldn't get an eye full of stubble if he was able to see down that low. I picked my jumper up from the floor and pulled it on over my camisole.

Eli walked into the kitchen just as I finished making the coffee. 'I was a bit optimistic hoping we'd find something here for breakfast. I found a jar of instant at the back of the cupboard that was only six months out of date.' I sniffed the murky contents of my mug before taking a tentative sip. Pulling a face, I tipped the contents of both cups down the sink. 'Looks like we're going out for breakfast, but on the bright side it'll give me a chance to *talk to people* and see if anyone else has seen my brother.' Talking didn't feel like such a fantastic super power to have when I was alone in a tiny cottage with a man with secret spy skills and a six pack.

Eli walked towards me, and I swallowed as he stopped mere inches from me. He leant forward and I closed my eyes, wondering if he were about to kiss me, but instead I heard the oak door next to my head open and close. 'You're right, not even a box of stale cornflakes. I'll grab my clothes and then let's head out.'

The cottage was even more spectacular in daylight. The rough-hewn wooden door opened onto a covered porch. The roof kept the fine mist from making my hair frizzy, as

I stood on the doorstep and took a lungful of crisp country air. I glanced across the fields and hills that stretched as far as I could see. Some of the distant hills had snow dusting their peaks. I hoped that wherever Ben was he was warm and safe.

Eli appeared next to me. He took a tentative sniff. 'Smells like …'

'Countryside?' I suggested.

'Dung.' Eli started marching past the bush where I'd seen the chocolate bar wrapper and let himself out of the gate.

'We have to make sure we shut this or the sheep will get in and eat the plants.' Eli didn't pause when I spoke and continued walking past his car and up the hill. 'Where are you going?' I called.

'To find breakfast. There's got to be somewhere round here that does a good fry up.'

'There is, but not within walking distance. Didn't you notice last night how quiet it was when we drove in?'

'I was just busy trying to keep my eyes open,' he admitted. He unlocked the car and I let myself in. 'Guide me to the nearest café. I need caffeine and bacon as quickly as possible.'

As Eli used the last of his toast to wipe clean his tyre-sized plate, I finished my coffee and spread some raspberry jam on my tea cake. He finally seemed more alert. 'So who do we talk to first?' he asked.

I showed the waitress Ben's photo as she cleared our table. She took the time to look carefully at his picture, despite every table being full of customers. I found myself holding my breath as she looked, but eventually she shook her head.

'Sorry love,' she said, tucking her pen into the wispy bun of white hair on top of her head. I stared at Eli, waiting for him to come up with a brainwave of what I should ask next, but he didn't. He was too busy hiding behind a newspaper and trying to look inconspicuous. It wasn't working. Most of the women in the café, and a few of the men, were glancing at him appreciatively. I wondered just how he stayed incognito when he worked. There was just no hiding how good-looking he was. I poked the edge of his paper down so I could see him. He had a grin on his face, despite how worried we both were about Ben. Mind you, it seemed he'd proved himself to be resourceful enough to get as far as the cottage, so hopefully he was okay. I just needed to see him to be sure. My brother didn't march to the beat of anyone else's drum and it was too ingrained in me to keep an eye on him to go without finding him now.

'Is he in trouble?' the waitress asked. I read the name badge with curled edges that was pinned to her white apron. The letters were lifting off as the plastic came away, and it took me a minute to decipher that it read 'Rhonda'. Most people in the cafe seemed to know her already, certainly no one looked surprised that she was chatting rather than taking orders, and no one shouted or called out anything rude to get her attention. The world outside of London was truly different, and I was beginning to appreciate it more and more. Even though she hadn't seen Ben, she wasn't in any rush to move on.

'No,' I assured her. 'He's my little brother. He's really clever and really, really kind. He can do anything with computers, he just struggles a bit in the real world.'

'We all know people like that,' she assured me, pulling over a seat from the table behind me and joining us. I was tempted to offer her the pot of coffee to make herself more comfortable. 'You don't live around here do you.' It wasn't a question. She could tell from our accents that we didn't. Besides, she probably knew everyone who lived within ten miles of the village.

'He got a bit upset at home the other day and we think he might have decided to come up here for a break. We have lots of happy memories here from when we were kids.'

'Have you visited recently?' she asked. I shook my head. 'It will have changed a bit since you were last here then. There's a new amusement park by the beach.' The elderly man sat at the table behind her sniffed and set his cutlery down on his plate with a clatter. 'We have a few problems with the kids who hang out sometimes, but if your brother likes computer games, maybe you should try there.'

I thanked her, paid the bill and left twice the tip I would have in London. We'd had more than twice the usual amount of attention we'd have got back home. It also still cost less than the last breakfast Lily and I went out for, and Eli had demolished the biggest meal on their menu. Outside, I stopped by Eli's car.

'Nothing is within walking distance here,' I said.

'I don't mind the driving.' *I* was beginning to mind however. The roads that led to the beach were winding. Eli grinned as he drove. I held onto the door with one hand and braced myself against the dashboard with the other.

'These roads are two way,' I pointed out. 'You might want to slow down a bit.' There were no pavements and if he judged a turn incorrectly we were liable to drive either into a tree or over the side of a hill. It was beautiful but utterly, utterly terrifying to a city girl. The biggest dangers I faced at home were getting in the way of incompetent cyclists trying their luck on a hire bike or getting stuck behind a crowd of slow-moving tourists. Mind you, having to wait behind a particularly leisurely group of sheep crossing the road at one point did seem a little familiar.

'I'm going ten miles slower than the speed limit,' Eli said, as I went into the brace position as we crested one hill. I shut my eyes until he parked, switched the engine off and turned to face me. 'You can take your seat-belt off now.'

'If I get out and kiss the floor like the Pope does when he gets off an aeroplane would you be offended?'

Chapter Sixteen

The lights were off when we arrived, lending the amusement park an air of being a deserted shell where pocket money and teenage romances came to die. The windows were covered in a thick film of grime, but I got as close as I dared and peeped inside.

'Is this the kind of place Ben might have come?' I asked Eli.

'He does like his games, though I'm not sure he'd enjoy the crowds of an arcade usually. This place could be perfect for him.'

I looked at the torn canopy that hung over the door and the hand-written sign, complete with spelling mistakes, which said that the arcade wasn't open on Mondays. 'Somehow I don't think crowds are going to be a problem here. Looks like we've got the rest of the day to ask around. If we don't have any more luck, maybe we can come back tomorrow.'

The thought of spending another night next to Eli wasn't unpleasant. In fact, it was a little too tempting. Crawling into bed after a long journey hadn't seemed too intimate, just sensible. We were exhausted and needed to sleep. The idea of doing the same when we were both awake enough to know what we were doing felt entirely different. I found myself blushing, then getting cross with myself for even thinking such thoughts when we hadn't yet found my brother.

'If you're worrying about your lack of pyjamas, I have no problem with you wearing that little set you had on last night,' Eli said. I cursed him for being able to read my mind. 'I didn't need to,' he said. 'Your cheeks are nearly as red as those knickers you had on last week. You didn't happen to bring those too, did you?'

I didn't answer, not least because there was a spare pair in my bag, and I didn't trust myself not to end up wearing them for him. I knew that I ought to suggest that one of us slept on the sofa, and yet the words didn't seem to want to leave my mouth. 'We're here to search for Ben,' I reminded him. And myself. Which is why we spent the rest of the afternoon visiting every shop, pub and café for miles around.

The people that we met made a stark contrast to those I'd tried to talk to in London. Without fail they listened to me explain why we were looking for Ben and looked at his photo, before shaking their heads and wishing us luck. The lady in the bakery had felt so sorry for me that she had given us free sandwiches and cakes, but by dinner-time my feet ached from walking, my throat hurt from talking and my eyes were sore from having to blink back tears.

'This is the last pub in this area that we haven't visited yet,' Eli said, opening the door and letting me walk past him. There was a roaring log fire set into the wall opposite the bar. Had I not been so distraught at running out of places to try it would have been a cosy and a welcome place to relax. Eli guided me to a comfy leather armchair and waited until I'd sat down before he went to the bar to fetch us drinks and menus. Coming back to the table he handed me a tall glass of sparkling wine. He opened the black plastic folder, took a quick glance before closing it and going back to the counter.

'What the hell, Eli?' I demanded when he sat back down. 'Do I have to order my own food now?'

'Relax,' he told me. 'They only had one vegetarian

option on the menu. You're having mushroom stroganoff. I already ordered it.'

'What if I'd wanted it—'

'—with chips instead of rice? Then you'd be in luck, because that's what I asked for.'

Sometimes it was nice to spend time with people who knew you so well. Sometimes it was infuriating for exactly the same reasons. I didn't ask how, despite sniping at each other for so long, he still knew exactly what I liked. I was scared he'd think that I was referring to the bedroom too. I tried to change the subject. 'Had they seen Ben in here?'

'The manager said the photo looked familiar, she thinks he might have been in here the night after we argued. Hence the cava. It was the closest they had to champagne. This could be our first break of the day. The waitress who worked the last couple of days is due in at eight. They reckoned she would know for sure.' He glanced at his watch. 'That gives us two hours. There's no point in running anywhere else in the meantime. We've already tried every other place nearby. I suggest we take the universe's hint and have a rest. I don't know about you, but I need one.'

When I finished my drink and went to the bar, I returned with a whole bottle of wine. 'To help us relax,' I told him when he cocked a questioning eyebrow. By the time the waitress came in, I'd drunk most of it myself, having conveniently forgotten when I had ordered it that Eli was driving. We'd cleared our plates and split a serving of sticky toffee pudding with ice cream.

'You're looking for your brother?' the woman said, taking her coat off and hanging it up behind the bar. She wore a T-shirt identifying herself as a student at the University of Gallifrey. If anyone would have noticed Ben and made him feel safe enough to chat, it would be her.

I nodded and showed her a bunch of photos of Ben on my phone. 'He looks like a grown man, and I know I shouldn't worry, but he's pretty innocent. I'm nervous that he'll get into trouble if we don't find him soon.' Not to mention that Dad would kill me if he got home to find that I'd lost my brother.

'He was fine when he was in here yesterday lunchtime,' she assured me.

'Are you sure it was him?'

She looked through some more pictures. 'Definitely, but he looked a bit more pale in person.' Yup, that was Ben.

I turned, threw my hands around Eli's neck and planted a kiss on his lips. His hands went round my waist, and he held me for a few seconds, before we pulled away and both took a sip of our drinks. The waitress began pulling a pint for the man stood next to me. I felt embarrassed at my display of affection for Eli, but no one else in the place knew our history or batted an eyelid at us. 'We've nearly found him,' I said excitedly, bouncing from foot to foot, the alcohol fizzing around my system.

'We're going to bring him home,' Eli said, putting his arms around me again. Still no one was looking, so when he kissed me again I didn't stop him.

It took a few minutes after we finished kissing before I could form a coherent thought that wasn't along the lines of 'wow'. Finally though, I pulled myself together and managed to ask a few more questions. Ben had only been in once, and the waitress only remembered him because he'd come to the bar to order a Coke and on hearing her complain about her phone refusing to unlock, he'd taken it from her and fixed it.

'I gave him his drink for free. He was chuffed. The girl sat next to him kept shooting me dirty looks, not that I talked to him any more after that. We were busy in, there was a game on the big screen. When I got back from serving some meals he was gone.' I assumed that she was mistaken about Ben being with a girl, perhaps he had sat next to one and she wasn't happy about it, but apart from that it sounded very much like my brother. I squealed again with relief and excitement that we might finally be getting close to Ben. Or perhaps it was the wine going to my head.

'Let's go,' I told Eli. I tugged on his arm, enjoying the feel of his biceps. It was easier to enjoy it now that I was less worried about Ben. I tugged again, or at least I meant to, I suspect really I was just stroking Eli's muscles. He grinned at me.

We stopped at a garage on the way home for petrol. When Eli climbed back in after paying he stopped at the boot to drop a bag in. When we pulled up in front of the cottage, he had to help me out of the car because the world was spinning too fast for me to walk by myself. He stopped to get his bag out of the boot.

Letting ourselves back in, I swore when I felt how cold the cottage was. 'Let me guess,' Eli said, 'a cottage this old doesn't have central heating?' He began to light a fire, but his city boy ways let him down again, and as I brushed my teeth upstairs I could hear him cursing as the fire refused to catch.

I took a quick shower, but had to hold myself up using the walls. It had been a while since I'd drunk so much. Pulling on a new pair of red knickers, I dropped the towel on the side of the bath and tucked myself into bed, ready for Eli to find when he came up. He must have been a while though, because the next thing I was aware of, it was morning. My head was pounding, and Eli was sat up, duvet down around his waist, grinning at me.

'I like the pants.'

Chapter Seventeen

'Did we …?' I asked Eli.

'I was a perfect gentleman,' he assured me. 'I assumed that you wanted to, hence the frilly red pants.' He lifted the duvet and had a second look. I screamed and batted the covers back down again. 'I was surprised that you weren't wearing anything else with them, I have to say.' I slunk down and pulled the cover up over my head, but he tugged it down again so that he could see my face. 'Sorry to disappoint you, but not only were you already asleep by the time I made it upstairs, but you'd drunk virtually the whole bottle of wine by yourself, and I didn't think you were in any fit state to decide if it was what you really wanted to do. I like vocal consent, not drunken fumblings. If we were together, I want to know that you really, really are enjoying what we're doing.'

This time he didn't stop me from pulling the covers up again, and I hid as waves of embarrassment and shame washed over me. I think Eli knew, as I could hear him chuckling as he pottered around the room getting dressed. I envied Lily's body confidence. If she wanted something and had a willing partner then she viewed sex as a perfectly good form of personal expression. She wouldn't have wanted the ground to swallow her up just because someone had seen her almost naked. Lily had tried to persuade me any number of times to learn to accept and enjoy my own sexuality. I thought about calling her to tell her what I'd done. She didn't bear Eli any grudges for the number of partners he'd had over the years – he had been free to do what he wanted technically – but she might still be cross about how upset I'd been at having to see the seemingly never-ending parade because I had never quite managed to move on in the same way. She would probably just caution me about risking having my heart broken again, and I wasn't quite strong enough yet to admit to myself that I was in very real danger of that happening if Eli didn't feel the same way as I did. As soon as Eli left the room I got out of bed and dug a couple of paracetamol out of my handbag. Sticking my head under the tap in the bathroom, I managed to get enough water to swallow them. It was easier to shower now the world had stopped spinning like a fairground ride, but not by much as the noise of the pump made my head hurt all over again. Eli tapped at the door and opened it.

'Get out!' I shouted. His hand reached just inside and set a cup of coffee on the floor though the rest of him thankfully didn't follow. The caffeine helped, and once the painkillers had kicked in I felt human again, though I didn't go downstairs immediately. In fact, I didn't go down at all, unready to face him after I'd made my need for him all too clear, until eventually Eli came to find me.

'Breakfast is ready.'

'When did we get food?' I asked, because it was easier to talk about that than to broach why I'd been waiting for him in just a slip of red silk and lace the night before.

'There was a small grocery section in the petrol station. You were so drunk I thought you might need a recovery breakfast today.'

'I wasn't that drunk.' I pouted.

'So you were sober when you dressed, or undressed, for bed last night?'

I shut up after that and continued to drink my coffee. 'Let's review where we're up to,' I said eventually. 'Ben was definitely in Wales, and probably stayed the first night here, so we're hopefully several hundred miles closer already?'

'And he was fine when the waitress saw him, that's reassuring.'

I tried to ring Ben's mobile yet again but he was still refusing to answer. I hung up, swore loudly and with no other ideas, began to draw up a list of places to revisit. Eli pulled the pad towards himself and read it out loud. 'The amusement arcade.'

I didn't say it was a long list. 'We tried everywhere else yesterday,' I reminded him. I wasn't as much of a whizz online as Ben, but I could use Google as well as the next person. I pulled up a list of hotels. 'Then I think we should come back and make some calls. Ben clearly hasn't been back since we've been here, but without a vehicle he's limited to how far he could have got.' We headed out to the car.

Eli was turning the key in the ignition as my brain finally sparked into life again too. 'I can't believe I've been so stupid,' I muttered, smacking my forehead with my open hand.

'If it's any consolation, if you had been sober then I definitely would have but drunkenness doesn't equal consent. You looked amazing. I had to have a very cold shower before I came to bed last night.'

I turned to face Eli, ignoring his response, though the butterflies in my stomach were evidence that my body was replying to his statement. 'How did Ben get to the pub? It took us ten minutes in the car. It must be three miles from here. The arcade is a good few miles on the other side. He's got to be getting around somehow.'

'He could have walked. He didn't have anywhere else he needed to be.'

'I'll call all the local cab firms when we get back here. There can't be many in the area. If one of them picked him up and took him to another hotel, at least we might have the next place to look. As things stand, we're risking falling further behind him again.'

The amusement arcade was no less depressing for being open and lit up. If a cleaning crew had been through since it had closed for the day, there was no evidence of it. The paths that twisted and wound between fruit machines, two penny slots and arcade games felt tacky under foot. A young man stood feeding coins into a machine which seemed to swallow his donations as fast as he could make them. His jeans were so baggy that not only was the waistband of his pants visible, but so was half of his bottom. Clearly he needed to buy some with new elastic. If he had any money left at the end of his session.

The rest of the arcade was deserted, though the flashing lights and beckoning noises of the games gave an eerie impression of a space that was haunted, the alarms and strobes flashing to entertain participants who were no longer present. I searched to find a member of staff without success. I was about to accidentally on purpose knock into a machine to see if I could set the alarm off to get someone's attention, when Eli yelled my name.

I raced over to find him pointing excitedly at a screen. 'I know you're chuffed to find Sonic the Hedgehog in an arcade, but please remember that we're here to find Ben.'

'I did,' Eli said, jabbing his finger at the display. 'Look'. He didn't step back, so I was forced to squeeze against him. The display read that we needed to add more credit if we wanted to play, but Eli made no move to drop coins into the slot so I stood next to him and waited until the screen changed again. 'There, see.'

And then I did. The top five scores were all attributed to somebody called Ben. Eli took me by the hand and led me to the next machine. This one not only had Ben as the top three scores, but it also gave the dates that the scores had been saved. The day after we had argued. Taking a quick run around the arcade, I checked all the other scores that I could see. Ben's name was on the majority of them. Whatever he'd been up to on his trip he'd clearly had time to spare, but I still needed to find him, apologise and bring him home.

The man in the baggy jeans wandered off and no one entered to take his place so eventually we gave up waiting to find anyone else to speak to. Presumably the place came into its own later in the day, but right now it was deserted.

Back at the cottage, I copied the list of mini cab firms onto my pad and began calling. The job would probably have been next to impossible in London. For a start there would have been an endless list of firms to ring, but also most of them would have doubtless been unwilling to track down individual passengers or drivers, especially as Ben was an adult who had left of his own free will. They wouldn't understand why Eli and I were so worried. Here though, my starting point of forty numbers was quickly whittled down. Five of the firms were listed twice, several more were so far away I didn't think they would travel this far for a five-minute journey.

It seemed that many of the businesses listed were in fact single driver operations. 'Probably farmers making a bit of spare cash by fitting in some driving for elderly neighbours and teenage drinkers on the weekends,' Eli suggested, setting a cup of tea next to my elbow and glancing at my notes.

As I crossed the last number off my list with no success

to show for it, Eli stepped behind me and began to massage my shoulders. It was hard to unwind, knowing that Ben was still missing, but the sensation of Eli's strong fingers touching me was hard to resist. I moaned, and he paused for a moment, before resuming his motion, this time in a more gentle and sensual action. He swept the hair from the back of my neck and kissed me.

When I moaned again, he gently lifted me from the chair and turned me to face him. He lowered his mouth to mine and kissed me until my knees buckled. I sat back onto the table, knocking my cup flying and spilling tea all over the floor. The sound of the china smashing made me jump, and Eli pulled back for a moment to check that I was okay. He leant in to kiss me again but I placed my hand on his chest.

'Just let me clean up or I won't be able to concentrate. I think living with my brother has rubbed off on me more than I realised.' I was half way to the sink to find the dustpan and brush before the blood returned sufficiently to my brain to allow the synapses to make a connection that I should have spotted two days and two hundred miles ago.

'The washing up,' I said.

Eli stared at me as if I were crazy. 'I'm giving you my best moves and you're thinking about the washing up?'

Chapter Eighteen

'I'm such an idiot,' I said, turning from Eli and beginning to pace as much as I could in the tiny kitchen.

'Are you still talking about the cup, or is this about me?' Eli asked, leaning against the counter-top.

'When Ben first left, we thought that he had been home because some of his clothes were gone but the washing up was still there. If Ben had seen it he wouldn't have left without doing it. And the passport, it was on the floor by the bin but not in the bin. He wouldn't have left it like that.'

Anyone else might have scoffed in the face of such scant evidence, but Eli knew Ben well enough to immediately realise the import of what I'd realised. He dug his mobile phone from his coat pocket and swiped the screen to wake it up. He lifted it to his ear, speaking to me as he waited for the call to connect. 'When we find Ben, and we will, you and I have some unfinished business.'

I gulped, and was trying to process how I felt about Eli, when he began to speak again. It took a second before I realised that he wasn't talking to me. 'Ben!' I shouted, reaching for his phone. Eli pressed another button and set it to speakerphone, before holding it in the middle between us.

'How are you doing, mate? We've been worried about you,' Eli said. It was more polite than the 'where the hell are you?' that I'd bitten back.

'I'm fine, just needed to get away for a bit.' My brother's voice sounded quite cheerful. It was a stark contrast to how worried I'd been and I felt my temper rise at his tone.

'You'd only just got back from holiday!' I pointed out. Eli shot me a look. 'I'm sorry Eli and I were arguing the other day. We didn't mean to scare you away.'

'I don't like fighting,' Ben said, 'but this trip is for me, I need it.' The relief I felt was palpable. Eli must have felt the same as he held his arm out and I ducked under it for a cuddle.

'Where did you go?' Eli asked him.

'Away,' Ben said, as if that were all the detail anyone might need. I stared at the phone, imagining that if my brother were in front of me right now I might hug him first then wring his neck for being so vague. Finally, Ben began to speak again. 'I was upset that you were shouting at each other. You two are my best friends. I hate that you don't get on.' I began to blush, aware of just how well Eli and I had been getting on recently.

'We've been … talking … a lot since you left,' Eli told him then winked at me. Ben couldn't detect the undercurrent of humour in Eli's voice, nor the amount that he'd left unsaid, and responded as if Eli had been giving him the full story.

'I'm pleased to hear it. Anyway, I had a good time when we were away but it got me thinking. Eli, I know you don't believe in forever love, unlike my sister who only needs to snog a guy and she starts fantasising about their wedding.' I blushed so red I had to turn away before Eli noticed. Ben continued, unaware that he was telling Eli more about my feelings for him than I was ready for him to know. 'I know you're very different but when you argue it feels like I'm being torn in two. I didn't know what to do so I left.'

'Where are you, bud?'

'Wales,' Ben announced with a flourish that would have amazed me, if I hadn't already known that he'd been here.

'Care to narrow it down a little?' I asked. 'That's only a whole country.'

Ben again missed my sarcasm. 'I went to our uncle's cottage, the one that Dad used to bring us to. It had a log fire, and the views from the garden were amazing. But it turns out that in the last ten years, they haven't added any wi-fi, not even the slow crap type that civilians use.' I could sense him juddering down the phone at the thought of slow connection speeds. 'I tried, I really did, but it was even worse than the broadband I could get in Cyprus, so I phoned around the hotels until I found one that offered fibre and booked in there instead.'

'How have you been getting around?' I asked, thinking that my brainwave about the taxis should have led to more results.

'What are you talking about?' Ben asked. 'I just get in the car.'

'You don't drive,' I pointed out.

'No, but ...' The call was interrupted by a high-pitched scream.

'Ben? Ben?' I shouted, grabbing the mobile and pulling it towards me, but it was no good. The call had ended. I handed it to Eli. 'Call him back, quick!' But Ben didn't pick up.

'Oh my goodness, oh my goodness, oh my goodness,' I cried, trying to pace again but not getting far without having to step around Eli or the table.

'Calm down,' Eli said. 'Ben said he was fine. In fact, it sounds like he's been having a nice break.'

'Did you not hear the scream?' I asked, my voice dripping with incredulity.

'I did hear it,' Eli said, pulling a chair out from the table and dropping into it. He covered his face with his hands. 'I just thought that if I could convince you that he was okay, maybe it would be true. That was not a good scream.'

'So now we're back where we started,' I said. 'We know Ben is here somewhere, but now he won't answer his phone, and he screamed. Now can we call the police?'

Eli shook his head. 'He admitted that he came here voluntarily. We've only got one scream to go on and they won't know him as well as we do to know he doesn't get worked up easily. Besides, I've covered for him at work but I need to have him back by the end of the week. He needs to show his face in the office before Christmas or they're going to notice, then they're going to investigate and if he's disappeared in mysterious circumstances they're going to rescind his security clearance. Bye Bye job.' Eli didn't need to tell me how bad that would be. Ben loved his job and he was amazing at it. Not to mention how much safer the country was for his efforts. 'He mentioned a hotel. Let's ring round, see if any of them have him registered.'

But half an hour later I was close to screaming myself with the frustration. 'How is this even possible? He's getting around in a car that he can't drive, staying in a hotel that he's not registered at.'

'Let's try again,' Eli said. 'Give me the list of cab firms, there must have been one on there who didn't pick up, that'll be who he's using. Or maybe the hotels are just saying no because they won't give out guest details, even if he is booked in.'

This time it was me shooting Eli a look. 'People talk to me. You said it yourself. If he was booked in a hotel in his own name, they'd have told me. They understood that I was worried.' I offered to make Eli a cuppa, thinking that I ought to make up for the one that I'd broken, even though I didn't actually feel like drinking it. There was something about the familiar action though of setting out the mug and tea bag that was soothing in and of itself, and once again, my brain finally put together evidence that should have been obvious. Refilling the kettle, I returned it to the counter and plugged it in, noticing the cables as I did.

'Ben's tattoo, it wasn't just wires. It was wires that fit together.'

'It was a male and female jack, I know, he told me.'

'And he'd been working out,' I said. 'I could see when he took his top off. He's not muscular like you yet, but he also wasn't the skinny runt that he had been.'

Eli finally caught up with me. 'The waitress yesterday said that there was a girl there giving her filthy looks. I assumed she was mistaken, but what happens if she wasn't?'

I grabbed my handbag. 'Get your keys,' I told him. 'We're going to the pub.'

Chapter Nineteen

The pub wasn't as deserted as the amusement arcade, though even here the slot machines were flashing despite having no one to attract. There was an old fashioned shoot 'em up arcade game next to the door of the gents. Out of curiosity, I checked the screen. Ben held the top score.

The waitress that we needed to speak to didn't start her shift until the evening, but the manager recognised us from our previous trip, and when I explained that I still hadn't found my brother, he offered to ring her so that we could talk.

'There's not much to report,' she said, when we got her on the line. 'She wasn't especially tall or short. In fact she looked pretty boring to me. Though your brother was obviously taken by her. When he wasn't shooting zombies or fixing my mobile.'

'What did she look like? What was she wearing?' I asked.

'Mousey hair, like yours,' the girl said, and I resisted the urge to hang up on her. 'And I can't remember her clothes. Honestly, I don't think there was anything eye-catching about her at all.'

I covered the mouthpiece with my hand. 'This is pointless, we're never going to find her,' I moaned to Eli. He took the phone from me and set it on speaker so that he could join in the call.

'Is there anything else you can tell us that might help?' he asked.

'You the cute guy that was there the other night?' she

asked. 'Come back on your own sometime and I'll help you.' I whacked Eli's arm so hard he yelped. I heard the waitress laugh down the phone. 'Yeah, the other lady was pretty jealous too when your brother helped me. He kept promising her that he hadn't looked at any other girls when he'd been on holiday which seemed like a strange thing to say given that they were clearly here together, but she seemed pleased to hear it. I took them the bill, I could hear them saying something about a wedding they'd been at, but I wasn't eavesdropping on purpose. I wouldn't have remembered at all except I was waitressing at a wedding the week before myself.'

'We need to ring round the hotels again now we know who he's with,' I told Eli after we hung up. He looked at me, confused. 'Stop thinking about the waitress. You're not coming back here alone.' He grinned at me. 'Ben must have been here with Erin,' I explained.

'How did you figure out that?' Eli asked.

'I don't like to comment on other women, but seriously, is there anything about her that you could remember or describe easily? Plus she was there at the wedding. And Ben said that they work together. Where else is Ben going to meet women?'

'There were some cute girls in the bar on holiday. No wonder he wouldn't come and talk to them,' Eli said. I stared at him. 'Of course I was only talking to them to be friendly myself.'

I decided that it was probably better not to ask or even to think about it. When we got Ben safely home, I'd be able to concentrate on working out whether there was anything between Eli and I. I hoped that Ben wasn't correct about Eli's refusal to commit and my need to, but that was a whole train of thought that wasn't going anywhere good, so I tried to push it out of my mind as I followed Eli back to his car.

He switched the engine on so that we could have some heating while we began to phone the hotels again, this time asking about reservations in Erin's name. We struck gold on the second call. Eli signalled left, and we were off. The hotel wasn't far, in fact we'd driven past it several times over the last few days to get to the pub, but it was set back from the road behind a huge gravel car park. There were only two cars in the enormous lot: a muddy jeep which looked more suitable for the hills and valleys of the surrounding countryside than the car park of a smart country hotel, and a small red Skoda with furry dice hanging from the rear-view mirror. 'Country cars.' Eli smirked, as he pulled his Audi into a space far away from them, as if he were scared that having a car suited to the area around here was catching. I didn't like to point out the thick layer of dust and mud on his usually pristine paint job.

Inside, there were brochures of wedding packages set up in a display, alongside a tower of dusty champagne flutes and a bouquet of imitation roses. The air reeked of boiled cabbage. If any of my customers had suggested having their nuptials here I'd have advised them to run a mile. The net curtains somehow managed to be both faded and discoloured which was a rare and unattractive combination.

Behind the desk, the receptionist stood to greet us. She was in her mid-fifties. Her bleached blonde hair was drawn back into a bun so tight that I bet no single strand would dare to escape. 'How can I help you?' she asked. The rictus smile on her face suggested that she neither wished nor cared to help us if she could help it.

'I rang a few minutes ago,' I explained. 'My brother is

staying here. I was hoping that you could tell us which room he's in?'

Her starched smile fell away quickly, and without it her expression looked as severe as her hairstyle. 'I'm afraid I can't give away personal details,' she said.

'But when I rang, the man I spoke to said that he was checked in.'

'You'll have spoken to Bryn, our trainee receptionist. I'll be speaking to him myself shortly after this.' Her mouth puckered so tightly it resembled a cat's behind. I wondered whether Bryn would still be her trainee by tomorrow.

'Then please can you ring my brother's room? Tell him I'm here and I'd like to see him.'

'I'm afraid I can't,' she said, standing up and resting both her palms flat on her desk. 'Is the manager in?' I asked. 'I want to talk to someone else.'

'I am the manager,' she said, straightening her pale pink cardigan and standing up to her full height of five-foot and not much more. It still didn't make it any more likely that I would come this close and give up without a fight.

'Listen, lady, I've been polite, I've been calm. But I really, really need to speak to my brother. Now would you please call him, before I start to get really fed up?' I didn't like losing my temper, and certainly I tried not to bully people usually, but her imperious manner was impacting on my usual level of manners.

Eli slung his arm around me and leaned in to speak to her too. 'I don't see Daisy angry very often, but smoke is about to start pouring out of her ears. I'd really advise you to call Ben's room.'

'I can't,' she said again. I took a deep breath, about to let her have both barrels for keeping me away from Ben when she spoke again. 'His girlfriend checked out shortly after you spoke to Bryn. You probably drove past their car on your way here.'

Eli swore loudly and creatively. A couple crept into the reception and hurried back out again as he cursed. Hopefully they were not in search of their dream wedding venue, but if they were then we'd saved them from making a mistake by booking in.

'Did they say where they were going?' I asked.

'Oh, I didn't see your brother, dear,' she said, her voice dripping with disdain, and though she had called me 'dear', there was nothing endearing about her tone. 'Just his girlfriend. She seemed in a terrible hurry too. Of course, all you city folk rush too much.'

I wanted to tell her that if she had hurried more I'd have been closer to finding my brother, but her sanctimonious expression was raising my blood pressure, so I left before I swore at her myself. I even managed not to knock over the glasses as I walked out. Which was easier to do because I knew that Eli wouldn't have the same level of control. Sure enough, a few seconds later I heard an almighty crash of broken glass.

'Sorry,' Eli shouted to her as he opened the door to leave. 'I accidentally knocked your display over in my rush to leave.'

Chapter Twenty

For lack of any other ideas we drove back to the cottage. 'So now what?' I asked, slamming the car door so hard that Eli winced.

'Now we try not to take it out on my car?' he suggested. I glared at him. He guided me into the cottage and tried to help me take my coat off but I slapped his hands away.

'I'm not staying,' I snapped. 'I should be looking for Ben.'

'But where are we going next? We need to regroup. There's no point running around the entire area again. We tried that once and all that happened was we ended up knackered.' I let him slip my jacket off and sat in the chair that he pointed to. When he placed a sandwich in front of me I ate it without tasting a bite. He fixed himself a plate and sat opposite me at the wooden table. He pulled the pad and pen from my handbag, turned to a fresh page and began writing again. 'Erin. What do we know? She works in our building. I think they brought her in to support Ben's work. To act as a link.'

'Between Ben and the other departments?'

'Between Ben and everyone else, except me. She understands more of what he does than anyone else I've ever met, but she's very good at blending into the background and making sure the office can run smoothly. I think Ben's been happier for having her around. He doesn't get into trouble for misunderstanding what he's been asked to do, and we get advance knowledge of any breakthroughs that he has made so we have the resources in place to act on his tips. They're actually a really good team and this country is lucky to have them.'

'So she works very closely with my brother and you didn't think to mention just how well Ben knew her before because?'

'We had no idea that he was with anyone. Besides, it's Erin. No one pays her much attention, she's very quiet, she just gets on with it.'

'Do you think that's why the washing up was left at home? Maybe she packed his bag for him and he never went in?' I suggested. 'Maybe she distracted him, or just lied and told him that she had cleaned up. Ben always tells the truth, he doesn't understand that other people don't.'

'So we argue, he goes to her feeling upset. She persuades him to run away with her,' Eli said, beginning to piece together the jigsaw to see if we could make it into a coherent picture rather than the jumble of assorted pieces that we currently had.

'She drives him here, then after one night they move on to the hotel with the wi-fi and dragon receptionist.'

'They go to the pub where he helps the waitress and makes Erin jealous.'

'But all is still well until he rings us.'

'Something sets her off.' I pushed my chair back and began to pace as I spoke. 'She gets spooked and leaves, but we don't know whether they're still together or not and Ben isn't answering our calls again. They came here because it was a place that Ben felt safe. Where would Erin go if she felt like she had to run?'

'Home?' Eli suggested. 'We need to find out more about Erin. Do we drive back to London?'

'It would be five hours before we get there. That's too long. What if she went somewhere else? We could be going in the wrong direction.'

153

'I can't phone into work and ask, they don't mind us taking a break when we need one, but you have to understand, Ben works on high level security projects. If they find out that he's gone AWOL, they'll panic.'

I had an idea but I knew that Eli wouldn't like it. Though whether his reaction would be due to personal jealousy or work competitiveness I wasn't exactly sure. The calculating part of my brain suggested that this could kill two birds with one stone. I could find out information to help my brother *and* push Eli into showing whether he was into me, or whether he just wanted to get into my red lacy panties. Then I kicked myself, because Ben should have been my sole concern, and I shouldn't have had any energy to spare wondering about how Eli felt about me. It was hard enough trying to process how I felt about him. It had been amazing to have a few days together where we had been getting on so well and not taking pot shots at each other. This was how I'd wished that we always got on. I'd forgotten how much fun Eli was when he wasn't teasing me and making me want to throttle him.

'I'm going out for some fresh air,' I told him, picking up my jacket again and letting myself out. The front door opened onto a porch that sheltered me from the wind. In the distance, the rain that had left us cold and drained had left the rolling fields green and lush, their edges lined with a thin strip of snow. Sheep grazed in a field so far away that they were reduced to fuzzy dots. I took a deep lungful of cold crisp air and dialled the number I'd been putting off calling.

'Taylor?'

'Speaking.'

'It's Daisy.' Now that I had him on the phone I felt guilty that I hadn't been in touch with him until I needed something. When I thought about how close I'd grown to Eli during that time, I felt even worse. I had never two-timed anyone before, not that Taylor and I had actually dated. I could never have lived with the guilt. It was compounded when he spoke again.

'Your name flashed up when you rang. Actually, I entered your name as beautiful girl in the green dress. I tried to call you again the other day.'

'I've been meaning to ring back,' I said, and I had. Initially I'd been meaning to get in touch to arrange a date. As Eli and I had grown closer, I'd wanted to wait until I had more of an idea of where that was going, but then I remembered how Eli had looked after me, his small acts of kindness, not to mention how it had felt to go to bed with him again. Even if there was no future for us, I couldn't in all conscience lead Taylor on when I was clearly not over Eli. 'There's a few things I need to tell you, and I don't think you're going to like it.'

Taylor didn't answer, and I hoped that he hadn't hung up as I began to outline the events of the previous few days, from finding Ben's passport on the floor and a bag of his clothes missing to us realising that he probably wasn't in London any more. I skimmed over the details of just how close Eli and I had become during our searching, but I'm sure that Taylor must have suspected. He worked with Eli and must have been aware of his reputation. I hated to think of myself as one of his harem, but it was impossible to deny that I was attracted to him. I cringed when I heard myself explaining that Eli and I had driven to Wales, and Eli and I had stayed in the cottage, and Eli and I had searched the whole area. When I explained that we'd finally found where Ben had been staying and discovered that he had been with Erin, he whistled through his teeth.

I breathed a sigh of relief that he hadn't hung up. 'So this isn't a social call?' he asked.

'I'm sorry,' I said. 'When I met you, I hoped that it could be. But right now, there's too much going on. I can't think about anything else. I need to find my brother.' *And then find out where I stood with Eli*, I thought to myself, and if it was just as I feared and that he didn't like me as much as I liked him, then I needed time to get over him. Because I could finally admit that he meant a lot to me. Ten years hadn't been enough to get over him fully before. I had no idea how I would even start this time if I had to move on.

'There's been lots of whispering going on in the corridors at work,' Taylor said. 'Now I understand why. If they've run off for a romantic break then they're in a world of trouble. We've got an international security session planned in the New Year. Erin and Ben were supposed to be introducing our European colleagues to a new IT package that Ben had designed. No one else in the office understands how it works exactly so we're not really going to be able to cover up if they're not here to show it.'

My heart sank. 'And if something has gone wrong and this isn't just an impromptu trip spurred on by a new relationship? I can imagine Ben not understanding why we'd be worried. But that scream, it was properly chilling.'

'Then it's even worse,' he said, echoing Eli's warning about Ben's security clearance if he were to disappear for long. Taylor promised to investigate and see what he could find out about Erin. I asked him to concentrate on finding out if there were any places that she might have run to. I was about to hang up when I realised I had one more thing to say.

'Taylor, for what it's worth, I'm sorry. I didn't mean to string you along.'

'No harm done,' he said. He didn't sound especially surprised or upset which was a relief.

Hanging up, I dialled Lily. 'I'm taking my break,' she called out to someone who must have been in the shop with her, though judging by the volume, not that close by. 'Sorry about that,' she said, as I rubbed my ear. 'How's Ben?'

I ran through our progress, or lack of it. 'Taylor's going to see what he can find out and let me know,' I told her.

'Can I be there for his de-briefing?'

'You do know that the phrase doesn't refer to him taking his pants off, don't you?'

'A girl can dream,' she breathed.

'He's all yours,' I told her.

'Trouble in paradise?'

'I'm not in a dating frame of mind right now.'

'Too worried about Ben? That's understandable, but Taylor would have been a great distraction.'

I told her about my growing feelings for Eli. 'Are you disappointed in me?' I asked her. 'I always swore I'd never be one of his hangers on. It's just that he's been showing this whole new side, thoughtful and kind. I don't know what to think.'

'I could never be disappointed in you, Daisy,' she said, but I could hear an undercurrent of pity in her voice. 'I just don't want to see you get hurt. Again.'

'I'm not sure I can avoid that,' I told her. I explained that we were going to stay in the cottage until we had more information about Erin, and asked her to keep an eye on the house and my shop in case Ben turned up back there again. I was scared though that he wouldn't, and frustrated that we had got so close to finding him only for him to slip away again.

'Don't do anything I wouldn't do,' Lily said.

'Too late,' I told her. 'You'd have had more sense than to sleep with Eli, and you definitely wouldn't have fallen in love with him.'

Lily fell quiet. She'd long suspected that I'd harboured feelings for him, and I'd long denied it, hiding behind my anger that he didn't feel the same way and paraded his string of girls in front of me, but spending time with him had lowered all of my defences. Finding out that he was a nice person, and how deeply he cared for my brother, had been the final nail in my coffin. I was head over heels for him and liable to get my heart broken all over again.

Chapter Twenty-One

Eli found me sat on the bench in the garden. He draped his jacket over my shoulders but I couldn't stop shivering. The sunset had been beautiful, but that was long since past and now it was dark, in the way that only the countryside can be with the lack of ambient lights. I'd never seen the sky so full of stars. Small wings fluttered past my face with a leathery flap. I jumped, and placing my hand over my heart, felt it racing. 'Bats,' Eli said. 'I saw one fly into the eaves of the house just now.' He noticed the tears that I'd tried without success to stem. It wasn't just the chill in the air that had me shaking. I was scared for my brother. 'We'll get Ben back, Daisy,' Eli said, drawing me into him and holding me tight. I breathed in the scent of his aftershave and found myself sobbing again. 'He'll be okay. Maybe I should drive us back to London, we can try Erin's house.'

'I phoned Taylor.' Eli's arms dropped away from me as I spoke but it didn't stop me. I would risk any amount of Eli's displeasure for my brother. 'He said that there's been some gossip going around this week as Erin's absence has been noted. They're not so worried about Ben yet as they think he's with you, but he was off last week and they're going to want to see him in the office again before long as they've got to get ready for their IT launch. I told him what we've found this week and that we'd been reluctant to leave, not knowing where to go next. He's going to investigate Erin from that end and let me know. Otherwise, who knows where we should try looking. We can't exactly phone every hotel in the country. Talking to people won't get me anywhere if I'm not sure who to talk to. So let's give

Taylor a few hours and see what he comes up with. This is his job after all.'

'You don't want to know what his job entails,' Eli growled. He was no longer touching me but was so close I could still feel the warmth from his body, which was lucky because the temperature was hovering around freezing. I pulled his jacket closer around me and he suggested that we go back inside so that we could light a fire.

This time it caught on the second match, and he sat back looking pleased with himself. 'You're getting the hang of this country business aren't you?' I joked.

He turned to face me and grinned, but it quickly faded. 'Maybe we should get some sleep, if Taylor comes through with some information we'd better be ready to take off quickly.'

We took turns in the bathroom, showering just in case we had to leave in a hurry. I brushed my teeth and shaved my legs, purely because I wanted to feel good and not in case this was my last night with Eli. I left my jeans and jumper next to the bed before stripping to my ivory silk French knickers and camisole. Again, just for myself and in no way because I couldn't wait to see Eli's face when he got into bed and noticed. I was bending over the bed straightening the pillows when Eli came in. He had a towel wrapped around his waist, but that was all. My eyes travelled over his toned stomach and down to the knot at his waist. I swallowed. At the same time, I saw his eyes taking in my nightwear. I pulled the duvet down and climbed in. 'Are you coming to join me?'

Eli's eyes travelled up and down my legs before he slowly shook his head. 'I think I'd better sleep on the sofa.' He left the room before I could say another word.

I thumped the pillow a few times before trying to get

myself comfortable, but it was no use. The discomfort was in my own mind and not in the bed. I tried to close my eyes and relax, but I kept hearing Ben's scream down the phone. The dragon lady hadn't seen Ben leaving with Erin, but he was no longer in the hotel. He couldn't have disappeared into thin air. Ben's skills were in cyberspace, not the real world. He had to be somewhere, and I had to find him and make sure he was okay.

And Eli was helping me to find him. Eli, who was currently sleeping on the sofa downstairs, when he should have been here, lying with me. Even if it was just for one final night before we found Ben, went home, and I had to watch Eli go back to his days as a dating supremo, always with a beautiful woman on his arm but never the same one twice.

I looked down, realising how desperate I felt, up here in my naughty underwear, not even able to attract a guy who had no standards when it came to who he would sleep with, except for me it seemed. The wind howled outside, shaking the windows in their loose-fitting wooden frames. I thought about Ben. I hoped that wherever he was he was warm and out of the elements. I began to cry again. I tried to stay quiet so that Eli wouldn't hear me, but there was no background noise to hide behind, no traffic or sirens disturbing the night's peace.

He stood at the door. I could sense him, even though I stayed with my head buried under the covers. Finally I managed to get my tears under control. Wiping my eyes with the back of my hand, I turned to face him. For a horrible moment I thought he was going to turn away, he swung his body as if unsure which direction to move in, before coming to climb in next to me.

He said my name, so quietly and gently, that I could

barely hear him, and he kissed my hair. I looked him in the eye, then propped myself up on my elbow so that I could kiss him back, but he pulled away. 'Have I done something?' I asked.

'You rang Taylor.'

'I needed his help. My brother is missing if you had forgotten ... wait, are you jealous?' I asked.

'I'm not jealous.' It was too dark to see his face, but I was pretty sure it wasn't happy. 'I don't like the guy. He's not as harmless as you think, not at work and not for dating. I've seen him in action and ... whoo.' Eli whistled. I guess if he'd seen things that shocked him then it must be pretty bad, but perhaps that was useful right now. I needed Taylor's skills.

'I'm not with Taylor. I was never really with Taylor.' Eli began to stroke my hair. I kissed his chest, and he took my chin with one finger and lifted it until we were face to face, whereupon he kissed my lips. 'It was you, Eli. Always.' If I'd been scared that my admission would put him off then his kiss set my mind at ease, even if it didn't come with any admission of his own feelings. I kissed him back, and then positioned myself so I was sitting astride him. His hands dropped to my waist and held me against him.

'We can't do anything else right now, so let me take your mind off it while we're waiting here.' His hands began to slip my knickers down and I paused.

'Condom?'

'In my wallet in my jeans,' he said.

'We used that one when you stayed over last week.'

'I restocked just in case. I wasn't sure you'd be able to resist me.' He was joking. Probably joking. I wanted to discuss his assumption further, but not as much as I wanted to find Eli's wallet. We could always talk afterwards. 'My jeans are downstairs.' I pushed him out of bed to go and get them. When he came back up carrying the little foil square, I beckoned him into bed. I didn't have to ask twice. 'Now, where were we?' he asked.

'I think you were about here,' I said, moving his hands to where I wanted them.

'Are you sure they weren't here?' he asked, moving them to somewhere even more interesting.

Afterwards, I lay with my head on his chest as we both got our breath back. I was slick with sweat and needed another shower. 'I'm glad you came upstairs,' I whispered.

'I couldn't bear hearing you cry, Daisy. I do care about you. It's just that ...'

I never got to hear the next part. The quiet night was broken by the sounds of a car engine, then a door slamming and seconds later a hammering on our door.

'Ben!' I shouted, stopping only to grab my discarded underwear before running to answer the door. But it wasn't my brother.

Chapter Twenty-Two

'Nice pyjamas,' Lily said, leaning past Taylor so that she could hug me. Taylor didn't say a word, but he grinned at me so I guessed that he wasn't mad, or maybe he too was enjoying the view. I tugged the neckline of my vest up but there was only so much the little slip of fabric could cover. 'We found out more about Erin,' Lily said. She barged past me into the kitchen where she found the kettle and set it off to boil. 'Cute,' she said, looking around her and taking in the brickwork and rustic wood. It wasn't clear if she was referring to my state of undress or the cottage.

'I wasn't expecting you,' I said.

'Clearly. Though if you had worn those for me I'd have been flattered.' She grinned.

I left her staring at the pitiful supply of nutrition available in the nearly bare cupboard while I went back upstairs to get dressed.

Eli was towelling himself dry as I walked into the bedroom. 'That was lucky timing,' he said. He pulled his jeans on quickly and reached for his jumper. 'I'll go down and see what they found out while you grab a shower.'

'I just need to grab some clothes then I'm ready to go,' I told him. Eli looked at me and shook his head. Instead of going straight downstairs I detoured to the bathroom and looked at myself in the mirror. I saw what Eli had seen. My hair was mussed, my cheeks were flushed. Even if I'd answered the door in a bathrobe, it would have been evident what we'd been up to. I followed Eli's example and took a shower. I needed the time to gather myself. I didn't ask him to finish the sentence he had started earlier. I'd finally admitted my feelings to him. I wasn't quite ready to hear the 'just' or 'but' which was apparently going to accompany any reply from him.

When I went back downstairs I found Taylor, Lily and Eli stood shoulder to shoulder at the table, leaning over a map. 'Erin's family have a house, here,' Taylor said, pointing at a location that I couldn't see. I elbowed Eli out of the way and stood in front of him.

'That's near Dublin,' I said.

'We just covered that part,' Eli told me, his tone droll.

'Excuse me for needing to catch up.' Taylor grinned when he heard us arguing, but Lily looked at me with concern. 'What makes you think she's headed there?'

'You mentioned finding Ben's passport on the floor,' Taylor said. 'It got me thinking, then after I spoke to you Lily rang me. We went back to your house. Turns out Ben's passport was nowhere to be found.' He took the diamante 'Shagaluf' cover from his back pocket and tossed it onto the table. 'I reckon she tossed this when she grabbed it.'

'Ben would never have left anything lying on the floor so it must have been Erin. Is she taking him to Ireland? Do you think she's taking him away? ' I was speaking so fast my words were running into each other.

'One question at a time,' Eli said. I took his advice and tried to take a deep, calming breath. 'I agree with Daisy. If Ben had seen her drop this, he'd have picked it up. So we know that she's been in the house, though Ben initially at least seems to have been with her by choice. The problem now is he won't answer his phone again and we have no idea where he is. Our boss is going to start causing a scene if he doesn't get back into work again soon, and then there's the scream. What would have made Ben scream?'

'Not to mention,' I added, 'my dad is due back from his holiday on Christmas Eve. That gives us just a few days to track Ben down. If Dad gets back and we're not there, with Ben, he's going to be devastated. He already lost my mum. I can't let anything happen to my brother.'

'We're not going to let anything happen to Ben,' Eli said. He reached out and drew me against him. I didn't care if he was just doing it to show off to Taylor. I wanted the comfort of being with him. Especially if it wasn't going to last once we found Ben again.

'What are these lines?' Lily asked, leaning over the map until her nose was almost touching it and pointing at a row of blue dashes. The lines extended from the western tip of Wales across the water to Ireland. 'There's a port near here. Do you think that's where she planned to go?'

'It might explain why she drove them all the way out here initially. Otherwise it seems a long way to go just to spend some time away. They already work together,' Taylor pointed out.

'Sometimes people can't see a good thing when it's right in front of them,' I said, and immediately began to blush. Clearly being able to switch off from whatever Eli had been about to tell me before we were interrupted wasn't going to happen.

'Sometimes what seems like a good idea to one person can feel risky to someone else,' Eli responded, letting go of me. Lily coughed to break the tension. 'I just meant that Erin's plan may have made sense to her, but I don't understand why she felt that she needed to sneak Ben away,' he clarified.

'Maybe she thought that the people closest to him wouldn't be supportive of him forming a relationship that lasted longer than ten minutes,' I muttered, half hoping that Eli wouldn't hear me as soon as I heard the words slipping out, but of course he did.

'My relationships last a lot longer than that,' Eli said. 'I thought I proved that to you at least twice last night.'

This time Taylor interrupted. 'That's all very interesting, but it doesn't solve the question of what to do now.'

Lily tapped the screen on her phone. 'There are no more ferries tonight. The next one leaves at about two a.m. tomorrow morning. I don't know about you, but I'm exhausted after that journey.'

'You can have the bed if you want it,' I told her. She shrugged. 'I'll go and change the sheets. There are spares in the closet.'

'Is there a spare room?' Taylor asked. 'I could do with a few hours kip too.'

'Sorry,' I told him. 'The cottage only has one bed.' If they hadn't already known full well what Eli and I had been up to before then that would have been a giveaway.

We pottered about, trying not to bump into each other in the cosy size of the living room as we moved around stripping the bed and fetching blankets. Lily and Taylor were grateful of the chance to sleep and soon headed upstairs. Lily had no qualms about bunking in with Taylor. I unfolded a blanket and began to make myself a nest on the sofa.

'And in your great planning session, did you work out where I was going to sleep?' Eli asked me.

I shrugged. 'I thought you had plenty of choices. There's the floor or your car for starters.'

'You're mean when you're cross with me,' he said, sitting next to me on the couch. He put his arm around me. It was soothing to feel the warmth of his body but at the same time it was utterly confusing. Had he been about to tell me that he didn't want to be with me any more? If so, why was he now running his fingers across the nape of my neck?

'What are you doing?'

'It's freezing out,' he responded. 'If I sleep on the backseat it'll take hours to defrost me in the morning. Now don't wriggle. I'm knackered and I could do with a kip.'

The sofa was soft and we sank into it. Eli winced as my knee accidentally collided with his delicate area. I apologised but he was too uncomfortable to hear it. Eventually he lifted me up and laid me down on top of him. He was far less soft than the couch, but somehow more comfortable. I laid my head back down on his chest and fell asleep as he gently stroked my back.

The alarm was too loud and too early. The cottage was so small that the one round was enough to wake all four of us. 'Time to get searching again,' I groaned, though I didn't move until Eli rolled over, dumping me onto the floor.

'You might be named after a flower, but you're not as delicate as one. I think you dented my ribs,' he complained.

'Wow, you weren't this grumpy last time I was on top,' I retorted.

Chapter Twenty-Three

'What happens if they're gone already? Erin could have taken him on the ferry yesterday,' I said as we headed for the cars. 'If only Ben were here. He'd be able to get into the system and see if she's booked tickets. Has she booked Ben a ticket? Is he with her by choice or is she holding him against his will?'

'You're doing that thing where you talk a lot again,' Eli said, dumping his bag into the boot of his car.

Taylor noticed us sniping at each other. 'Why doesn't Daisy come in my car and you can drive Lily?'

'No!' we all shouted together.

He stepped back. 'It was just a suggestion.'

'So, the plan is, we drive to the port and hopefully arrive in time for the first ferry of the day.' I looked around me at the sky which was still pitch black. 'Well, of the night. We see if we can spot Erin and Ben, and if not we ask around to see if we can find out if she was on the ferry yesterday. If we get any sign that she's taken him on a ship, we buy tickets, head to Ireland ourselves and carry on searching. There's just one problem' I pointed out. 'We were all too tired to think of it last night. Erin has Ben's passport, but what about ours? We can't travel without one. Mine's back in my flat. In London.'

Taylor reached into his jacket pocket and fanned out a pair of burgundy covers. Lily tapped her own pocket to show that she had hers too. 'I picked Daisy's up from her flat when we realised that Ben's was gone,' she said.

'And I had no idea where Eli's would be so I got one of my contacts to sort one that he could use,' Taylor added.

We took our passports and slipped into Eli's car. He started the engine, turned the heating up and we drove away from the cottage.

The roads were deserted, the darkness broken only by the beams from our headlights. If I hadn't known that we were driving down a road that carved and wound its way through the hills, I'd never have placed where we were. It was unsettling to have such a complete lack of light to see our surroundings, especially because I knew how steep the drops by the side of the roads could be. When we finally merged onto the main carriageway that hugged the edge of the coastline, I finally spotted another car. The driver was sipping from an insulated mug, and it reminded me of both my sleep and caffeine deprivation. I'd have mentioned it to Eli, but his lips were pursed in concentration as he followed the curves of the road.

Glancing behind me, I could see Taylor's car not far behind. It was a cherry-red, low-slung sports car, and I had to admit that I was more excited by the car than I had ever been about Taylor. Turning my body away from Eli, I closed my eyes and tried to fall asleep again. It was no use, despite my fatigue. My brain was far too busy worrying about Ben and trying to understand Eli's reaction to me calling Taylor for help. I'd assured him that he had no reason to be jealous. If anything, his history with the opposite sex was far more extensive than mine.

So what was the reason for his reticence towards me now? It wasn't a lack of chemistry, that was for sure. I thought back to Eli's behaviour towards me even before I'd met Taylor. He had seemed to enjoy the sight of me in the green dress at the wedding, and no one had forced him to swap his food at the wedding to ensure that I could eat. In fact, he hadn't needed to invite me to join them at all. He'd done all of those things just to be kind. Why, after years of sniping at each other things had begun to thaw, I had no idea, but I was relieved. I turned back to look at him, only to find that he was already glancing at me. He turned his face away quickly, and I could see the tension in his jaw. Was he every bit as confused about our bond as I was?

'We'll be there in a few minutes,' he said. I sat up straighter and began to look around me. Presently we approached the port area. For the first time since we'd left London, we were suddenly surrounded by other people, though they were all as subdued as we were, given that the time was not yet two a.m. It was odd being awake when you knew that the vast majority of the rest of the country was fast asleep, tucked up all snug in their beds. I pulled my coat tighter around me. Taylor drew up and parked next to us. Lily bounded out, apparently the only person in the vicinity who was not feeling wrecked.

'Come on Dais,' she said, taking my arm. 'Let's leave these guys here to watch the cars. We'll poke around and see if we can find anyone who can help us. Try not to kill each other before we get back,' she told them as we walked away. Taylor laughed at her suggestion. Eli looked a little put out, as though she had ruined his plans.

A weathered-looking man wearing a bright yellow work coat with reflective strips was waving lorries into lines as they waited for the ferry to be ready for them to load. We waited until he had guided a muddy-green ten-wheel truck into position, then gestured to get his attention. I explained about our search but he was shaking his head before I'd finished speaking.

'I only work the early shift, my love.'

I elbowed Lily to take the dreamy look off her face when she heard his Irish brogue. He was easily old enough to be her father, but if he carried on talking it would take more than that to put her off. 'Is there anyone else we can ask?' I suggested.

He gestured to a small portakabin on the other side of the car park. 'Yer main office won't open til a few minutes before the ferry goes, but you can get a coffee and ask in d'are if you's a mind to.' We thanked him and went to stock up on supplies. 'Feel free to bring an extra cup back for an old man,' he shouted after us. Lily turned to wave that she had heard him.

The wind blowing off the water took the frigid temperatures even lower. We were glad of the respite inside the cabin. The man behind the counter wasn't much younger than the guy that we'd left outside, but he had a similar accent and Lily swooned as we ordered drinks and explained about our search. Sadly he was no more useful, apart from as a source of sustenance, and all too soon we were back out in the fresh air, albeit this time laden with supplies. Lily took a drink over to the man shepherding the lorry lines, and I went to tell Eli and Taylor about our lack of progress.

'Do we try and get a place on the next ferry in case they've already gone? For all we know they travelled yesterday. Or do we wait for a later ferry and see if anyone here remembers them? The main office should open soon.' I shook my head as I tried to think through all of our options.

Eli tried to sort through all of the options I'd suggested. 'I vote that we go,' he said. 'We have her address, we might as well check it out. If she catches a later boat we can be there to greet her.'

'I agree,' Taylor said.

'We've got no proof that she still has Ben with her,' I pointed out.

'She's planned all of this so far to be with him. She's got his passport. Why else would she have it if she weren't planning to take him somewhere?' Taylor asked.

I handed them steaming cups of coffee and we took turns to lace them with little pots of milk and packets of sugar. Eli raided the paper sack that I carried and helped himself to a bacon roll before handing another to Taylor. Lily came back from her mercy run and took a third. They smelt divine, but I had to be content with just the aroma. They didn't stretch to veggie bacon alternatives so I had a plain bun. I considered covering it in ketchup just to add some flavour, but my stomach felt delicate on so little sleep so I ate it plain.

'Our friend turned out to have more information than he knew,' Lily said as she chewed. 'They had a security alert yesterday afternoon. There was a loud bang sometime in the afternoon. Someone thought it sounded like an explosion and the whole port was closed down until they discovered that it was some fireworks. They reckon some kids set them off as a joke.' Eli and Taylor both winced and shook their heads. I realised that they'd probably spent too much time surrounded by guns and explosives to find pranks like that offensive rather than just a bit stupid. They knew only too well that weapons were not a thing to joke about. 'Anyways,' Lily continued, 'there were no ferries in the time after Erin was seen checking out of the hotel. So they definitely haven't left yet.'

'That's great news,' I said, jumping up to hug Lily. 'We're not far behind them after all.'

'There's also some bad news,' Lily continued. 'All of the passengers who weren't able to travel yesterday were offered the chance to go today. We might not be able to get a ticket.'

Chapter Twenty-Four

'I've never been in a queue at this time of the morning unless it involved alcohol,' Lily said, stamping her feet to try and stay warm.

'I remember.' We'd been in a club and the queue for the ladies' toilet had been ridiculous. Lily had used the gents instead.

'They had no right to kick me out,' Lily reminisced.

'You were caught shagging the bouncer in there. You broke the cubicle door.'

'It was hard to fit. He was massive. Not as big as Taylor though.' She licked her lips. 'But that's my point,' she said, looking at me as if I were stupid. 'If I was with the bouncer, who did they find to kick me out?'

The line in front of us shuffled forward and we finally came into sight of the ticket desk. Unfortunately, there were still another twenty people ahead of us. 'So the plan is, get tickets for whichever ferries we can for today, if any, then just hang around and get on whenever we see Erin?' Lily asked.

I nodded. 'And if we don't see her, then you and Taylor take the last ferry of the day and check out her house. Eli and I will double back and check her flat in London again. But hopefully we'll see her.'

'And if we do but we can't get tickets?' Lily asked.

'I don't even want to think about it,' I told her.

When we finally made it to the front of the queue, I was nearly as grumpy as the woman behind the counter. She typed away on her keyboard for a good few minutes before she even looked up at us again, and when she did I swore that her eyes were so distant that she stared straight through us. 'I know that you're very busy,' I started, and she looked like she was about to cry. 'We just wondered if you had any tickets left at all for today. I know it's not likely, but we'd really appreciate it if you could find some. We have to find my brother …'

She held her hand up to halt my begging. 'I've got a few seats left on the next ferry. After that what with Christmas coming there's nothing until Wednesday.'

She stared behind me at the queue before tapping on her keyboard again. She didn't seem bothered whether we booked or not, she just wanted the waiting crowds to disappear. 'We'll take four tickets please.' I handed her my credit card and hoped that I had enough on my limit to cover the cost.

Eli and Taylor were arguing when we made it back to the cars. We were able to hear them before we saw them. 'Dial it down before I knock some sense into the pair of you,' Lily shouted. Given how they both towered over her, I almost hoped that they would continue to fight just to see her try. I'd seen her control a room full of overexcited and undersexed young men in the past when a new batch of magazines was delivered to her shop so my money would have been on Lily for the win.

The men seemed to realise this too, as they quit arguing and got into their respective cars. Eli slammed his door, and Taylor left his open, his long legs splayed out to the side as he stared into space. Lily's friend in the yellow coat jogged past us, and a few minutes later the line of lorries began to move.

Lily climbed into Taylor's car and I re-joined Eli. 'If you're going to stay this cheerful I can get out and travel with Taylor,' I told him, as he continued to sit in silence.

He reached past me and switched the stereo on. 'Better?' The upbeat music was a stark contrast to the frosty atmosphere inside the car.

This time I ignored him. We were well into our stand-off when I spotted Erin. She was in the lane next to us but because it was moving slightly faster than our lane, when she halted she was stopped a couple of cars further ahead than we were. I shot upright and pointed out of the window. 'There, look, she's over there.'

Eli waved me back down. 'Subtle, Daisy. If she didn't hear you shout then most likely she saw you almost jumping out of your seat.'

'Next time you run a class in surveillance let me know and Lily and I will sign up, given that you're such an expert. I don't suppose you could spot whether Ben was with her?' I wanted to jump out immediately but the car in front of us began to creep forward so I put my belt on and tried to both sink down in my seat and stare out of the window at the same time. 'She's in that row over. They're going to be on the same ferry. We could try and overpower her now,' I suggested.

'It's not like there would be many witnesses,' Eli scoffed, gesturing at the sea of cars around us.

'So what? We get on the ferry? What if we do and Ben's not with her?' I picked up my handbag and began to rummage through it, just in case any James Bond style gadgets had mysteriously appeared that might allow me to capture Erin without risking being arrested myself. It was no use. Apart from my toothbrush, a comb and an emergency sanitary towel, all I carried was my purse and the teddy bear with an enormous boner.

Eli drove forward another foot, and the cars paused again as we waited for the ramp to be lowered for us.

Before I could think of a reason not to, I'd opened the door and climbed out. The driver of the car next to me noticed and frowned so I gave her a quick smile to reassure her that I was okay and hoped that she wouldn't draw any more attention to me. I dropped to the floor and wriggled my way towards Erin, hunched over so that hopefully she wouldn't spot me in her mirrors. I could hear Eli hissing my name but I ignored him. Clutching the teddy in my left hand, I waited until I had reached the back of Erin's car. I wedged the bear as far into the exhaust pipe as I could. Then I raised my head, took the quickest peep I dared and hurried back to Eli.

'What the hell were you thinking?' he shouted.

'I've got a plan. Put your fingers in your ears. There's going to be a bang. Any second.' I covered my own ears and waited. Eli looked at me as if I were crazy. Eventually I had to agree with him.

'What did you do, shove a potato up her exhaust?'

'No,' I told him, rolling my eyes. 'I didn't have a potato. So I used a toy.' I didn't mention which part of the teddy had fitted into the pipe.

'You do realise that that only works in movies?'

'Damn,' I said, slamming my hand against the dashboard. 'I thought it would blow up. The port was shut yesterday because of the fireworks. I thought that they might freak out and close it again if they heard a loud bang. Then I was going to chase Erin somewhere quiet and get Ben back. I'm sure that he's asleep on her back seat, there's a blanket and I thought I saw something that looked like Ben's Incredible Hulk T-shirt sticking out the side of it. So, what is going to happen?'

'The car might stall, if you shoved it in far enough,' he admitted.

'Allowing us to sneak over in the confusion and rescue Ben.'

There was a small pop and something furry and blackened flew over the roof. I glared at Eli, before slipping out of the car again. I could hear him hissing my name, but I ignored him. Following the trajectory, I found the teddy next to the bumper of an old VW campervan. His fur was singed and he looked very sorry for himself. I waved him to show the couple in the van that I'd found what I was looking for, and they waved back, until they spotted the furry protrusion under his leather pants. The driver's mouth fell open, and I crept away hoping that the darkness would mean that they wouldn't recognise me later.

Climbing back into Eli's car, I showed him the bear and I saw the first smile that he'd had since Taylor and Lily had arrived. A couple of rows away, the cars began to creep forward again, all apart from Erin's. 'It worked,' I said, 'quick, let's go and rescue Ben.' I opened my door, just as Erin must have tried the ignition again. Her line was soon loaded on to the enormous ship and the car ahead of us restarted their engine to follow on.

'Well done, Miss Marple. You cracked the case.' Eli started his own engine, and I quickly closed the car door before we drove onto the ferry.

Chapter Twenty-Five

I lost sight of Erin as we were directed on board by Lily's friend in the yellow coat. He waved as he saw her and sent both of our cars to the front of a new line. Eli eased his way down the narrow lanes and parked behind Taylor's car. There was barely a body width to spare between the cars, and I wondered how Taylor would fit. I watched him open his door gingerly and squeeze himself out, as slowly and carefully as he could, until he made it to the front of the parking area where a pedestrian path was marked out. Lily jumped out too, narrowly avoiding denting the door on the little blue Polo in the next row.

'Oops,' she said, not looking behind her to see the terrified expression on the men's faces. 'So, what's the plan?'

I wanted to walk up and down the rows until we spotted Ben, but a pre-recorded message announced that all passengers were required to leave the parking zone and go upstairs to the main deck. I tried to fight against the tides of people streaming past, but when I nearly got knocked over by a kid dressed as Superman, I had to admit that all of my plans were falling to pieces.

Lily slung her arm around me and pulled me along. 'Don't worry. They're trapped on a ship. There's no exit now, we can't lose them again.' She had more faith in our skills than I did.

She led us up to the main deck. We found portholes where we could watch the ferry slowly pull away from the shore, or we would have if it had been light yet. As it was, there was one streetlight on the pier that gradually grew smaller, until it seemed that we were alone on the sea, surrounded by nothing but fog.

'There's a map of the ferry,' Eli said, spotting a display board screwed to the wall. 'We're here.' He gestured at a massive arrow which echoed his words. 'How about we split up. Lily, you take the café, shop and the seating area. Taylor, you search the decks outside. It looks like there are a bunch of private cabins. If I were Erin, I'd be trying to lie low and she'd have more privacy if she had a cabin. We might need to try and talk our way into them, and if she's there then it could get messy, so I suggest that Daisy and I search those together.'

I checked my mobile. 'I still have a little signal. Try and message if you find them, but we'll arrange to meet back here in an hour just in case we lose reception once we're further from shore.'

Taylor glanced at the windows that were covered in beaded drops of water from the rain that was now lashing the boat. He lifted his hood up to cover his head and made for the door. 'Thanks Taylor,' I said, 'we owe you one.' He gave me a mock salute to show that he appreciated my words, but his usual cheery smile was missing.

'What are you going to do when he comes to claim it?' Eli muttered.

'I'll sacrifice myself on your behalf,' Lily said, fanning herself with a sick bag that she plucked from the counter.

'Shouldn't you be off looking for Ben?' Eli asked her.

'I'm on my way, and if I'm full of coffee and cakes when I return from the café, that doesn't mean that I haven't also been searching,' Lily said. It seemed that we were all a little more relaxed now that Ben was so close. All we had to do was find him.

She wandered off in search of caffeine, and Eli and I

made for the corridor which led to the cabins. As the ferry drew further from land, the wind and waves picked up and the floor began to pitch and heave.

I rolled with the motion, steadying myself with a hand on the wall when the movement grew too extreme. I turned to Eli. 'This is fun. It reminds me of going to Alton Towers with you and Ben to celebrate passing our A-levels.'

'Have you forgotten that we had to leave early when Ben threw up over the third set of spare clothes?' Eli gripped on to a door handle with both hands as the ferry took an especially big dip. He hung his head and groaned. 'How are you coping with this? It's horrible.'

I shrugged and swayed my hips more than I needed to as I walked. 'It's not that bad.' Turning to see how grey his skin had become made me realise that he didn't agree. 'We're so close to finding Ben,' I reminded Eli. 'He was in Erin's car, I know he was. There are four of us searching a ferry. How far can she go? Any minute now, one of us is going to spot her and then we're getting my brother back. And if she hurt him then she might find herself accidentally falling overboard on one of these swells.'

'Remind me never to hurt you,' he muttered.

I shut up before I could point out that he was ten years too late. 'Come on, there's another corridor that runs off the top of this one. Let's see if there's any sign of them down there.' But there wasn't. Eli suggested that we knock on the cabin doors to see if we could trick Erin into opening up, but when we got shouted at for the third time because we'd woken up a couple of small children, we retreated back to the café to try and find Lily.

We arrived back at the same time as Taylor struggled in through the door from the outside deck, complete with a gust of frigid wind and a spray of salty water. If I had thought that Eli was struggling with the swells, Taylor was almost green. 'No sign of them,' he moaned, throwing himself into an empty chair. 'And they've closed the decks now the wind has picked up, so I don't need to go out there again'. He was probably relieved but his face was too green for me to be sure.

He laid sprawled out, deep breathing with his mouth open like a fish as we headed back to the café. 'I'm hungry. Anyone else fancy some more breakfast? Daisy, you can get some beans on toast.' Taylor sat up, clapped both hands over his mouth before getting up and running to the toilet as the ship rolled and dipped once more. 'Something I said?' Lily asked, before pulling a face when we heard heaving noises coming through the closed door.

Lily and I had finished our second breakfast before Taylor emerged. Lily handed him a bottle of water and apologised for making him sick. 'You heard, huh?' he groaned, rubbing his face with both hands.

'It sounded pretty bad,' Eli told him, clapping him on the shoulder a little harder than was strictly necessary. 'I'm glad I didn't do anything embarrassing, you know, like puke on my shoes.'

We all glanced down at the suspicious splodges on Taylor's otherwise impeccable brown loafers. 'Yeah, you looked really cool trying to pretend you weren't about to puke when that last lady shouted at us,' I told him. 'Turns out waking up a couple of toddlers who've been really sick themselves doesn't endear you to people.'

'The smell.' Eli shuddered. The ferry pitched so hard that we heard a crashing coming from the direction of the café.

'You'd have thought that they'd use plastic in weather like this,' Lily commented. 'The guy I was chatting to behind the counter was saying that the winds are due to pick up later this morning.'

'You mean this is just the start of the storm?' Eli asked, his eyes wide and his skin growing paler than I'd ever seen it.

The overhead speaker blasted to life with a tone so loud that I jumped, spilling coffee all over my hand. I licked it off and tried to make sense of the announcement. 'Something about engine parts?' I hazarded.

'Wow, hasn't a life of trying to decipher announcements on the tube taught you anything?' Lily asked. 'I thought all those years on the underground should have been good practice for you. He said that one of the engines has developed a fault. They're sending out a smaller boat from the Irish port to meet us with a spare part, but it can't leave until the wind dies down, so we're here for the foreseeable.'

Taylor stretched out even further in his chair. 'If anyone needs me, I'm going to be dying quietly over here.'

Eli laid his head back in his own chair. 'I would take the piss, but I feel sick too.'

Lily and I looked at each other. 'I guess it's down to us to save Ben,' I said.

Chapter Twenty-Six

The wind howled as though it were a living creature in agony, sounding especially loud and unsettling now that the engines had died and there was no mechanical hum to drown it out. Lily's friend from the port flung the door open and threw himself inside. His gasped to catch his breath, his face every bit as red as his coat was yellow. 'Outside is clear, I'm locking the doors,' he announced, as if anyone was stupid enough to want to go outside in the pouring rain. Even Eli wouldn't have made Taylor go out if the weather had been as bad as this when we first boarded the ferry. Probably.

Lily returned from her search. 'They're not in the café,' she said. 'I talked to Aidan who works there. He says he hasn't seen anyone matching their descriptions.'

'No one remembers Erin,' I pointed out. 'It was a couple of days before we even realised that she had anything to do with Ben disappearing.'

'Let's try the shop again.'

'I don't think they're going to be in there stocking up on duty free,' I said, but in the absence of any other great ideas we tried the shop nonetheless. The girl behind the counter stood up straighter when we came in, but sank back down to rest her head on her palm when she recognised Lily again. Clearly my friend had already been in several times to ask about my brother. The girl's long, blonde hair fell over her face, and she looked so bored that she couldn't even be bothered to move it from where it blocked her view.

'Quiet night in here?' I asked. She didn't bother to answer.

'At least when I have a shift this empty I can try watching the new DVDs,' Lily said, finger walking her way through the display of comedy T-shirts. 'Did I ever tell you about the time I saw my neighbour in one? Honestly, I had no idea he was into things like that. I took him home some brochures for a better quality range of bondage equipment that we stock. His wife went mental. I was only trying to be helpful. How was I supposed to know that he hadn't told her about his new job?'

If the girl was trying to make out that she wasn't eavesdropping then she failed miserably. She moved her hands away from her ears so that she could hear Lily more easily. 'I told you about the items my doctor came in for once, didn't I?'

I shook my head. 'But please feel free to save that tale for another day.'

'You can tell me,' the girl said. I read the name tag on her white blouse. Beneath the four-leaf clovers in the corners of her badge was delicate writing in black calligraphy. Orla stood up and Lily and I put down the cut glass whisky tumbler and walked over to talk to her.

Lily leaned over the counter and whispered in her ear. Orla's face grew flushed. 'People really do that?' she asked. Lily nodded.

'If you help us find Daisy's brother, I'll tell you a whole lot more.'

We explained our predicament, yet again. We were becoming so well-rehearsed with the story that we were finished telling it in no time. 'Is there any way I can get down to the car decks to search her car?' I asked.

Orla thought for a moment before she answered. 'I think they lock the access doors once we're at sea. It's for passenger safety in case the cars roll.' I'd been desperate to go and hunt around until she said that, but the thought of being squashed by a vehicle was enough to convince me to try all other options first. This wasn't exactly the steadiest of journeys to begin with. 'If I were them, wanting to retain my privacy, I'd have booked a cabin,' Orla continued.

'I wish we'd booked one, then we wouldn't have to watch Sick and Sicker seeing who can look most in need of medical attention whilst spread-eagling themselves in chairs. I swear Taylor tripped about three people with his stupid long legs just now,' I moaned.

'They usually save one or two cabins for people to book up on the day,' Orla told us. 'Of course, those might have gone by now, but you might as well ask. There's a counter on the cabin desk, it's quite hidden away at the end of the corridor, but Niamh might well be there still.'

Lily and I raced out of the shop, as fast as we could when we were bouncing off the walls with every wave and trough. The queue at the counter wasn't as long as the one that we had been in for ferry tickets earlier, but it was longer than I'd have liked considering that Orla had suggested that there might only be a handful of cabins up for grabs. I looked at Lily. She looked back at me. I shrugged. I was out of ideas and almost out of hope.

'Everything is half price at the café?' Lily asked me, her voice incredulous and much louder than usual. 'I guess they have too much food due to the bad weather. I think they were about to sell out of coffee though.'

Two of the couples ahead of us glanced at each other before slipping away towards the café. 'The staff are going to kill you if they find out you started a rumour like that,' I whispered.

'I sneaked into the stock room with one of the chefs whilst I was looking for Ben earlier. I think he'll forgive me,' she said, and winked. 'You know the saying, "it's not the boat you float, it's the motion in the ocean"? Well, it turns out that when you have a big boat and the ocean is moving like this, it's pretty epic.' Then she mock-whispered loud enough for the group of students ahead of us to hear her every word. 'I hear they're giving out free whisky shots at the bar to help with travel sickness.'

'No one is going to believe that,' I said, keeping my own voice to an actual whisper. But Lily was right, and sure enough the students also dropped out of the queue, mysteriously announcing to each other that they thought they might just get one more drink before they tried to score a bed. Before I knew it, we were in front of the desk.

'Do you have any cabins left?' I asked.

The harassed lady behind the desk wore a name tag that identified her as Niamh. We had found the person Orla had mentioned. She sighed and typed a few buttons on her desk, then a few more. Then she sighed again, rolled her neck in such an exaggerated fashion I heard it crack and stared at the screen for so long I wondered if she had fallen asleep with her eyes open. 'Cabins?' Lily prompted. Niamh jumped, her pink blouse coming untucked from her navy skirt.

'We have two left,' she said, pushing her tortoiseshell glasses back up her nose. She mentioned a price so astronomical that I cringed. Just then Eli and Taylor rejoined us, as did an overwhelming odour of seasickness.

'They have double beds and private bathrooms with showers,' she added.

'We'll take them,' Lily said, her nose wrinkling. We handed over my credit card and our passports. Niamh spent another few minutes typing into her system, though I wasn't clear how much she would have needed to add apart from our names and payment method before handing them back, along with two keys.

'Mr and Mrs Kirk, you're in number fifty-seven, that's down the hall to your right,' she said, handing me the receipt. I didn't look at the total again. I was going to have to get Lily to pull some more of her bumper shifts in my shop to help me recoup some of the expenses of this trip already.

'Mr Kirk?' Eli asked.

I shushed him, wondering whether this was where we'd finally find out whether Taylor was a first name or surname. 'Miss Lily, you and your partner,' she looked down her nose at Taylor who was stood with his eyes closed, leaning against the wall, 'are in number sixty.'

'Mr Kirk?' Eli asked again, following me as I began to count off the room numbers.

'Lily and I will take this one,' I said, opening the door and dumping my handbag on the bed. 'You guys can take the cabin down the hall.'

'We are not sharing,' Eli said, gesturing at Taylor.

I rolled my eyes. 'Fine, you can share with me. Lily will share with Taylor. It's not like we're going to sleep, anyway. Let's get our heads together once you guys are feeling better and we can think where we're going to look next.'

'Daisy, I think we can afford to take a little break. We're not going anywhere,' Lily pointed out. 'The engines are still off. What harm could there be in having a quick nap. I'm a little tired from all the … motion on the ocean.'

Chapter Twenty-Seven

'I bet he thinks he's hilarious,' Eli complained, as soon as Lily and Taylor left us alone.

'What are you talking about?' I asked, looking around me at the stark bedroom which I'd just paid a small fortune for. We were below the main deck, just above where the cars were parked. As such, the odour of stewed coffee from the café met with the lingering exhaust fumes in the corridor outside our cabin. Thankfully the door was a sufficient barrier, keeping those fragrances in the hallway, leaving only the scent of stale bodies and disinfectant. Presumably the crossing before ours had been rough too and the staff had been left with a serious cleaning job. Perhaps that explained why the room was so bare, it made for quicker clearing up.

There were no windows, only bare walls coated in a wipeable plastic. A bathroom was accessed through a door set into the right-hand wall. It was so small you could practically sit on the toilet and take a shower at the same time, but it was still far nicer than the loos upstairs. Those had been used by many queasy passengers already and I shuddered at the relief of not having to use them again. The rest of the room was dominated by a double bed. The sheets were thin, again probably for ease of washing, but as the ferry was heated so thoroughly I was feeling warm enough without them. Eli hadn't noticed. He was too busy feeling sorry for himself. I wished that he would snap out of it. If everyone else was determined to have a nap when they should have been out looking for Ben, then the least they could do was stop moaning.

'Taylor said that he couldn't get my passport so he had one of his contacts make one quickly. He didn't mention that he'd given me your surname. Congratulations, we're married,' Eli complained. 'I suppose he found that hilarious.' He tossed the passport to me. 'Catch.'

I didn't know whether to laugh or cry. I wasn't surprised that Taylor was having a joke about commitment phobia at Eli's expense, but I was surprised that he was relaxed enough about me not following up on our flirtation at the wedding to include me in his ruse. Behind me, Eli stripped his T-shirt off and dropped it onto the bed. 'I'm going to take a shower, then I'm going to sleep for an hour. After that I'll be ready to search for Ben again. If the ferry hasn't sunk by then. And assuming I haven't slipped into a coma from being so poorly,' he said. How did he cope on missions if he felt this sorry for himself when he felt ill?

I opened the passport and stared at the picture of Eli that Taylor had used. Remembering back to when he had last had his head shaved almost bald, I guessed that the picture was at least five years old. Taylor must have copied it from Eli's Instagram account. Eli had paired his look with a goatee and had looked rugged. Ben had done the same but had looked like he was ill. Dad had made him grow it out when they received the third get well soon card. It wasn't a bad photo, but Eli had broadened out and put on some serious muscle tone since it was taken, and I had to wonder if that was why Taylor had used such an old shot.

Just thinking about Eli's physique was enough to get me hot under the collar, and when the man himself emerged from the bathroom stripped down to just his pants with beads of water rolling down his chest, I licked my lips. 'They don't provide towels apparently,' he said by way of explanation. 'The shower is pretty decent though, if you want one. I feel better for it. I'll be ready to help you search again soon, I promise.'

There was no natural light in the cabin to judge his hue by but at least Eli did look less like he was about to collapse. I couldn't begin to think about how rough I might look. I didn't want to stop searching long enough to shower, though to be honest I probably needed one. It was just an hour's sleep did seem very tempting as an alternative. 'They can't go anywhere,' Eli said, as if he could read my mind and sense that I was wavering.

I sighed in frustration. 'This is the slowest chase ever. How come in the movies it's all top speeds and shoot outs? We've had queues and now a broken-down ferry. And we're still none the wiser for how to find Ben.'

'Which is why I'm going to grab a nap,' Eli responded. 'I can't think straight right now. Maybe I'll have a brainwave whilst I'm asleep.' He climbed under the covers, laid his head down on the pillow and was snoring before I could ask him to budge over. I wondered if this was what it would be like to really be married to Eli. Then I tried not to think about it because I was fairly sure I'd be able to cope if so and that was scary.

I lay next to him so that I could close my eyes and try and think where to search next instead. That was a much safer topic and a useful distraction, that was until Eli turned over and threw his arm around me, drawing me against him. It grew more difficult to think straight after that. Especially because it wasn't just his muscles that were hard.

He rubbed his lips against the back of my neck, I wondered if he was awake until I heard another gentle snore. It amazed me that he had managed to switch off so completely. Only a few minutes ago he had been fuming at Taylor, now he lay completely relaxed next to me. Well, most of him was relaxed. I tried to force my mind to consider the problem at hand, finding my brother, but it was difficult to concentrate. Eli had been so angry at Taylor. Was he pissed off because he was the butt of a joke, or was the idea of being married to me so awful?

I had loved him for so long. Even though we had been teenagers when we first got together, I knew that my feelings for him had been real from the beginning. I'd spent years trying to get over him, with no success, watching him hook up with countless other women without ever making a commitment to any of them. Occasionally I'd seen him with the same girl twice, but it was only ever due to him bumping into her again at the same club rather than a purposeful arrangement. Clearly some of them had also found that he was addictive once you'd had your first taste. Others were upset to see that he had clearly moved on quicker than they had, and I'd seen more than one drink thrown in his face. It was possible that in private he also had a little black book to refer to if he ever needed company. If he did, was I in there?

We had spent several days together now, and I was quite sure it was the closest thing Eli had ever had to a relationship, but we still hadn't spoken about whether there was anything more between us, any chance at the future I hoped for with an ever-increasing longing. He'd not mentioned any specific feelings towards me. Was I just a convenient booty call while we were on the road? But if that was the case, why had he displayed such antagonism towards Taylor? True, he had never liked any of the men I had dated previously either, but in the past I had put that down to his belligerent personality. It hadn't even crossed my mind that it might be anything else. Now I began to wonder.

Was that why he had been so grumpy with me whenever I'd mentioned Taylor, or was he really just blowing hot and cold on me? And why was I spending so long questioning this yet again? Hadn't I wasted enough of my teenage years doing just that? Fed up and needing a break, I swung my feet out of bed and got up again. There wasn't room to pace so I left Eli to his nap and headed back out to the deserted corridor.

I turned the corner, building up a huge head of steam as I planned to walk the ship until Erin emerged, at which point I'd hit her over the head with the sodding teddy bear and its freaky bulge until she told me where she had stashed Ben. I was daydreaming about pulling her stupid mousey hair until she squealed, when I almost walked into Lily.

'You know they don't give you towels in these cabins?' she huffed. 'Taylor just took a shower and just stood there with the water dripping off him, looking like he was asleep on his feet until I dried him with his top and put him to bed. He didn't even ask me to join him.' She looked put out by his lack of interest.

'Didn't you get enough action when you went to the café?'

'You didn't see Taylor naked. I'm pretty sure it would have been enough to tempt even you to look past Eli for once.' She was clearly not offering the distraction I had hoped to find by leaving my cabin.

'Come on,' I told her. 'Let's go and see if there's anyone else we can talk to. If nothing else maybe Orla will still be in the gift shop and we can score Taylor a clean T-shirt. If they sell any that would fit him.'

We strode down the corridor, bouncing off the walls

with the sway of the boat. There were fewer people around than there had been even half an hour earlier. Those that were still in the main passenger area lounged in the chairs, sprawled just as Taylor had been before we had booked the cabins. The crew were walking around handing out sick bags, though several looked like they had better hang on to a few for their own personal use.

'I need something to drink,' I said.

'I hear you. A shot of tequila would be pretty medicinal right now.'

'I meant water,' I told her. 'We need to stay sharp.'

'No one else is,' she replied, gesturing at the passenger who had given up trying to find a seat and was now lying prone on the floor.

'I left my purse in my room. Come with me to grab it and I'll go to the café so that you don't need to see your personal chef again. Unless you want to?'

She shook her head. 'It was fun, but it was pretty cramped in the back room. Maybe I'm growing up, but I think I might wait for somewhere a little more comfortable next time.'

'Lily,' I said, staring at her in shock, 'I never thought I'd hear you say something so sensible. Please tell me that I haven't broken you?'

She laughed and threw her arm around me. 'Don't worry, Aidan gave me his number. Once we've rescued Ben I might look him up. If Taylor doesn't make me a better offer.'

We didn't get as far as the cabins. Heading back downstairs to the lower deck, we passed the counter, only to see the lady who had booked us our rooms, Niamh, now leaning forward across her desk with her head on her hands. We hurried over. 'Let's try and get her talking, see if she's seen Ben or Erin,' I whispered to Lily.

'Are you okay?' Lily asked her, taking in the pallor of Niamh's already pale skin. As we got closer I could see that the journey was taking its toll even on the most seasoned staff.

'How are you still walking around?' she asked us. 'Half of the crew have gone off sick and we're supposed to be used to this. You took the last two free cabins, which means that everyone who came to ask for one after that has been shouting at me.'

I tried to apologise but she waved it away. 'It's not your fault. It's always like this during rough crossings.' Her speech was punctuated by the contents of her desk rolling off the side and crashing to the floor. She bent and picked everything up as if it were a frequent occurrence. 'What can I do for you?'

I thought back to Lily's description of Taylor attempting to dry himself after his shower and shuddered. 'I was just wondering if we could borrow some towels?'

She moved her chair back from her desk and opened the doors to a cupboard on her left. The ferry rolled again and instead of reaching down to pass us the supplies, she clapped her hand over her mouth. Lifting the counter, she moved from behind it and ran past us to the loos.

'Do you think she meant for us to help ourselves?' I asked Lily.

'She didn't lock up so I guess so.' Lily and I glanced at each other before making our way into her domain. Lily counted out four towels whilst I scoured her desk quickly. 'What are you doing?' Lily whispered, as if Niamh might reappear any second. Given the speed at which she had legged it to the bathroom I wasn't expecting her back in a hurry. Still, I tried to speed up my search.

'If Erin is squirreled away in a cabin, there must be a

list here somewhere of which one they're in.' There were no paper lists on the desk and I looked at the computer. Luckily Niamh had run in such a hurry that she hadn't logged out. I stretched my fingers and began to try and navigate my way to the list of cabin users. 'Keep an eye out,' I told Lily.

'I've found an extra stock of sick bags,' Lily said, exploring the contents of the cupboard again.

'That wasn't what I wanted you to look for, but it sounds useful, we'd better take half a dozen. But would you please now watch for her to come back? I don't want to get caught hacking her system.' If searching on a computer that had been left logged in and unattended counted as hacking. Ben would have scoffed at the idea, but this was probably just about my skill limit when it came to computers. I tapped a few more buttons and found myself looking at a list of crossings that the boat had made over the last few weeks. I clicked on that day's date and was greeted by a list of numbers. 'How does Ben do this?' I muttered, cursing as I clicked on the first one to see what happened.

'Hurry up,' Lily hissed. 'She might be back any second.'

'I'm not being slow on purpose,' I spat back. 'I don't exactly want to get caught and locked in the brig.' That thought gave me pause. 'What are we going to do with Erin once we find her?'

'That assumes we ever do,' Lily said. I shot her a look. 'Oh, don't look at me like that. Of course we'll find her, and Ben. Any minute. And hopefully before the lady comes back.'

'These numbers relate to the cabins. Look, this is yours. Ooh, I know Taylor's full name,' I squealed.

Lily put down the box of ferry-line branded

toothbrushes and peered over my shoulder. 'No wonder he uses his surname.'

I found mine and Eli's cabin next. I carried on clicking down the list as quickly as I could. 'Here,' I said, pulling Lily over to stare at the screen next to me. 'They've been two doors down from me all this time!'

'Let's go,' Lily said, picking up the towels.

'Let me close this screen so that she can't tell what we were looking at' I said, pressing a few more buttons and cursing as the screen turned black. 'What the hell?'

The door to the bathroom opened and Niamh returned, heaving herself along hand over hand against the wall. 'Did you get everything you needed?' she asked.

'We did,' Lily assured her.

'But I'm afraid I accidentally leant on your keyboard,' I lied. 'I'm not exactly sure what I pressed but I think I've switched it off.'

'Don't worry,' she said, waving me away. 'Stupid thing does that all the time. I might use it as a good excuse to close up and have a little lie down behind the desk. There isn't much more I can do here anyway.'

We came out from behind the counter and she took our place, dropping the counter back to its original position before pulling down a metal shutter and closing up shop.

Chapter Twenty-Eight

'That was lucky timing,' Lily said. 'If we'd got to Niamh's desk any later she'd have shut the office and we'd never have found out where Erin is. So now we go and knock on Erin's door and beat Ben's whereabouts out of her.'

'Yes,' I confirmed. 'If we were characters in an action movie. But we're not. So we'd better come up with another plan.'

'I don't know why,' Lily muttered, put out that I clearly wasn't planning to kick any doors down. 'Everything else that we've done so far has pretty much been down to luck.'

'Not to mention our great people skills,' I added, hoping Lily wouldn't be offended by my sarcasm.

'Hey,' she replied. 'I do have great people skills. I'm telling you, there was hardly space to swing a cat in the stock room and I still managed to make Aidan pretty happy. I've got a few little things in my bag that helped of course.'

I nudged her to move her on before I had to think any more about what she had said. 'What exactly have you brought with you?' I asked.

We went via Lily's room to retrieve her handbag, sneaking in so that we didn't wake Taylor. Pausing in the hall outside, we looked through it to take stock of our supplies. It didn't take long. 'Are you sure we shouldn't wake the guys to come with us?' Lily asked.

'Given how rough they've been feeling I'm not sure they'd be much use. Plus they're spending too much time bitching at each other,' I told her. 'We've got this far on our own.'

'Apart from driving hundreds of miles. Taylor and Eli did that for us.'

'But we've found all the evidence that guided us to get this far. We don't want to freak Erin out and have her try and run all over again. Not that there is anywhere to go on this godforsaken boat. But it took us this long to find her once.'

We passed the door to the room where Eli was sleeping, and stopped two cabins down. I knocked gently, pressing myself to the wall on the left, as they do in every cop movie I'd ever seen. I was completely unsure what I would do if Erin were to open it up as I was severely lacking in the gun department. Action heroes never had to storm an entry carrying only a bottle of glittery body spray.

'What am I doing with this?' I hissed to Lily.

'When she opens up, threaten to spray her with it. She won't know what it is and she'll step back, we force our way in, rescue Ben ...'

'And spend the next few hours hiding in our own cabin until they get the engine re-started and we can get to port,' I finished.

Lily rolled her eyes at me. All our planning, what little of it that we'd managed to do, was in vain as there was no answer to our knock. 'What if she's not in there?' Lily asked.

'We searched the ship already,' I reminded her. 'There's nowhere else she can be.' I tried the handle but the door was locked. I'm not sure why I thought it might be open. If I was kidnapping someone and taking them to another country, I'd be sure to keep them locked in. 'We should have searched for a master key when we were behind the counter,' I moaned. 'There must be one. I bet people get locked out all the time.'

Lily gasped, and I turned to ask whether she was okay when she reached into her bag and withdrew a small black velvet pouch. 'I can get us in,' she said, excitedly. 'You'd be amazed the things my customers get themselves locked to. After the millionth time I had to saw someone out of their handcuffs, I took a course.'

I stepped back so that she could get at the door. She withdrew a long silver pick from her bag and hunched over the lock. I hoped it worked quickly because to me it seemed far too obvious what we were doing to be easily explained to any passers-by. The ship rolled under our feet and it seemed like we were getting some help from the universe. I could hear groaning coming from several of the cabins and no one seemed willing or able to leave them. There was more cursing from Lily too, and finally a delicate click. She stepped back, and I rested my hand on the door. 'Are you ready? I'm going in.' I threw the door wide open, and charged into the room, spray can held out in front of me. 'We're here to rescue Ben,' I shouted.

No one answered. Lily entered the cabin so close behind me that when I stopped abruptly, she bumped into my back. Ben was lying on the bed, snoring. The room was shadows and shade, but there was no mistaking the guttural sound. The relief that he was okay washed over me, and I dropped a kiss on his forehead. He brushed me away and turned over without even opening his eyes. It wasn't a lot of gratitude to show for the hunt that we had been on, especially one that had gone on over several days and a good few hundred miles, but given that I'd spent a chunk of it distracted by the sight of his best friend naked, I couldn't really complain. The light in the bathroom was on and I crept to the door, expecting Erin to emerge any second. I peeked into the room, sweeping the shower curtain outside and spooked myself when the cubicle was empty.

'You thought she was lurking like a stalker, didn't you?' Lily whispered in my ear. I jumped hard enough to knock my head on the shower rail. 'You need to stop watching horror films like *Psycho* and start buying some from me. I bet I could find something that would float your boat.'

'After this I will happily never get on a boat again,' I told her.

Behind us we heard a muffled groan. I pushed past Lily to get back to my brother. I brushed his hair from his face and felt his forehead with my lips to check if he had a temperature. I had a gut memory that my mum used to do this to us when we were sick, but I couldn't remember any specific examples. He felt cool.

'Erin?' he moaned. 'I'm sleepy.' He turned over again and resumed snoring.

'I don't mean to be rude, but are you sure she kidnapped him?' Lily asked. 'He doesn't seem unhappy to be here.'

'You didn't hear the scream,' I told her as I shook Ben's shoulder and tried to wake him. He stirred but didn't open his eyes. 'Why won't he wake up?'

Lily sat next to me on the bed and lifted one of his eyelids. 'Daisy, look. His pupils are dilated. He's stoned.'

I hunted around the bathroom to see if I could find what he'd taken, or perhaps been given, but there were no bottles. Returning to the bedroom, I hunted for any sign of a bag but was unsuccessful. 'I bet she left everything in the car. She wouldn't have known how rough this crossing would be or how long it would take. Maybe he'll wake up soon. Now we need to get Ben out of here and then we can come back and beat the crap out of her for scaring me like this. Not to mention putting Eli through hell too.'

I looped my arm around Ben and tried to lift him but he was too heavy. Lily copied me and took his other arm. Between us we got him sitting up, his head lolling forward onto his chest. 'On three,' I said, counting up. When I reached three we both stood, but Ben was a deadweight, and we collapsed back onto the bed.

'Let's go and get Taylor. He could carry Ben no problem,' Lily suggested.

'I'm not leaving him.'

'You stay,' she said, jumping to her feet. 'I'll be back in a sec.' She made for the door and opened it, before slamming it shut and pressing herself against the wall, her hand over her heart. 'Shhh,' she cautioned. 'Erin just came round the corner. I don't think she saw me.'

We hurried into the bathroom, and for lack of a better idea hid behind the shower curtain. The cabin door opened and closed again. I held my breath, waiting to think of my next move. Fabric swished and the bed creaked. Erin must have sat next to Ben. I heard the gentle sound of her kissing him and whispering his name. Her voice was quiet and tender. Lily motioned towards the door. I'd come to hate Erin over the last few days, but now I could hear the affection in her voice, I waved Lily back.

She began to sing him a lullaby, her voice hauntingly soft in her native Gaelic. I couldn't understand a word, but I didn't need to in order to experience the emotion. She loved him, I could tell. The tune ended, with her humming the last few lines. She kissed him again, and this time when she spoke I could hear every word.

'We'll be home soon,' she told him. 'Then we can start over. Just you and me. Away from that slut of a man you call your best friend.' Her voice grew harder and she spoke of Eli, the anger spilling out. I knew how it felt to be angry with Eli about his womanising ways, and it made me realise how much my feelings for him had changed. This was no time to hope that his had too though, because when Erin spoke again I lost my temper.

'And your sister,' she continued. 'She thinks she's so cute, with her little shop selling its stupid scented candles and overpriced chocolate. As if that's real romance. It's what card companies want us to think we need Valentine's Day for, that's not real love. Not like we have. And she doesn't even have a fella herself.'

I threw myself round the corner and flew at her, knocking her off the bed and landing on top of her on the stained and threadbare carpet. She screamed as I knocked the air out of her. I felt pretty winded myself, but not enough to give me pause. I was so angry that I wanted to slap her, but I'd heard the way she spoke to my brother and I dropped my hand. I was angry at her, probably more angry than I'd ever been with anyone except Eli, but if Ben did love her then I couldn't hurt her.

Turning her over, I pulled one arm up behind her back and pinned it as I straddled her. 'Lily,' I shouted, 'I've got her, quick.' Lily burst into the room, clutching a toothbrush as if it were a knife. I stared at her. 'It's not a dental emergency. She doesn't have sweetcorn trapped between her teeth. Get me something to tie her up with.'

Below me, Erin twisted and bucked. I jacked her arm up higher until she groaned but held still. Lily upended her handbag onto the bed and began to paw through the contents. 'I've got tampons, fifty pence in change.' She swept her hand on the bed as she sorted more. 'Tights?'

'Perfect, tie her arms together,' I instructed.

'Even better.' Lily uncoiled the ball of tights to

reveal something metallic, trimmed with pink fake fur. 'Handcuffs.'

Quickly we secured Erin, using the cuffs on her arms and the tights to bind her legs. I sent Lily to fetch Eli. I sat next to Ben while I waited, stroking his hair and checking his eyes to see if the medication had worn off at all. It hadn't, and as Erin rolled on the floor, cursing at me, he continued to snore.

Lily was back within minutes. Eli pushed past and ran to Ben. He swept up his sleeping body and hugged him. Ben was unresponsive, and Eli lowered him slowly back to the bed before going to stand and glare down on Erin. 'If you've hurt him, I will end you.'

'And I'll help,' said Taylor from the doorway. He was leaning against it and still looking pretty grey, but the glare in his eyes was unmistakable. 'I've done it before. I know where to hide bodies.'

After that Erin stopped struggling. 'So, what do we do now?' Eli asked me.

I was about to answer when the floor began to vibrate and the air was split by a mechanical groan. The engines had started again.

Chapter Twenty-Nine

'We need to find Ben a doctor,' I said again.

'He'll be fine,' Taylor told me, ignoring the daggers that I shot at him with my eyes. 'I've had training about subduing unwilling travel partners.'

'You mean you've been trained to kidnap people?' I asked in disbelief. 'What are you?'

Behind him Eli grunted. I took it to mean that I didn't really want to know.

'My point was, I've seen people sedated. Ben will be fine. His pulse is steady and he's breathing well.'

'Then we should call the police. I'm sure the captain can radio to shore. They can have someone waiting to arrest Erin the minute we reach land.'

'And risk Ben losing his job?' questioned Eli.

'What the hell are you talking about?' I asked, amazed that he was even considering letting Erin get away with capturing Ben.

'Think about it,' he said, his voice patient but firm. 'Ben has access to very secure data. If the boss finds out that he was kidnapped ...'

'By a girl,' Taylor interjected. Lily whacked him. 'I meant, by a woman.' Lily smacked him again. 'Ouch, okay, by Erin, who was previously assumed to be the quietest person in the office, it doesn't really look good for him does it? They'll get scared of how easy it would be for him to get picked off in the future.'

'Do you want me to hit him again?' Lily offered. I did, but I shook my head. I figured that I ought to try and act like a grown-up, though it was hard to feel like one, with six of us crammed into a tiny cabin, including one person still asleep on the bed and one trussed up on the floor. Erin grunted and wriggled, trying to free her feet from the tights, not that she would be able to get very far. Taylor was so broad he basically blocked the door without really trying. I glared at her and she lay still and quiet again.

'So what do we do?' I asked Eli.

'Get Ben home, then work out what do with Erin,' he said, decisively. For want of a better plan I agreed with him.

'Next question,' Lily said, as she packed the remnants of her crap from the bed back into her handbag. 'How do we do that? We can't exactly stroll up the desk, announce that we've changed our mind about our holiday and can we please stay on the ferry to go straight home?'

'I for one, want off of this godforsaken ship,' Taylor said.

'We're not getting off the ferry,' I told him. 'I know you're a muscle head, but seriously, how are we going to get Ben out of the cabin? You going to carry him to the car? How are we going to explain that? We're going to have hundreds of witnesses and there goes any chance of keeping this quiet.'

'Fine, we stay on board,' Taylor accepted, throwing his hands in the air in surrender. 'But no one touches my car.'

'And what about Ben?' I shouted, the frustration getting to me.

'What about me?' Ben asked, sitting up in bed and rubbing his eyes. Eli and I both leapt over to hug him, knocking him flat on the bed so that he had to push us off in order to breathe. 'Where the hell am I? Why is the floor moving? Am I drunk? Why are you all here, and why is my girlfriend wearing pink fluffy handcuffs?'

'We're here to rescue you,' I told him. He rubbed his eyes again as if to clear them, but still looked confused so I filled him in with the details of our search. When we finished, he asked for his laptop. We searched the room but couldn't find it anywhere. Erin ignored him asking her repeatedly where she had put it, so we threatened to throw her overboard until she admitted that it was in her handbag. Lily glanced at us nervously. She wasn't keen on hurting Erin, but Eli, Taylor and I would have had no problem with it. Even Ben looked distressed until he was safely back behind a screen again.

He typed away on his keyboard. 'I've booked us on to the return journey, and logged into their cabin booking system so that they won't hire this room out again,' he announced.

'What about my car?' Taylor asked. Eli appeared to squirm at his tactlessness, before admitting that he too wanted to make sure that his car also made it home safely. 'They're going to get in the way when they start unloading the ferry once we reach shore.'

'I can sort that out,' Lily announced. 'I'll go and find my friend from the dock with the yellow coat.' She slipped out of the room, and I was sure that she was going as much to escape the tension in the cabin as to be helpful.

'What was the last thing that you remember?' I asked Ben.

He thought for a moment before answering. 'Erin told me that she was taking me home. I thought she meant London. Then she handed me a tablet saying that it would help my travel sickness. I'd thrown up all over her car on the way here you see. I swallowed that, and then I woke up here. My head hurts now though. I think I prefer the tablets you usually give me, Daisy.'

'But before you hung up, you screamed,' I reminded him.

'Erin was putting my laptop in her bag and it nearly slipped out.'

I shook my head, amazed by how this seemed to be a perfectly rational action to him. 'And you didn't think to call me back and let me know that you were okay?'

'Erin said she had,' he replied, and I wanted to throw her overboard all over again.

'Did she? That was kind of her,' I said. Even Ben managed to spot the sarcasm in that one.

He looked sheepish when he spoke. 'She didn't call you, did she?' I shook my head. 'You said that you had to guess where we were. Didn't you find the note? Erin said that she would write one after she'd done the washing up.'

'No note,' Eli growled. 'Would have saved me a night of walking round London searching for you.'

Ben looked even more downcast at that. 'I'm sorry.'

'It wasn't your fault,' I assured him, keen as always to protect my brother. 'She didn't do the washing up either.' That was the first time that I'd seen him look genuinely hurt and I began to feel guilty. It was bad enough that his first ever girlfriend had drugged and taken him away from us, but to realise that she had left a mess behind her was more than I should have dropped on him without warning.

We fell silent after that, each lost to our own thoughts. I was relieved to see Ben again. Now that he was sitting up in bed and playing on his laptop, it was just like he'd never been away. The waves had dropped, and Eli was beginning to look a lot better. Even Taylor finally relaxed enough to lose the scowl.

Finally, the hum dropped and the engines fell quiet. 'Please don't tell me that we've broken down again,' Eli moaned.

'I think we're docked,' I told him.

'Are you sure we need to turn around and head straight back?' Taylor asked. 'We're only a few minutes away from the best pint of Guinness you've ever tasted.'

'Weren't you the one who told us that we needed to get Ben home before he was missed at work?' I pointed out.

'That was before I lost everything I've eaten in the last three weeks. A man needs sustenance.'

At that point there was a tap on the door. We all froze. When the door opened and Lily came in carrying three huge brown paper bags by their handles, I breathed an enormous sigh of relief. Especially when she opened the bags and began to hand round cups of tea. 'I threatened to tell Aidan's boss about how unhygienic his stock room is if he didn't hook us up with supplies,' she said.

'That was your fault for dragging him in there,' I pointed out.

'He didn't need much persuading.' Lily opened the second bag and began to hand out foil parcels.

'I think I love you,' Taylor said when he opened his and found a sausage sandwich.

Lily offered Erin a sandwich. I glared at her but she handed it over nonetheless. 'You need to feed her. Even prisoners have some rights, don't they?'

She looked at Eli and Taylor who both shrugged as if to say they neither knew nor cared what rights Erin ought to have. 'I'm pretty flexible about whether she needs to get home in one piece,' I muttered.

Chapter Thirty

We spent the first hour arguing about who was travelling in which car to get home. Now that I knew that Ben was okay, I wanted some time to talk to Eli, but equally I didn't want Ben on his own in a car with Erin. She was still sulking and silent, but she had drugged him and dragged him on board a ship. I didn't want her to try and talk him into thinking that that was a normal part of a relationship.

And so eventually, twelve hours after we first left Holyhead, we were back again, more tired and dishevelled than when we'd left. Six hours after that we finally parked outside my shop. We'd made it back with Ben just in time. Tomorrow was Christmas Eve and Dad was due back from his trip. I climbed out of Eli's car and stretched until my bones clicked back into place. 'Eli, thank you for driving,' I told him, 'And no offence, but I hope that it's a really long time before I need to travel anywhere again.' Eli opened the boot and handed me my bag. Ben took his own, and they did a complicated handshake that took at least three minutes to complete. I don't know how they concentrated on it as I could barely keep my eyes open.

'What do I do with her?' Eli asked, gesturing to Erin who was still sulking on the back seat.

'I have some ideas,' I said. 'I think Taylor might know some places we could get rid of her.'

'Just let her go,' Ben said, leaning in and untying the tights from around her ankles. Erin climbed out, and she and Ben hugged until I growled at her. Releasing him, she scurried away and was soon lost to the twilight shadows and crowds of last-minute Christmas shoppers. Ben let himself in to his flat and slammed the door shut.

'I'm going to get a lift home before I collapse,' Lily said, giving me a quick hug and sliding back into Taylor's car. Taylor tapped two fingers to his forehead in a mock salute and drove off. Eli and I were finally alone, Ben was safe and it should have been a prime opportunity for us to finally talk, and yet now that we were here, I could barely form a coherent thought, let alone begin to ask Eli what was going on between us. Not least because if he were to walk away, I didn't think I'd have the strength left to deal with it. Instead, I opened the door to my flat and walked in, leaving it open behind me so that Eli could choose whether he wanted to follow me inside or not.

My heart would have raced when he did, but it didn't have the energy, so instead we headed straight for my bedroom where we kicked our shoes off, climbed into bed fully clothed and fell asleep. I woke the next morning to find a cup of coffee waiting on the trunk next to my bed, and heard my shower running.

I sat up, sipping slowly and trying to get my head around the previous few days. When Eli walked into my room with just a towel wrapped around his waist, I almost forgot that I had wanted to talk before we ended up in bed together again. I licked my lips, purely because they were dry and not because he looked so good. A drop of water ran down his chest. When it reached the towel and was swallowed up, I finally managed to look up and meet his eyes again. He grinned at me.

'Wait here,' I told him, partly because I was desperate for any opportunity to procrastinate in case he didn't share my feelings, and partly because it didn't seem fair to talk when I felt scuzzy from all the travelling and he looked totally edible.

'Daisy,' he called. I figured he wanted to leave soon. He hadn't been home in days, not to mention that he would be due in the office briefly, but he'd be so much less likely to run away from me if I were in fresh clothes so I called back that I'd only be a moment and carried on into my bathroom. I was just rinsing the conditioner out when Eli appeared in my bathroom. 'I need to go to work,' he said, but given that he was still wearing just the towel and that he looked at me rinsing the soap off for longer than he needed to filled me with confidence. When he finally left the room, I made sure that I shaved my legs too.

Eli had only got as far as putting on his tight grey boxer trunks, and as tempting as it was to talk to him when we were both half naked, I wanted to move on from the physical aspect of our relationship, which, without being boastful, was already pretty smoking. I shooed him out of my bedroom to make us some breakfast and dressed quickly in a red tartan skirt, black tights, white blouse and tight black jumper. There was a slight psychological boost from being more put together.

When I finally emerged, my hair loose over my shoulders and lips slick with gloss, Eli handed me a plate of cold toast and brushed past me as he ducked into my room. I took a bite of toast and sat on my bed as he emptied his holdall, searching for anything clean enough to wear for the office. He sniffed a shirt before grimacing. 'Can we talk?' I asked him.

'I need to go home before work and grab some fresh clothes.' He sighed.

'I wanted to thank you for helping me find Ben,' I began,

ignoring the way that he was now tossing his dirty gear back into the bag in a heap.

'It was partly my fault too that he left,' Eli said, taking a black T-shirt back out of the tangle and pulling it over his head. It was tight enough that the wrinkles were smoothed out by being stretched across his broad chest. 'I was arguing with you. I don't want to be like that with you any more.'

It was just the lead-in that I'd wanted and filled me with hope. 'I don't want to fight either,' I said, setting my plate down on the trunk. I clasped my fingers together and stared at them as I spoke. 'I've really enjoyed this time with you, Eli. Apart from the whole not knowing where my brother was and having to rescue him from a nutter who had drugged and abducted him.'

'I had fun too,' Eli said, zipping his jeans up and leaning over to kiss the top of my head. 'Why don't you go and see if Ben is ready to go? It's Christmas Eve. We've got half a day to make up three days of missed work before they close the office for the holidays. Not to mention that we really need to show our faces before they send a team out to try and retrieve us.'

I hoped he was joking, but as he threw his bag over his shoulder and left the room I had to concede that this conversation wasn't going according to plan. I'd hoped that he would sit and listen as I reminded him of how well we had worked together. Instead, he was stood by my front door pulling his jacket on. I tried again. 'Spending time together in the cottage was pretty cosy.' That made him stop and smile, briefly, before he bent over to tie his laces. He had one hand on the door when a knock from the other side made me jump.

I glanced at my watch. It was a little after eight a.m. and

I didn't usually open up for another hour, not that I had any more appointments booked in. Having been out of the office and away from the phone for several days, I'd missed out on the chance to book in anyone who had left their gift buying to the last minute. The income from these last gasp sales would have been nice, especially given the cost of our trip, but I'd manage without. It was worth it to get Ben home safely.

Eli opened the door. He probably meant to slip out, but Mr King blocked his path. Straightening his paisley tie he coughed, and I found myself snapping to attention. 'I apologise for being here without an appointment,' he began. He coughed again gently, and I sensed that he was fighting an embarrassment that he hadn't wanted to display. 'Yesterday morning I left the house to fetch my morning paper only to find a vintage Bentley parked outside.' Eli paused in his preparation to hear more about the car. 'It's beautiful,' Mr King continued. 'Bottle-green, black running board, chrome lights, leather seats. It's from 1937, still runs like a dream.'

'That sounds beautiful,' I said, wondering where he was going with his story.

'I can't give Mrs King a collection of stuffed toys when she's been out and bought such a beautiful present for me. We usually swap token gifts, but I can't do that now. I was hoping that you could come up with something spectacular for me to give her in return.'

'With no notice? On Christmas Eve?' I spluttered. Now Eli was truly grinning, his arms crossed as he leant back on the door watching how I would deal with the situation. I could sense his smug satisfaction at my failing to come up with a romantic gift. He'd never been convinced that my boutique served a real purpose. It's true that my job didn't keep the country safe or prevent violence anywhere in the world, but my little shop brought a lot of happiness to the people who visited it, and in a world where terrible things happened to people who didn't deserve them, it was so important to me that opportunities to spread love and bring joy were valued. This was a prime opportunity for me to demonstrate a service that only I could offer, and nothing was coming to mind. It was only a few days since Mr King had looked through every item in my shop and found them wanting.

Mr King noticed my hesitation and drew his wallet from his pocket. 'If it's a question of cost, I can assure you that there's no limit,' he said. I could see a wad of cash neatly folded inside. There was easily enough to cover the cost of the ferry tickets and the cabin hire.

'I'm just thinking about what might best suit your needs,' I assured him. I ran through in my head what I already knew about his wife. She liked jewellery but had a vast collection of rings. She couldn't eat chocolate any more and had questionable taste in teddy bears. It wasn't much. Across the road, I noticed Cody open her front door and begin to fix a holly wreath to it. The long sleeves of her purple kaftan dress kept getting in the way and she pushed them up to her elbows and hurriedly looped the wreath over a nail before they slid down again. I had the beginnings of a brain wave.

'Where did you get married?' I asked.

'Scotland,' Mr King answered.

'That sounds romantic,' I commented, feeling hopeful that he would agree.

'It rained.'

'Anywhere that you've been on holiday that was of special significance to you? Your honeymoon perhaps?'

'Our honeymoon was in a tiny bed and breakfast. The owner slept in the adjacent room. We had twin beds with awful polyester sheets. I got static shocks every time I rolled over.' That would have seriously put a stop to any amorous adventures. No wonder he looked so grumpy at the memory.

'And it rained?'

'Every day,' he said.

'How about a second honeymoon?' Eli suggested. 'You could whisk her away to Paris. What could be more romantic than that?'

I stared at him, both surprised by his attempt at being helpful and annoyed that he was suggesting something so obvious. Mr King was already shaking his head though.

'Our first grandchild is due in a fortnight. Mary would throttle me if I suggested that we leave the country now.'

I snapped my fingers. 'Let's go,' I said, pointing across the road at Picture Perfect, and tugging my front door shut behind me.

Chapter Thirty-One

Cody let us in and offered refreshments, but I jumped straight to the point. 'Mr King needs a gift for his wife and I think you might be just the person to help,' I told her. She looked surprised but heard me out nonetheless. 'I was wondering whether you had thought about offering family portrait sessions?' I turned to Mr King. 'You could wrap her up an empty photo frame and explain that once the baby is here, you could all meet with Cody one day and have some photos taken of your wife and her first grandchild.'

Mr King clapped me on the back. I had to take a step to steady myself. He might have been in his early seventies, but he was clearly still as strong as he had ever been. 'Genius,' he boomed, glancing at Cody to see what she thought of the idea. 'I'd make it worth your while,' he told her. He named a price that would have paid my bills for two months at least.

Cody blushed, then reached across and shook his hand. 'I'll print you out a gift certificate,' she said. 'You can put that in the frame.'

'And I'll take those diamond studs that you showed me last week,' Mr King said to me. 'You wrap those up nicely and I'll give her them to wear in the photo shoot. That's the least she deserves for putting up with me all these years. Do you know, I'd been injured in a motorbike crash shortly before we met? I was in a terrible mess, physically and emotionally. Not that men talked about such things in those days. I often think I wouldn't have made it through without her. She has been the best part of me for a long,

long time, and I needed to find a way to show her that despite my gruff exterior.' And at that he cocked an eyebrow at me, as though challenging me to correct him or to agree that he was indeed fairly scary. 'I love her, very much. Yes, I think that'll do nicely.' Eli tapped his watch and Mr King spotted him. 'Mark my words, young man. If you find someone who loves you, don't waste your opportunity. You feel invincible right now, I did at your age. But life has a way of throwing curve balls at you. Having someone at your side to help bat them away, well, that's worth more than a vintage Bentley.'

We left Mr King with Cody to arrange the final details and I let Eli back into my shop. He picked up his bag. 'But our talk?' I asked him, as he opened the front door yet again.

'Ah Dais,' he groaned, glancing at his watch. 'Can we do this another time?' There was clearly no point in trying to find out if he had any feelings for me when he had one foot out of the door, so I kissed his cheek and handed him his bag. 'See you later,' he said, taking it from me.

There was a lump at the back of my throat as he walked away, and when I found myself blinking away tears I tried to give myself a little shake. He hadn't turned down my affection, but neither had he given me any indication that he shared it.

I was about to shut the door and begin the hopeless task of trying to distract myself, when a black taxi pulled up and my dad climbed out. Eli paused long enough to shake his hand, then continued on until he turned the corner and was lost from sight. Dad lifted his suitcase out of the cab, and I hurried out of the door to help him, wishing as I did that I'd stopped long enough to grab a coat too. I may have only been outside for a few minutes, but it was long enough for my teeth to start chattering and for me to wonder how Lily coped when she usually had at least twice as much flesh on display.

'Daisy!' Dad said, drawing me in for a hug. He'd only been gone for a week and a half but already he looked better for the break. His skin had a tan that looked so much healthier than the grey pallor he had left with. His hair was just a fraction longer and it suited him. He looked taller too, and it took me a minute to realise that it was just because he was no longer hunched over under the weight of his grief.

'Are you busy today?' he asked, and I assured him that I had time. Any jobs that he came up with would help distract me from hurting over how easily Eli had walked away from me. 'I need some shopping,' Dad said as I opened the door to his house and carried his suitcase up the stairs. 'I've learnt some recipes. I thought we could have a little pre-Christmas meal tonight. Eli said he'd be back around five. We'll start with cocktails. I've got a bottle of Cypriot brandy that we can serve after dinner too.'

I barely had time to wrap Mr King's earrings and deliver them to him at Picture Perfect where he and Cody were happily chatting about locations and lighting, before Dad met me at my front door and ushered me straight back out with a list and a handful of cotton bags to carry the groceries home in. Ben caught up to me as just before I turned the corner. Thankfully he looked none the worse for his travels. 'Dad said to tell you that Lily is welcome too. He said to buy an extra box of filo pastry for the Spanakopita. Said you'd know what that meant?'

We said goodbye as he turned right and walked to work, whilst I turned left in search of fresh spinach, feta cheese and olives. Dad had been very specific about several of his ingredients, and I had to ring him three times to check whether I'd found the correct things. Finally spotting the last bunch of mint, lying forlorn and forgotten at the back of the greengrocers' shelves, I picked it up and hurried to the till, just as a harassed lady in over-sized sunglasses asked the girl behind the counter if she had any fresh mint. I looked in my basket and decided that mine barely qualified for that description. I was about to offer to split it nonetheless when she pushed the glasses to the top of her head, leant forward and began to ask the girl if she knew that her party would be ruined, simply ruined and awful, if she were unable to offer her guests a mojito. When her voice reached a shrill pitch that only dogs and small children would be able to hear, I covered my ears with my hands. Before she could calm down enough for me to approach her, she swirled her scarf around her neck with a flourish and left the store.

When I paid for my purchases I apologised to the girl that she had copped an earful. She waved away my words. 'If she can't plan ahead then it serves her right. Though she seemed like she could do with a good drink to loosen her up a bit.' I had to agree. 'Good luck to her finding some anywhere else today,' the girl added. 'I'm locking up in a minute and we don't open again for two days. In fact, if you can use any of these,' she gestured to a box of assorted veg that was bagged up for disposal, 'seems a shame to waste it.'

I agreed, and when she wouldn't charge me full price for everything I picked up, I added a couple of coins to the total and handed over some cash. The bags were heavy, and by the time I got back to my road my arms were aching and I was kicking myself for not taking a cab. Dad was pleased with my finds though, and it was worth the effort to see him looking excited about cooking. In fact, it was staggering to see him excited about anything at all.

I made us each a cup of tea, and I watched as he danced around the kitchen chopping spinach and folding filo parcels. He hadn't moved with so much energy in years. As angry as I was with Eli for walking away, I was grateful to him for the gift that he had given my dad by taking him on holiday. I tried to tell myself that even if Eli didn't have feelings for me that I would try to accept it and not be too hurt, but I knew I was lying to myself.

Dad slid a tray of small pastries into the oven and handed me an empty mixing bowl to wash. He hummed as he moved around the room, tidying away jars and packets and adding a stack of chopping boards and frying pans to the pile awaiting my attention. I sighed, and he offered to take over. 'It's not the washing up,' I told him. 'I'm thrilled to see you cooking again.'

'I lost the hunger for it before, I know,' he said, putting his arm around me and giving me a quick squeeze. 'I lost a lot when I lost your mum. My partner, the future I had hoped to have. I'm sorry that I wasn't in a better place for you and Ben growing up.' He let go and went in search of a tablecloth. His voice floated out from the back of the cupboard. 'I have some making up to do, I think. Starting with a Christmas that is actually merry, for once.'

'You were always there when we needed you,' I told him but he emerged triumphant, holding a length of golden fabric, and shook his head.

'Physically maybe, but you have to understand, your mum was the love of my life. When she died, I only got out of bed in the morning because I knew that you needed breakfast and to get to school on time. As you got older and you needed me less, I found it harder to make myself function.'

'What changed?' I asked him. 'You seem so much happier after your holiday.'

'I've been watching you and Ben find your places in the world,' he told me, picking up a tea-towel and beginning to dry the pile of plates that I'd washed so far. 'You've both found roles that make you happy. I started the holiday as I usually did, wishing that your mum was with me, thinking about how she would have enjoyed sketching the views, painting the beautiful sunsets, and it hurt to be there without her. Then Eli arranged the cooking classes, and at first I was annoyed because I hadn't agreed to go, but it was actually fun. There were a couple of women there who had recently been widowed themselves.'

'Did you meet someone?' I asked, hearing my voice go all squeaky as I said it. 'If you did, we'd be okay with that,' I assured him, though in truth even the thought of it felt strange.

'I didn't meet anyone,' he continued, and for a second I had to admit that I was relieved, until I realised that this meant that he was still on his own and I began to feel guilty. 'One of them had been widowed for a few years, and like me, she was still struggling with missing her partner, feeling guilty for enjoying life without them. Her friend though had only lost her husband a couple of months earlier, after a long illness. She was much younger, and you could tell that she was hurting. She came down to breakfast every morning with red-rimmed eyes like she had woken up crying. But she was trying, you know, she signed up for a bunch of classes. It turned out that she couldn't cook, and even after several sessions with the hotel instructor she could hardly swim, but she never stopped trying. One day I asked her how she had the energy to try so hard, and she told me that she didn't have the energy not to. If she didn't fill every minute then she spent the time feeling sad, and her husband had made her promise before he died that she would look after herself. She said that if she didn't exhaust herself before bed then she didn't sleep well for missing him, and he would have hated that. So she was throwing herself into all the opportunities that he would have encouraged her to try had he been there, and then when she went to bed, she could imagine herself telling him all about her day and she could go to sleep knowing that he would have been proud of her. I thought about how your mum would have felt if she'd seen me, sitting there feeling sorry for myself. The next day I decided to copy her example. Your mum would have wanted me to. The chef said that my pies were the best he'd ever tasted.'

I dried my hands on his tea-towel and reached over to give him a hug. I giggled when he told me that they'd asked him to stay and teach the baking class when the old chef had been found drunk and sobbing in the corner after one of the guests had set fire to her shirt trying to bake fairy cakes. I realised that not only was it the longest speech I'd ever heard him give, but it was also the first time I remembered laughing with him in years too.

'Would Mum have been pleased about my shop, do you think?'

'She would have loved it,' he assured me. 'She believed in true love. She would be thrilled that you're helping people to celebrate that.'

'Eli doesn't believe in happy ever after love,' I said, concentrating on a pan that needed some elbow grease so that I didn't need to look him in the eye as I spoke.

'Eli was older when he lost his mum,' Dad said. 'He was old enough to know what he was losing, and he didn't have any other family to look after him. I did my best to make him welcome here, but I was pretty hurt myself. I didn't have the skills to help him either.'

'Do you think he'll ever heal enough to be able to fall in love?' I asked.

'Do you think he is worth taking a chance on?' Dad asked.

I nodded, and then the tears started. Dad held his arms open and I went to him. He held me as I sobbed. 'Give him time,' my dad told me. 'You can't put a time limit on grief, but know that you will find love, whether that's with Eli or not I can't predict. But if you're open to love then it will come. I promise.'

Chapter Thirty-Two

Dad had sent me down to get cleaned up and changed before dinner. I'd called Lily to invite her and she promised to stop by for a quick snack before her shift started at work. I'm not sure what kind of people wait until late night on Christmas Eve to go shopping for last-minute sex toys as gifts, but apparently there were enough of them that Lily was expecting to work until midnight.

When she arrived at five, it was already dark. I'd turned my overhead light off and lit my room just with the hurricane lamp. It was dark and sombre and suited my mood perfectly. She grimaced when she saw my floor length and shapeless black dress and turned me around, ushering me back into my room and raiding my wardrobe herself until she found a navy-blue, mid-length dress. It was sombre enough that she could persuade me to wear it, but with the cap sleeves and lace detail around the neckline, I had to admit that it was a little more suitable for a party than my original outfit.

'I'm not sure why I'm dressing up,' I moaned, as Lily guided me to a chair and switched the light on so that she could apply my lipstick.

'You're dressing up because you fancy the pants off Eli and you want to show him what he's missing,' she reminded me.

'You're supposed to be my best friend. You're meant to be on my side.'

'I am,' she assured me. 'I'll be there to look after you if he decides that he's incapable of forming close bonds with another human being. Other than with Ben, obviously.'

'You don't think there's any chance for us?' I asked, hating the whine that I could hear in my own voice.

'Of course I do, he'd be crazy to let you slip through his fingers. Now, turn around and let me fix your hair.'

We let ourselves into Dad's flat at half past five, just as he finished pouring ouzo into a selection of small glasses. 'There's olives on the table and home-made bread and houmous, but don't fill up on that. I've got about half a dozen different meze dishes for you to try in a minute.' He went off to get himself changed, and Lily and I ignored his warnings and dug into the starters. The bread was still warm, and he'd added his own touch with a light sprinkling of smoked paprika on top of the dip which was delicious and smoky on the tongue.

The front door downstairs clattered shut, and shortly afterwards Ben and Eli appeared. I handed Ben a shot of ouzo, admiring his T-shirt as I did.

'What do all those numbers mean?' Lily asked him.

'It's binary,' I told her. 'Look, they're all zeros and ones.'

'I Googled it at lunchtime,' Eli said, taking a glass from me and knocking it back in one. 'It says "I've read your emails".'

'And on the back it says "they were boring",' Ben told us proudly. 'I designed it myself.'

'Has he read my emails?' Lily asked me in a whisper.

'Probably,' I told her, refilling her glass after she knocked her shot back too. 'Though I'm sure yours were a lot more interesting than mine.'

Eli had swapped his dirty jeans for a slate-grey suit and a shirt that was barely a shade lighter. He had added a thin black tie and shiny shoes. When he caught me staring, I held eye contact as I emptied my own glass, and yet when he winked at me my mouth still felt dry.

Dad came back into the kitchen and clapped him on the back. Then Dad insisted that we all join him for another glass of ouzo as he toasted Eli and thanked him for the holiday. 'The main course will be served in a few minutes,' Dad announced. 'There's lamb moussaka for the meat eaters, aubergine for you Daisy.'

I thanked him and swiped a small filo triangle containing spinach and cheese. The alcohol was going to my head already and I found myself blushing whenever Eli's eyes reached mine. When it kept happening, I gave up and reached for the wine.

Dad had just set the dishes, covered in melted cheese and still bubbling away on the table when the doorbell rang. 'Is that yours or mine?' Dad asked. I wasn't expecting anyone but I went to answer it anyway. Dad was busy slicing a loaf of bread and I couldn't bear to take him away from his cooking when he had so recently rediscovered it.

I opened the door to find Cody stood there, her hair loose over her shoulders. She handed me a bottle of red wine so I invited her in to join the party. Dad handed her a plate of aubergine moussaka and beamed as she raved about it. 'I didn't mean to gatecrash,' she said as Ben topped up her glass. 'I just wanted to thank Daisy for sending a customer my way this morning.'

The doorbell rang again and this time Dad went to open the door. When he came back upstairs he looked confused. 'Is this one of your friends?' he asked, looking between Ben, Taylor and myself. Every time he glanced at Taylor he had to tip his head back to look up high enough.

'I just wanted to check how Ben was after the weekend. Your dad kindly invited me to join you for dinner,' he explained. Lily got up and fetched him a drink and plate before shoving Ben aside to make room for him next to her chair.

'What happened at the weekend?' Dad asked.

I coughed, and Taylor got the hint. 'Oh, we just went for a little ride in the car,' he said.

'Did Ben get sick again?' Dad asked.

'It wasn't my fault,' Ben said, and I kicked him under the table to shut him up before he put his foot in it. He glared at me, but Dad was used to us bickering and ignored us, concentrating instead on Cody.

'So how did you meet Daisy?' Dad asked her.

'I've just opened up across the road,' she explained. 'It's more of a gallery than a shop at the moment, but I'm hoping to start selling more once the word gets out. Daisy kindly sent me a customer this morning. He's booked me in for a series of family photo shoots, not to mention that he bought several of my framed prints. I was so nervous about launching my own business and it was just the confidence boost that I needed. Now I can take a few days off for Christmas, maybe even treat myself to one of those scarves you showed me downstairs, Daisy.'

I only had a couple left in stock, both of which would clash with her hair, but as she was currently wearing a purple and pink tie dye dress and looking amazing in it, I figured that if anyone could carry it off, Cody could. 'I was thinking that I should offer a commission on the work. I wouldn't have got it if it weren't for you,' she added.

'And to think you were nervous about her shop putting you out of business,' Ben said, picking up his glass to toast us. 'Maybe it's lucky that our surveillance didn't turn up anything juicy.'

I kicked him again, this time hard enough to make him jump. He knocked over his wine glass and Dad had to jump for a tea-towel to mop it up before it dripped off the table.

'Just kidding,' I said, hoping that Ben wouldn't correct me.

'Are you okay, Cody dear?' Dad asked. 'Did any wine get on your lovely dress?'

'No one would notice a few wine stains on this old thing.'

'It's very pretty and it suits you very well,' Dad told her.

My mouth dropped open and I couldn't think of anything else to say, until Lily recovered and asked Cody about her most recent photographs. Thankfully Taylor had a few more social skills than my brother and decided not to mention the pictures from the drone flights, and so instead we were soon hearing more about Dad's holiday.

We'd finished the main course and Ben had cleared the table, when the bell rang again. I looked around, wondering who else could possibly be dropping by given that most of the people I knew were already in the room.

Ben jumped up, leading Eli and I to reach the same conclusion at the same time.

'Ben, please tell me you haven't been stupid enough to invite Erin too?' I asked him. Ben blushed, and with his colouring being the same as mine, he couldn't hide it either. It was evident that he really had been that stupid. 'What were you thinking?'

The bell rang again, and when none of us made a move to answer the door, Dad wiped his mouth on his napkin before getting up himself. When he walked back in with Erin behind him, I worked hard to bite my tongue. Dad had gone to a lot of effort to cook tonight, and it was so amazing to see him interacting with people and not just hiding out in front of the football game on the telly. I didn't want to scare him away, but when Ben stood up and kissed Erin on the cheek, I couldn't help but growl at her.

'Daisy,' Dad said, the warning evident in his voice.

'Dad, she's not good for Ben.' I thought that I was being very restrained in my explanation. Ben evidently did not agree.

'She loves me,' he said. 'In fact, before you so rudely interrupted our trip, I was going to ask her to marry me.'

'She kidnapped you,' I said, pushing my chair back so hard that it fell over.

'She took me in when I couldn't bear to be around you and Eli arguing yet again. What the hell was going on this time? Was it because you're sleeping with him and going out with Taylor?'

'Actually, *I'm* going out with Taylor,' Lily said, glancing at me. 'That's why he's here now. We wanted to ask if you minded, Daisy. I figured he was single so why not? But I just wanted to make sure. Given that you and Eli had been hooking up anyway, I mean. We got to know each other when we were looking for Ben but I thought that he was hung up on you. We didn't get together until he dropped me home the other day and came in for a shower, and well, one thing led to another.' Taylor reached across and squeezed her knee. She stroked his thigh as she waited for my response.

'Help yourself,' I told her, and she squealed and threw her arms around Taylor's enormous neck. I watched for a minute to make sure that she could actually reach the whole way around, before staring at my brother again. No one had reacted to the information about me and Eli hooking up, and I realised that no one else must have been very surprised to hear it. Cody must have been wondering what on earth she had walked in to. Dad sat and calmly topped up both of their glasses with more wine.

'You can't trust Erin,' I said, turning again to speak to my brother.

'I know she loves me,' Ben said.

'I do,' Erin added.

'Shut up!' Eli and I shouted at her.

'There's no need to be rude,' Dad said, jumping to his feet. 'Cody, if you don't mind, I'd quite enjoy a tour of your gallery.' He turned to speak to the rest of us. 'When I get back, I want the full story of what was going on here while I was away.'

Chapter Thirty-Three

Dad led Cody downstairs, and we all waited until the front door closed before we really let rip. 'What on earth were you thinking?' I asked Ben. 'She's criminally insane. How the hell could you think you were going to marry her?'

'There was a jeweller next to this arcade when we were away. I had a big win on one of the machines, and when I went out to treat myself to a bag of chips, I walked past and saw this diamond ring.' He reached into his pocket and I groaned as he pulled out a small burgundy leather box. 'Dad is going to go mad when I tell him what happened,' I warned him.

He ignored me and got down on one knee. 'Erin,' he said, 'I don't always understand people, but I understand you and you understand me. Please will you do me the honour of marrying me? I promise that I will always love you.' He opened the lid, where a thin gold band held diamonds which glistened and danced in the light. 'Just please promise me that you'll never drug me again. And that you'll always do the washing up when you say you will.'

I got up and headed for the ouzo. 'And there was me thinking that you liked romance,' Eli scoffed as he watched me pour and down another shot.

'Don't tell me that you're happy about this?' I asked him.

He turned to Ben. 'Your sister is right. What are you thinking, mate? She had you doped up and locked in a cabin.' Ben stood up and hung his head.

'It wasn't locked from the inside,' Erin whispered. At

232

least she had the common sense not to answer his proposal. I guess she knew that if she had said yes right then she'd have been in trouble.

'It didn't need to be,' I roared at her. 'He was unconscious.'

'Ben, be serious,' Eli implored. 'You can't marry Erin. What is she going to do, lock you up in your bedroom every time you do something wrong?'

'I was trying to give him a break from you,' Erin said, just her head poking out from behind my brother. He reached behind him and guided her to his side. 'He was so upset when he called me that night. He said you were yelling at each other. I had to drive over and pick him up. He didn't calm down until we were half-way to that tiny cottage, though that could have been because he'd taken a travel sickness tablet by then and fallen asleep. And he took that one himself, before you ask.'

'Which is where you got the idea?'

'We were so close to the port, I just wanted to give him some space to think. We had the car, I thought, why not?'

'Because you never asked him if he actually wanted to go,' I pointed out.

'Her car, which she had to pay hundreds of pounds to have towed home again from the port,' Ben pointed out, as if I hadn't spoken.

'Don't even think about asking me to pay towards that,' I spat. 'You've caused enough trouble already.'

'You didn't have to come looking for me,' Ben shouted, slamming his hands against the table, but given his slight size it didn't make much of an impact.

'Did you expect us to just leave you? To have no idea where you were? We spent days worrying and searching.'

'Yeah, I bet you were so worried that you didn't fall

into bed with Eli again the first chance you got?' I blushed as he spoke and he turned to Erin. 'Looks like you were right about that.' He turned back to me. 'So now that you can't manage your own love life, you decide that you need to rule mine? You might think that you're the queen of romance, but let me tell you something. You've fallen in love with someone who won't commit to you. At least Erin and I feel the same way about each other.'

I wanted to tell him that he was wrong about Eli, but I couldn't. There was a strong possibility that he was correct. But Ben wasn't finished. He turned to Eli and continued with his speech. 'You're supposed to be my best friend. You think that you're so great with people, but you couldn't see that I'd fallen in love. You insisted on dragging me round that wedding to look at all these skeezy women, when the one I loved was left alone watching us. Why do you think she faked the computer problems at work? She was trying to rescue me.'

'I didn't know,' Eli said.

'And you didn't stop to notice or listen when I tried to tell you. You dragged me on holiday when I wanted to be with my girlfriend, just because you'd got yourself exhausted and needed a break. Then, when I get a tattoo to remind me of Erin, you both treat me like I'm a little kid who didn't know what he was doing.'

I began to realise that Ben had grown up more than I'd given him credit for. Apart from the whole wanting to get engaged to his kidnapper thing. But he was on the money about Eli, which didn't bode well for hoping that Eli had any feelings for me above and beyond the physical.

'And you,' Ben said, turning to me, just in case the damage to my ego hadn't already been done. 'You don't need to panic every time I leave the house without you. If you understood the projects I organise at work, you'd see how much other people trust me.'

I swallowed, unsure how to respond because he was correct. I'd got so used to having to be the person who looked out for him as Dad had got increasingly distant, I'd never given Ben the space to grow himself. 'I'm sorry,' I told him. 'I'm glad that you've met someone, but can you understand why I'm worried about you being with Erin after what happened?'

He nodded. 'And we've talked about it. Erin is going to have some counselling, and then after that, if Erin says yes, we're going to get married.' He turned to Erin and she nodded at him. I guess that was her way of accepting his proposal without saying anything in case we jumped on her again. 'I hope that you can be happy for me. At least I've found someone who is emotionally available.'

'What is that supposed to mean?' Eli asked him. 'You're the one who told me that I wasn't allowed anywhere near your sister.'

'We were sixteen,' Ben told him. 'She had been mooning over you for months, you slept with her without thinking about how she would feel afterwards. You can't blame me for telling you to be careful with her. Daisy always wanted to fall in love like my mum and dad did. Were you ready for that back then?'

I wasn't even sure that Eli was ready to fall in love now. And I wasn't sure how much I liked that Ben was making it obvious how I felt about him before I'd had chance to talk to him myself.

'I didn't say that I was in love with him,' I pointed out.

'But you are. Even I can see it. And how many other long-term relationships have you had in your life?' Ben asked.

'A few,' I responded.

'That weren't because you lived miles from each other, or knew that he'd be moving away to university and wouldn't be wanting you to commit, leaving you free in case Eli ever changed his mind? In case you were wondering, he isn't going to change his mind. Eli thinks he's so mature, but I don't think he'll ever be brave enough to risk falling in love. He's too scared of losing you and being on his own again.'

When Eli slammed his own fists on the table, the noise was deafening. Ben jumped, Erin hid and even Taylor stepped back a pace, drawing Lily against him in case she was nervous. Lily was the only person who didn't look scared. I asked her to explain why she seemed okay when no one else was.

'You need to hear this,' she told me, 'even if it hurts. Hell, maybe especially if it hurts. You need to know whether you have to finally move on. You must be the only person who runs a romance shop who is perpetually single. I know how much you want to be in a relationship. Maybe it's time you found out whether that can ever happen with Eli.'

We all turned to face Eli. His eyes flashed with anger. This didn't bode well for him declaring long hidden feelings towards me.

'This looks serious,' Dad said, walking back into the kitchen. Eli turned and left the room. Dad called out after him. 'Don't forget our Christmas lunch tomorrow. Cody is coming too.' He looked at Lily and Taylor. 'The more the merrier, I guess.'

'Thanks,' Lily said, planting a quick kiss on his cheek. 'We'll see you tomorrow.' She and Taylor left too, and Dad looked at Ben and I.

'You'd better sit down and tell me everything.'

Chapter Thirty-Four

Christmas morning dawned clear, crisp and cold. I pulled the duvet around myself and tried to go back to sleep but without success. Dad had been shocked to hear about Ben's adventures, though I think that he was relieved to hear that Eli and I had tried so hard to find him and make up for fighting.

He'd been angry at Erin for how she had treated Ben, but had shown more grace than Eli and I had for listening to her reasons. He understood better how Ben being dragged around to look at other women had hurt her feelings and that Ben had grown angry with Eli and me for not seeing how much he was capable of by himself. He had stopped short of welcoming their engagement but had promised to consider giving his blessing once Erin had undertaken some therapy.

For his part, Ben had apologised for running away and refusing to answer his phone to let us know that he was okay. In his defence, he had thought that Erin had told us. Erin had stayed long enough to try to explain. She'd wanted some time for Ben and her away from what she saw as Eli and my overbearing influence over him. That stung because I could see the truth in it. When they had turned to me, I had burst into tears and run down to my flat. Dad had followed and hugged me until I stopped crying, but then he had given me space to think and not pressed me for any further explanations yet. Which was lucky as I had none to give.

I took a shower, using my most expensive lotions and creams but even the heavenly scents failed to lift my moods. Looking in the mirror didn't help. I could see how bloodshot my eyes were from crying. I brushed my hair out and applied a bright lipstick to try and distract from it, but I kept remembering Ben's words about Eli's inability to love me as I loved him and crying all over again.

Choosing a halter-neck dress from my wardrobe, I slipped it over my head. The fabric was black which suited my mood, but it had a delicate pattern of blossom which I hoped would allow everyone else to see it as a little more festive than I really felt. In deference to the frost on the windows, I slipped a pair of sheer tights over my legs. Opening my jewellery box, I sorted through earrings until I found a pair of pearl studs that had belonged to my mum. I rarely wore them for fear of upsetting my dad, but he had seemed stronger the day before than I ever remembered seeing him, and I needed to feel close to her.

Moving the lamp from the box next to my bed, I lifted the lid and began to unpack my stash of presents. I had a selection of suitably rude T-shirts for Ben. There was a set of silk underwear for Lily. They were black, and whilst Lily would doubtless complain that they covered too much skin, I knew that she would look stunning in them. I took out my pen and wrote Taylor's name next to hers on the gift label as I was sure that he would be getting the benefit of them too.

For Cody, I had wrapped one of the silk scarves that she had admired, as well as a bar of my favourite lavender-scented soap for relaxation. I'd originally planned to give Dad a pair of the leather slippers that I stocked, as his old pair were getting worn out and tatty, but as I looked at them I realised that this wouldn't suit his new, more positive demeanour. As a shop owner who prided herself on going the extra mile to find special gifts, I couldn't bring myself to give him such a meaningless present now. Pulling over my laptop, I began to search for a replacement gift.

I'd just found what I needed and printed out his enrolment at a local college for an evening class of Italian cookery lessons, when my doorbell rang. Expecting it to be Lily, I didn't look out of the window before I opened it. Eli was stood there, holding out a package. It was the size of a shoe box, bright red and tied with a green ribbon.

'Can I come in?' he asked. I stepped back and let him walk past me, hoping that he wouldn't notice how red my eyes were. He did, of course. 'I'm sorry,' he said. 'I never meant to hurt you Daisy.'

'It wasn't your fault,' I told him, letting him in on the realisation that I had come to in the middle of the night. 'It wasn't your fault that I cared about you. It's not your responsibility to protect my heart.'

'Even if it's me that's putting it at risk?' he asked. He swept a lock of my hair between his fingers. I stepped back, bumping into the counter. Turning away, I headed for my kitchen.

'Did you want a coffee?' I asked him. He accepted, and I busied myself fixing us drinks. When I carried the mugs out he was stood, staring at the items under the glass in my counter.

'You don't just sell memories, do you?' he asked.

'No,' I told him, waiting to see where he was going with his thought processes.

'You offer a celebration of lifetimes spent together. These items are thank yous for years of love and caring.' He picked up a small cut-glass rose that laid on my shelf. I'd been thinking of putting it away for Arthur in case he wanted it for his wife's next birthday. 'This might be a promise of love still to be shared in the future.' Eli set the flower down and picked up a small bud vase. 'This might hold the first flower a girl was ever given, or one from her wedding bouquet. Flowers bought as a symbol of a meaningful bond between two people, not as an after-thought or an apology.'

I waited until he had finished looking around. 'Ben was right,' he said, and I could feel my heart beginning to break as he spoke. 'I didn't think that I could ever love anyone as you wanted to be loved. Even ten years ago, the first time I ever held you and kissed you, I could feel how badly you needed to be loved, and as much as it excited me, it scared me too. When Ben told me that I shouldn't go near you, I took it as a get out clause. He was my best friend and I couldn't risk losing him.'

I sipped my drink and tried to hide behind the mug so that he couldn't see the hurt on my face.

'Then my mum died.' Eli's voice broke, and I could see his eyes fill with tears. I placed my mug on the counter and took him into my arms. Even if he couldn't love me the way that I loved him, I couldn't leave him to grieve alone. 'I was scared that if I loved someone as much as I had loved her, it would kill me to lose them.'

'I understand that,' I told him. 'Losing my mum nearly killed my dad too. It's taken him years to begin to deal with it. I have to thank you for helping him.'

'And what about you?' he asked.

'I'll live,' I told him. 'You don't need to worry about me. It's not your fault that I fell for you.'

'But I wanted you to,' he told me. 'I told Ben that we ought to invite you to the wedding. Then when Taylor started to flirt with you, I nearly cracked up with jealousy.'

'You never told me.'

'I didn't think Ben would approve,' Eli said. 'Plus he was

right, I didn't think I could love you as you deserved to be loved.'

I began to cry, and it wasn't pretty. I'd cried so much the night before that instead of just weeping a few delicate tears, I passed straight to great heaving sobs.

'I'm sorry,' Eli said again. 'I really never meant to hurt you.' He handed me the box he was carrying and turned to leave.

'Wait,' I told him, and went to pick up the small box that sat on my bed. Eli followed me in, sitting next to me on my bed to open the parcel that I handed him. Tearing off the tissue paper, he lifted out a series of small photograph frames. The first was a picture of him, Ben and me. We were maybe seven or eight. His mum had taken the three of us to the National History Museum, and we had posed for a photograph in front of the huge dinosaur skeleton in the entrance hall. It showed how long he had been in my life, and how much a part of our family he was. The second photo was of him and his mum. I'd taken it just before we had found out that she was ill. She'd been so full of life and energy in the picture, laughing as if she'd just been told a joke. Next to her, Eli had stood tall and handsome, a hint of the man that he would soon become. He looked happy and proud of himself.

There was a small black velvet box which made him roar with laughter when he opened it. 'James Bond cufflinks,' he said, lifting them out. 'What do you think of me?'

'I thought Ben had made my feelings public,' I muttered, not looking up to meet his eyes.

He gestured at the box he had handed me. I opened the lid and pulled out a CD. 'What's this?' I asked him, reading the title on the side.

'It was playing on the radio the day you brought me

down here. Do you remember? The room was still cluttered with your dad and grandad's old baking equipment. You hadn't even moved your bedroom down here yet. There was just a mattress in the back room, and a radio that your dad used to have in the kitchen. You put it on, this song was playing, and you made me lie down while you shut the door.'

'I was pretty confident, wasn't I?' I said, remembering how it had felt to be with him that first time.

'You were beautiful,' he said. 'You still are.' If he was trying to let me down gently, it was working. My heart still ached for him, but it helped to realise that he was letting me know that it was his hang-ups that had held him back, and not anything that I had done wrong. Maybe this was his true Christmas gift to me.

'There's more in there,' he told me, lifting another small wrapped item from the box. I unwrapped it. 'Juicy fruit chewing gum. You'd been chewing it before you kissed me. I could taste it on you. I haven't been able to chew it since without thinking of you.'

There was one more small box, about an inch square. The same size as the box that Ben had pulled out of his pocket yesterday. My pulse began to pick up, but Eli took it from me quickly and held my hand. 'It's not an engagement ring,' he cautioned, but as he traced the line of my cheek with his finger, I could only wonder what it was. Opening the box, he revealed a small silver ring with two interlinked hearts. 'It's a promise ring. Well, a question ring first, I guess. Daisy, I do love you. I don't know if that's enough. I don't know how to deal with this fear of losing you, and I can't promise that I will always be romantic enough for you. But I'd like to try, if you will have me?'

He barely caught me as I launched myself across the

bed and flung myself into his arms. I covered his face with kisses as he laughed. 'So you liked my gift?'

'It's the most romantic thing anyone has ever done for me,' I assured him.

He pumped his fist. 'I knew it, you can be the queen of romance, and if you'll have me, I can be the king.'

'I'll have you,' I said, and he took a small bunch of crushed mistletoe out from his pocket.

'I guess I won't be needing to use this then,' he said. I took it from him, and standing on my bed, I fixed it to the ceiling above my bed with a drawing pin.

'Let's go and celebrate Christmas with everyone upstairs. You can kiss me underneath it tonight.'

Thank You

Dear Reader,

Thank you for joining Daisy on her epic road trip. I hope you enjoyed her adventures to save Ben and that you fell in love with Eli just as she did.

If you have enjoyed reading this story it would mean a lot to me if you had a few minutes to share a review. As a new writer, this is a great way for people to find out about my books.

If you have any thoughts, comments or questions you can contact me via the details at the bottom of my author page.

Hannah x

About the Author

Hannah Pearl was born in East London. She is married with two children and now lives in Cambridge. She has previously worked as a Criminology researcher at a university in Leicester, as a Development Worker with various charities and even pulled a few pints in her time.

In 2015 she was struck down by Labrynthitis, which left her feeling dizzy and virtually housebound. She has since been diagnosed with ME. Reading has allowed Hannah to escape from the reality of feeling ill. She read upwards of three hundred books during the first year of her illness. When her burgeoning eReader addiction grew to be too expensive, she decided to have a go at writing. In 2017 she won Simon & Schuster's Books and the City #heatseeker short story competition, in partnership with Heat magazine, for her short story *The Last Good Day*.

Hannah is a member of the Romantic Novelists' Association.

Follow Hannah:
www.dizzygirlwrites.wordpress.com
Twitter: www.twitter.com/HannahPearl_1

More Ruby Fiction

From Hannah Pearl

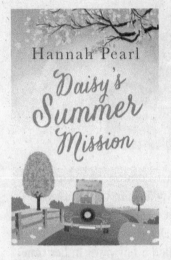

Daisy's Summer Mission

Daisy's job as a gift shop owner may involve selling chocolate truffles and lacy knickers but, this summer, she finds herself turning her hand to a slightly different profession ...

Daisy's boyfriend, Eli, works for a secret government agency and, try as she might, Daisy can't seem to help getting caught in the middle of his missions, which take her on a thrilling ride from the streets of Paris to a remote health retreat where carbs are banned!

But when she finds that Eli might be in danger, Daisy has to stop playing at being a spy and become the real thing. Teaming up with her pensioner customer, Mr King, Daisy embarks on her most important summer mission yet. Can she save the day?

Sequel to Daisy's Christmas Gift Shop

Visit www.rubyfiction.com for details.

Evie's Little Black Book

Is hunting down every man you've kissed the answer to finding Mr Right?

When Evie is invited to the wedding of the guy she'd fancied throughout her teens, it's the final straw. What's wrong with her and why can't *she* keep a man?

In between consoling herself with ice cream and chocolate, and sobbing her heart out to her cousin Charmaine, Evie has a brainwave – and it all centres around her 'little black book' (well, more floral patterned notebook really) – which contains the details of every man she's ever kissed or dated. Perhaps the cure for her disastrous love life has been nestled within its pages all along …

Does Evie's little black book really hold the answers, or will learn she learn that exes are exes for a reason?

Visit www.rubyfiction.com for details.

It's My Birthday

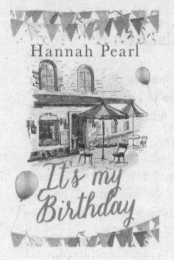

Hannah Pearl

Oh boy, another birthday …

Karen could be excused for crying on her birthday, especially as it's the first one since her husband got on a plane to the States and never came back. Then there's the fact that her workmates were practically bribed to attend her birthday meal. But when a restaurant double booking leads to her sharing a table with single dad Elliot and his daughter, things start looking up.

As Karen gets to know Elliot she experiences feelings she thought she'd never have again. But is it enough? Or will the thing that destroyed Karen's previous relationship also ruin things with Elliot?

Visit www.rubyfiction.com for details.

Burn

**There's no smoke
without fire …**

Jess has always held a candle
for Dex – so when he comes
back into her life after a
school reunion, she couldn't be
happier.

But something happened to
Dex before he mysteriously
left the area all those years
before – something that still
gives him terrible nightmares and makes him seem cold and
distant.

And then there are the rumours – rumours that Jess can't
bring herself to believe. But when the truth finally comes out,
can Jess be the one to help Dex fight the demons from his
past before they consume him completely?

Visit www.rubyfiction.com for details.

Introducing Ruby Fiction

Ruby Fiction is an imprint of Choc Lit Publishing.
We're an award-winning independent publisher,
creating a delicious selection of fiction.

See our selection here:
www.rubyfiction.com

Ruby Fiction brings you stories that inspire emotions.

We'd love to hear how you enjoyed
Daisy's Christmas Gift Shop. Please visit
www.rubyfiction.com and give your feedback or
leave a review where you purchased this novel.

Ruby novels are selected by genuine readers like yourself.
We only publish stories our Tasting Panel want to see in
print. Our reviews and awards speak for themselves.

Could you be a Star Selector and join our Tasting Panel?
Would you like to play a role in choosing which novels
we decide to publish? Do you enjoy reading women's
fiction? Then you could be perfect for our Tasting Panel.

Visit here for more details ...
www.choc-lit.com/join-the-choc-lit-tasting-panel

Keep in touch:
Sign up for our monthly newsletter Spread for all the latest
news and offers: www.spread.choc-lit.com. Follow us on
Twitter: @RubyFiction and Facebook: RubyFiction.

Stories that inspire emotions!